TRANSACTIONS IN A FOREIGN CURRENCY

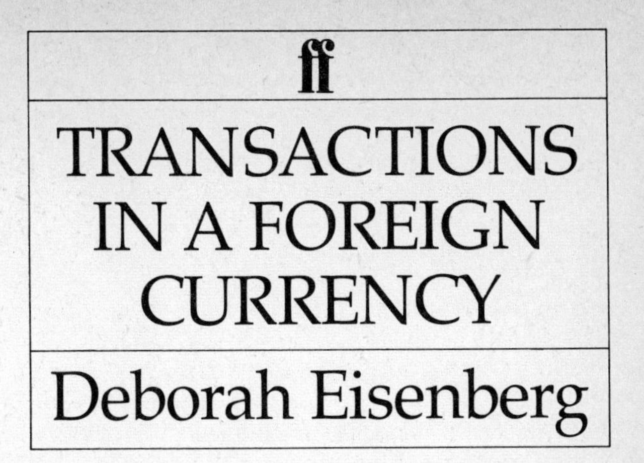

TRANSACTIONS IN A FOREIGN CURRENCY

Deborah Eisenberg

faber and faber

LONDON · BOSTON

First published in the United States of America in 1986
by Alfred A. Knopf, Inc., New York
and simultaneously in Canada by
Random House of Canada Limited, Toronto

First published in Great Britain in 1986 by
Faber and Faber Limited
3 Queen Square London WC1N 3AU

Printed in Great Britain by
Butler & Tanner Ltd, Frome and London

"Flotsam", "What it Was Like, Seeing Chris", "Transactions in a Foreign Currency" and "Broken Glass" originally appeared, in somewhat different form, in the *New Yorker*. "A Lesson in Traveling Light" appeared in *Vanity Fair*.

British Library Cataloguing in Publication Data

Eisenberg, Deborah
Transactions in a foreign currency
I. Title
813'.54[F] PS3555.I7/
ISBN 0-571-13798-9

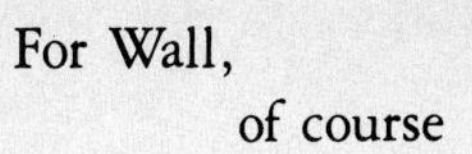

For Wall,
of course

Contents

TRANSACTIONS IN A FOREIGN CURRENCY

Flotsam

The other evening, I was having a drink with a friend when the sight of two women at the next table caused me to stop speaking in midsentence. Both of the women were very young, and fashionable to an almost painful degree. They were drinking beer straight from the bottle, and they radiated a self-conscious, helpless daring, as if they had been made to enter some baffling contest and all eyes were upon them.

"Earth to Charlotte," my friend said. "Everything all right?"

"Fine," I said, and it was, but for a moment that seemed endless I had been pulled down into a forgotten period of my life when I, too, had strained to adhere to the slippery requirements of distant authorities.

I had just come to New York then, after breaking up with a man named Robert. At first, everything had gone well with Robert. We lived in Buffalo, on the ground floor of a large house, and while he taught at a local university and read and worked on his dissertation in the study, I tried to make things grow in our little patch of a garden and did some part-time research for a professor of political science. At night, we cooked dinner together or with other couples from Robert's department, or once in a while went dancing or to a movie, and I thought Robert was happy.

But after a while Robert seemed to lose interest in me, and part of what I had been was torn from me as he pulled away. And the farther he pulled away from me, increasingly the only thing I cared about was that he love me, and there was nothing I would not have done to be right for him. But although I tried and tried to figure out how I ought to be, my means for judging such a thing seemed to have split off with him. So while Robert seemed to grow finer and more fastidious—easily annoyed by things I said or did—I seemed to grow coarser and more unfocused, and even my athletic tallness, which Robert had admired when we met, with the dissolving of his affection came to feel like an untended sprawl, and my long blond hair, which I'd been proud of at one time, seemed insipid and childish—just another manifestation of how unequal to Robert I had proved to be. And after a time I was overtaken by a paralysis that spread through every area of my life, rapidly, like an illness.

One day, Robert and I had been sitting in the living room reading when I noticed that he had put down his book and was just staring out with a little frown. "What are you thinking about?" I said before I could stop myself.

"Nothing," he said.

"Sorry," I said. "I'm sorry."

"Then why did you ask, Charlotte?"

"Sorry," I said.

"Then why do you always ask? Always," he said.

I didn't say anything.

"You know what?" he said. "You're like the Blob. You remember that movie *The Blob*? You're sentient protoplasm, but you're as undifferentiated as sentient protoplasm can get. You're devoid of even taxonomic attributes."

"Robert," I said.

"Have you ever had an intention?" he said. "Have you ever

had a desire? Have you ever even had what could be accurately described as a reaction?"

My ears went strange, and I heard my voice say, "You always want me to be different. You want me to be some other person, but if you don't tell me what you want, how can I know what to do?"

"Jesus," Robert said. He looked at me, his eyes narrowed.

The moment locked, and I felt a harsh tingling across the bridge of my nose, and I knew that if I didn't turn away fast Robert would hit me.

I went out carefully, as if trying not to startle something from a hedge, and drove to a drugstore where there was a telephone, and eventually I got ahold of my friend Fran.

"Sit right there," she said. "Don't move. I'll make some calls and get back to you."

So then I sat on the little wooden seat and waited. A pretty girl with dark hair came into the store, and I watched as she chose a lipstick at the counter, looking very pleased with herself. What was going to happen to me, I wondered. After a while, Fran called with the number of someone named Cinder, who lived in New York and was looking for a roommate.

"Great," Cinder said when I reached her. "I'm desperate. The girl who was living here disappeared a few weeks ago with about half my stuff. Ex-stuff now. I had to get myself a live-in junkie, right? And of course she stuck me for all of last month's rent. I know it's a sign that you called today, because I was just about to advertise, which I really hate to do, because you get these guys saying their name is Shirley and can they come over and shit in your ear or rupture your asshole, kind of thing."

"Well, I got your name from Franny Straub," I said. "Her friend Lauren took a design class with you."

"Whatever," Cinder said.

"Listen," I said. I felt ill with apprehension. "Could I move in tonight?"

"Sure," Cinder said. "You wouldn't be able to bring the rent in cash, would you?"

I'd never been to New York before, and I remember so clearly how the subway looked to me that night. How gaudy and festive it was, like a huge Chinese dragon, clanking and huffling through its glimmering cavern. Even though it was very late, the cars were full of people. They sat there, all together, and their expressions were eased in that subterranean lull between their different points of embarkation and destination. It seemed to me that I was the only newcomer.

Cinder came down and helped me lug my suitcase upstairs. She moved with brisk precision, and her blond hair was cut like a teddy bear's. "Cinder," I said. "It's an interesting name."

"Lucinda, actually," she said. "But—you know." She opened two bottles of beer and handed one to me. "So, hey, welcome to your new home, which is what my seventh-grade teacher said to our class the first day of junior high, scaring us all out of our *wits.* So you're just coming down from a bad thing, huh?"

"Yes," I said, looking around unsuccessfully for a glass. "Well, not exactly." I didn't know how to put into words to this able person my failure with Robert.

"Anyhow," she said, "tomorrow we'll talk and talk and talk, but there's some stuff I have to take care of now, and, besides, you probably want to sleep. If you go out before I'm up, just leave the rent on the kitchen table."

Cinder gave me a tiny room to myself, but I spent most of my time in the kitchen with her and men she was seeing and her friend Mitchell. Most of my belongings were in the kitchen, too, which had shelves and a closet and a bathtub in which things could be kept, and Cinder had told me to put anything I wanted on the walls. In a place of honor, looking down over the kitchen table, I tacked a snapshot I'd taken of Robert one day in our garden. He was smiling—a free, simple, lifted instant of a smile that I never saw again.

The apartment was in the East Village, and although the neighborhood had long since lost its notoriety, it glittered to me. Cinder and Mitchell seemed so comfortable there. Mitchell moved with an underwater languor that was due to a happy combination of grace and drugs, and his black hair was marvelously glossed. But even though he and Cinder were so different in appearance, they both dressed in meticulously calculated assemblages that reached from past decades far into the future. Together their individual impact was increased exponentially, like that of twins, owing to a similarity I now understand to be stylistic, in addition, of course, to whatever similarity underlies all acute and self-conscious beauty.

Next to them, I felt clumsy and hideous, but it seemed to me, I suppose, that the power of their self-assurance would protect me, that my own face and body would learn from it, and that soon things and people would alter in my path, as they did for Cinder and Mitchell. It seemed, in short, that I would become fit for Robert.

But nearly five months passed, during which I sat around Cinder's kitchen table under Robert's picture, and my face and body remained the same. And then I found one day, that what I'd become fit for was, in fact, something quite other than Robert.

Everything seemed to change on that one day, but really, I think, things had been changing and changing over the course of many previous days, and perhaps what eventually appears to be information always appears at first to be just flotsam, meaningless fragments, until enough flotsam accretes to manifest, when one notices it, a construction. In any case, there was a day when I started out as usual by going uptown to the office where I'd gotten a job as a secretary, and around lunchtime Cinder called. She was at her store, a tiny place around the corner from the apartment, where she sold clothes, some of which were used and some of which she designed and made herself, and she was in a terrible rage, having just had a big set-to with John Paul, a man she was going out with. "Can you come down?" she said. "I need you."

I was always gratified and astonished that it was I in whom Cinder confided and whose help she asked for, but when I arrived at the store that day Mitchell was already there, lying on the couch, and Cinder was laughing. "Charlotte!" Cinder said. "I know what this looks like, but I was an absolute wreck when Mitchell got here—wasn't I, Mitchell?—and he literally glued me back together. You know what we should do, though. I'm absolutely starving. We should get some pirogi. Hey, I've learned this interesting new fact about men. The more weight they make you gain, the more attractive it means they are. God. Why can't I be one of those little twitching things who shred their food when something goes wrong? I wish I were willowy and thin like you, Charlie."

"You are willowy and thin," I said. "I'm bony and big, like a dinosaur skeleton in a museum."

"Dinosaur skeleton." Mitchell centered me slowly in his gaze, and I faltered. "It's been a long, long time since I thought about one of those," he said.

"Mitchell, darling," Cinder said, straddling him to massage his shoulders, "how could I get you to go next door and get us some pirogi? Like three orders, with extra sour cream. I am *ravenous.*"

"That stuff I glued you together with sort of absorbed my liquid assets," he said.

"I have money," I said, handing him a ten.

After Mitchell left, Cinder told me about her fight with John Paul. "He called and said he wouldn't be able to go to the concert tomorrow night, and I said why, and he said it was work, but I mean, how could I believe him, after all, Charlie? So he said, right, there was this girl, and then, stupid me, I got just incredibly pissed off, and naturally he ended up saying he didn't think we should see each other anymore. I mean, Charles, I really don't care, you know, about his *girls.* Heaven help us, I'm hardly in a position to complain about that sort of thing. It's just that he makes me feel like some . . . doddering nagging haggy old *wife.* And the worst thing is, though, I think a lot of it has to do, unconsciously, I mean, with revenge. I mean, I bet that what this is really about is Arthur."

"Arthur?" I said.

"Oh, you remember," she said. "That guy I met at that party John Paul and I went to last week. Oh, fabulous," she said to Mitchell, who was walking in with an immense load of pirogi. "But I really don't see how he can get so upset about a thing like Arthur. The guy was boring, he was stupid, and he wasn't particularly attractive, either. In fact, I really don't know why I did it. Just to assert myself, I suppose. Have some pirogi, Charlie." She held one out to me, speared on a plastic fork.

"No, thanks," I said.

"Really?" Cinder said. "Hmm. Mitchell?"

"*No food,*" Mitchell said.

"Wow. Well, what are we going to do with all this shit?" She looked helplessly at the pirogi. "Anyhow, I don't mind that John Paul likes women. I know he likes women."

"Likes women," I felt, was an inexact description. Something happened, even I could see, between John Paul and women, that didn't have all that much to do with what he thought about them. One evening recently, while he and Cinder and I were standing around in the kitchen talking, he rested his hand on my arm, high up, where a slave bracelet goes. Later, in my room, when I got undressed for bed, I looked at the place in a mirror, before I remembered what had caused it to burn like that.

"Oh, get real," Cinder said to a roach that was sauntering across the pirogi. "God. This place is such an ashtray."

"Oh—are you open?" said a girl in a very short skirt, hesitating at the door.

"Definitely," Cinder said. "Come in. Look around. Have some pirogi."

"Well, I don't think I will, really." The girl looked at the plate sidelong. "I'm on a diet. Goodness," she said, drawing nearer, "they're awfully pale. What exactly are they?"

"An acquired taste," Mitchell said, lying back and shutting his eyes again.

The girl looked from one of us to another.

"Well, I suppose all tastes must be acquired, really, musn't they?" I said nervously. "It's a confusing term. To me, at least."

"I've never encountered a taste I haven't acquired in about one microsecond," Cinder said, staring flatly at the girl, who shifted under the scrutiny. "Besides, why are you on a diet? You don't need to lose any weight, does she, Mitchell?"

The girl looked over at Mitchell. He unlidded his green, stranger's eyes and stared at her for a moment before the suggestion of a smile appeared on his face. She began to smile then, too, but bit her lip instead and looked down.

"Everything's half price today," Cinder said.

"Great," the girl said neutrally. She glanced at Mitchell again and then turned her back to us and moved the hangers along the rack with a rhythmic precision. Why were we watching her like that, I wondered. I felt terribly uneasy.

"That peacock-blue one would look really sensational on you," Cinder said.

"Really?" the girl said. "This one?"

"Are you kidding?" Cinder said. "With those legs of yours? The light in the dressing room's broken, but you can just slip it on over there.

"See? That's great," Cinder said. Next to the brilliant blue of the dress, the girl's legs gave off a candied gleam, as if they had never been exposed to the light before.

"It is good," the girl said, watching herself approach the mirror. "But it's very—I don't know if I could really carry it off."

"What you need is something like these with it," Cinder said, putting one of her own earrings to the girl's ear.

"Hmm," the girl agreed to the mirror, with which she had established a private understanding.

"You know what, Cinder," Mitchell said. "You should wear that color yourself." The reflection of Cinder's face floated behind the mirrored girl.

"I really like this dress," the girl said. "It's really good. The only trouble is, I'm looking for something to wear to dinner with my boyfriend's parents."

"I used to have a boyfriend," Cinder said. "Up until about an hour ago."

"Really?" the girl said. "You just broke up with some guy?"

"Broke up," Cinder said. "Fantastic." She related her story to the girl with as much relish as if it were the first time she'd told it. "He says he doesn't even care about me," Cinder said.

"He said he didn't care about you?" I asked.

"Well, that's what he meant," Cinder said.

"But maybe he meant something else," I said.

"I know what he meant, Charlotte. I know the guy. When you're in love with someone, you know what they're saying to you."

"That's terrible," the girl said, looking at Cinder round-eyed. "That happened to *me* once."

"So you understand," Cinder said.

"Oh, God," the girl said. "I really do."

Cinder stepped back and looked at her for a long moment. "I'd really like you to get that dress," she said finally. "You'd be a fantastic advertisement for my stuff. But let's face it. I mean, your boyfriend's parents! They'd have you out the back door in a couple of seconds, bound and gagged."

"Well," the girl said, looking into the mirror.

"Look." Cinder turned to me. "Would you wear that dress to your boyfriend's parents', Charlie?"

"What about you?" the girl said to Mitchell. "How would you react if I showed up in this dress?"

"I'd run amok," Mitchell said, lying immobile on the couch, his eyes closed. "I'd go totally out of control."

"See, I might as well, though," the girl said, examining the mirror again. "Jeff wouldn't care. Actually, his parents are fairly nauseating people anyway. In fact, his sister just cracked up. She tried to stab her husband with her nail scissors, and they had her put away. Anyhow, if I don't use it for dinner I can always wear it someplace else."

"Oh, shit, though," Cinder said. "I just remembered. That's the one with the crooked seam."

"Where?" the girl said. "I don't see it."

"Well, I wouldn't want anybody wearing it around. Listen, come back next week. I'll be making up some more, and I've got this incredible bronzy-brown that would be really good on you."

"Well, I really like this blue, though," the girl said.

"Yeah, but I'm out of that, unfortunately," Cinder said.

"What a sweet kid," Cinder said after the girl left. "And wasn't she pretty? I really hope she doesn't get hurt."

"Sweet!" Mitchell said, and snorted. "No!" he shrieked, twisting, as Cinder leapt onto the couch to tickle him. "Much too stoned!"

"You are such a cynic!" Cinder said. "Isn't he, Charlie?"

"Yes," I said. "Cinder—how did you know that girl would look good in that dress?" I asked.

"Well, that's interesting," she said, releasing Mitchell to devote her full attention to this question. "See, I always know. I'm always right about how people look, and how they're going to look in different things. That is, if they're worth looking at in the first place. And the horrible truth is, I can do that because I'm such a jealous person!"

"What do you mean?" I said.

"No, it's true," she said. "Really. My jealousy is a tool for looking at other people, and now John Paul is my special, sort of, lens. I look at other women through his eyes, and I know what it is in them that he would find attractive. It's awful. I'm completely subjugated to his vision."

"But, Cinder," I said. "It's a wonderful talent!"

"It's not a talent, Charlotte," she said, "it's an *affliction*." She looked furious.

"Cinder," I said after a moment. "Could we—do me up sometime? Make me look—I don't know, like that girl?"

"Oh, you don't want to look like that girl, Charlie, honey. Mitchell's right. She was a boring little thing. You don't want to look like everybody else anyhow. You've got your own looks."

"I know," I said. "But could we fix them?"

"You've got incredible potential, you know, Charlie," Cinder said. "I could spend hours on you. Sure, O.K., we'll do the whole thing—clothes, face, hair—"

"Don't do anything to her hair." Mitchell's voice floated into our conversation with an otherworldly pallor. "It's soft."

"Soft, yeah, but it's got to get cut or something," Cinder said.

"Like Big Bird," Mitchell added faintly.

"He's asleep," Cinder said.

"Cinder," I said, "could I try on that blue dress?"

"Oh, let's not get into it today, Charlie," she said. "I'm so destroyed. You must be exhausted yourself—I've kept you for hours. Mitchell, would you take me out to get drunk and disgusting? Then maybe you could take advantage of me, if you could stand it." Mitchell's eyes remained closed. "Oh, never mind," Cinder said. "That was a joke."

"Well, goodbye." I stood up. "See you at home later."

"They need any extra roaches at your office?" Cinder asked. At our feet, the plate of pirogi swarmed.

When I got back to the office, I just sat and sat and my mind kept wandering back to the store. Why was I so sad? After all, Cinder had said I was more interesting than that gleaming girl.

"Hands off!" a voice said suddenly from behind me.

"Oh, hi, Mr. Bunder," I said, noticing that my hands were in my hair. Well, it *was* soft.

"You look to be, say, in orbit." As Mr. Bunder sat down on a corner of my desk, the fabric of his trousers pulled against his thigh. It looked extremely uncomfortable, but I couldn't stop staring at it.

"Not concentrating, I guess," I said.

"Listen." He leaned in toward me. "Want to get something to drink?"

"Right now?" I asked. He had a pinkish, stippled look, as if he'd just gotten something to drink.

We settled down side by side in a booth near the bar. "So you're worried about your roommate, huh," he said.

"Yes," I said. "Well, not exactly." How hard it was to figure out how to say anything to anyone! "Well, actually, though," I said, "she does get these terrible headaches, but I think they're from tension in her back. She's upset about a man she's been going out with."

"Well, maybe I'll come over and check it out. I give a bad back rub." Mr. Bunder poked me on the arm. "But seriously," he said. "There are a lot of hard-noses out there. They get some poor little girl going—it gives them a big boost in the ego department. Then they see something maybe a bit better.

Some knockout just sitting at the bar licking her chops. Beautiful women going begging in this city. Dime a dozen." He kept looking around the room. I wondered if I was sitting too far away from him and he was feeling insulted. On the other hand, perhaps I was sitting too close to him and he was feeling embarrassed.

"I'll get us a couple more of these," he said. "You like the olives, huh?" He held his olive in front of my mouth and I ate it, like a seal. For a moment, I was terribly hungry, but then I thought of the roach-capped pirogi, and I lost my appetite.

"So what brought you to New York?" he asked.

"Well . . ." I said. What had brought me to New York? "I split up with someone in Buffalo."

"Busted marriage, huh?" Mr. Bunder said. "Too bad."

"Oh, no. It wasn't a marriage. We were just trying it out." I searched my mind for something that would be interesting to Mr. Bunder. "He was an assistant professor." Mr. Bunder blinked. "Well, not that that has anything to do with it," I said. "But we weren't very compatible."

"Guess not," Mr. Bunder said. He sighed, looking around, and tapped with his glass on the table.

"Have you ever been married?" I asked, to be polite.

"Have I?" Mr. Bunder said. "Yeah. I have. I'm married right now." I wondered if I should leave. Mr. Bunder didn't seem to be having a very good time.

"You know," he said, perking up. "You look a little like that what's-her-name—Meryl Streep. You know that? Around the—the—mouth, or something. Olive! Olive!" He held his olive in front of me, but I was committed just then to pushing a little globule of water on the table from one side of my glass around to the other without breaking it up.

"What's the matter?" he said. "Need another drink?"

"No, thank you, I'm already drunk," I said, surprised. "I'm sweating."

"Terrific," Mr. Bunder said. "Well, maybe you want to go sweat at home. Check up on that little roommate of yours. I'll get you into a taxi before you fall over."

"Thank you, Mr. Bunder," I said outside.

"Call me Dickie, would you?" he said. "When you girls say 'Mr. Bunder,' I think you're talking to my father."

I had trouble getting past Mr. Bunder to climb into the taxi he'd hailed for me. Or perhaps he was planning to get into it, too. "Did you want to share this someplace?" I asked.

"Thanks, honey," he said, "but I think I'll hang around here for a while. See if any of the ladies at the bar is interested in an evening of fudge packing."

It had been nice of Mr. Bunder to ask me to join him. He must have seen that I was lonely, too. I felt sorry for him as I watched him go back into the restaurant by himself. He looked so pink and tender in his bristly little suit, and from behind he seemed to move choppily, as if propelled by warring impulses, like a truffle hound going back to work after a noon break.

"Where have you been, Charles?" Cinder said to me. "I've been desperate."

"I was having a drink with Mr. Bunder," I said.

"Mr. Bunder!" she said. "Do people still name their kids Mister? Oh, right. He's one of those cowpats you work for, isn't he?"

"Yes," I said. "Well, I mean . . . Oh—Cinder, does 'fudge packing' mean something?"

"What? How should I know?" she said. "Christ, where do you hear this vile shit? Anyhow, listen. I really need your help. If you'd come half an hour later, you probably would have found me in a pool of blood with a machete between my ribs." She looked at me blankly for a moment. "Between my ribs? Is that what people say? It sounds wrong. 'Between my ribs,' 'among my ribs'—doesn't 'between my ribs' make it sound like you've only got two ribs? It's like people say 'between my teeth'—'I've got something caught between my teeth'—and it sounds like they've only got two teeth. I think you should say, 'I've got something caught *among* my teeth.' Well, no, that doesn't work, either, does it, because you can really only get something caught—oh, weird—*between two teeth!*"

"Cinder," I said, "what happened?"

"What?" she said. "Oh."

It seemed she had called John Paul back, and he'd agreed to come over, but then she'd remembered she already had a date with someone else.

"Oh," I said, and looked at her. "So why don't you call John Paul and say you made a mistake—tell him you can't see him tonight?"

"Charlotte," Cinder said. "We're talking John Paul here."

"Well . . ." I said. "What about the other guy? Could you call him?"

"Hmm. I didn't think of that," she said. "But anyhow I don't know how to reach him. I don't even know his name."

"You don't know his name?"

"He's just some guy I met on the street," she said. "Some Puerto Rican or something."

As we looked at each other, concentrating hard, the doorbell rang.

I crouched next to Cinder at the door, where she was peering through a crack. She plucked me back, but I'd seen a very young man, dark and graceful, in a crisp shirt. "Shit," Cinder whispered.

"How many years before someone is older than someone else?" I wrote on a little pad of paper we kept for lists.

"4 if yr a man 2 if yr a wman," Cinder wrote back. "But so wht?"

We sat absolutely still under Robert's photographed happiness while the footsteps outside the door continued back and forth and the doorbell rang again, and then, as Cinder and I stared at each other in horror, a second set of footsteps mounted the stairs. But it was Mitchell who spoke, not John Paul, and Cinder and I both let out our breath.

"Hey," Mitchell said. "Something I can help you with?"

"I'm a friend of Cinder's," the stranger said. "I was supposed to see her tonight, but she doesn't seem to be home."

"That's weird," Mitchell said, as Cinder muffled a gasp behind her hands. "She said she'd be in all evening."

"Well, if you see her," the other voice said, "tell her Hector was here."

I peeked out and watched the men walk together toward the stairs. How nice men were with each other, how frail and trusting, I was thinking, and just then an explosion of hilarity escaped from behind Cinder's hands, and the two men halted and turned back toward the door in perfect synchronization. "What was that?" Hector said.

After a moment of utter motionlessness on both sides of the door, the two men began to discuss the possibilities of marauders, gas leaks, and overdoses, and Mitchell decided to climb over the roof and down the fire escape into Cinder's room. "If I don't open the door for you in about fifteen minutes," he said to Hector, "just chop it down, I guess, or something."

Cinder and I scrambled silently back to her room. "This is a catastrophe," she said.

"Yes," I said. "It is."

"Mitchell is so sweet, isn't he, though," she said, "to go up over the roof like that. It's pretty hard. He did it once before, when I flushed my keys down the toilet at some ridiculous party."

"How did you do that?" I asked.

"Well," she said. "I mean, it wasn't on purpose. But he's the sort of person that would do that sort of thing."

"I don't think he'd climb over any roofs for me," I said.

"Mitchell isn't nice to you?" she said. "God. If I ever saw him not being nice to you, I'd beat him senseless. Oh, I mean, I know he can be sort of a snot sometimes," she said, "like a lot of those really great-looking men. It's not like women, you know. We're brought up to be able to handle being beautiful, but those really beautiful guys are brought up like hothouse flowers, and they're not taught what to do with all that stuff. They just get super aware of all that potential for, you know, damage, and they get sort of wooden. A lot of them can't even speak to a woman who isn't absolutely gorgeous herself. It's sort of like rich people, or people who are famous—they like their friends to be rich or famous, too, so that everyone understands everyone else on a certain level and no one has to worry about anyone else's motives."

Usually I enjoyed learning things from Cinder, but today everything she said made me feel worse. It wasn't fair of her, I thought, to call Mr. Bunder a cowpat without knowing him. Of course, she would have called him a cowpat even if she did know him. Robert would have called him a cowpat, too. Well, except that Robert would think that "cowpat" was a stupid thing to call someone. And actually, come to think of it, Robert wouldn't like Cinder one bit, either. And Cinder wouldn't like Robert. Well, Mr. Bunder was always nice to me.

"And men like Mitchell just worry and worry, you know?" Cinder was saying. "They're afraid they'll either be contaminated or unmasked if they get too near a woman who isn't beautiful. They're afraid their own beauty is all they have, and that it isn't really worth anything anyhow, and that it misrepresents their real inner disgustingness, and that they're going to lose it—all that stuff. Thank God John Paul isn't like that! He just loves being beautiful. He thinks he *deserves* to be beautiful, and it's like he's got this big present for anyone who happens to be around—drunks on the corner, women with baby carriages, the grocer."

The little claim John Paul had staked on my arm asserted

itself again, just as, with a huge thud, Mitchell climbed in the window. "Oh, don't get up," he said. "I was just passing by."

"I'm really sorry, Mitchell," Cinder said. "I'll explain all of this later, but right now please, please get out there immediately and grab that kid before he does something really dumb."

"When is John Paul supposed to get here?" I asked when Cinder had dispatched Mitchell.

"Pretty soon. Now, to be precise. But he's always late," she said. "Actually, he probably won't come at all."

"Oh, I'm sure he will," I said. I would have liked to put an arm around Cinder, as she so easily did with me when I talked about Robert, but I could only sit there next to her with my hands in my lap.

"You know," she said, "I think I've just figured out why men treat me so badly. It's karma. I really think it is."

I could figure out a few things about men myself, I thought. I could figure out, for instance, that men who said you looked a little like Meryl Streep meant that they didn't find you attractive but they thought someone else might. And I could figure out that men who said you looked like Big Bird or a dinosaur skeleton didn't think anyone would find you attractive.

"You're lucky that you're so nice," Cinder said. "Men are going to treat you really well in your next life."

"You know what?" I said after a moment. "I think Mitchell and Hector are in the kitchen."

"Jesus," Cinder said. "You're right! What on earth is Mitchell doing, that maniac!"

"Does he know that John Paul's supposed to come over?" I asked.

"Good point. I guess I didn't get a chance to mention it." She sucked air in through her teeth. "Well, Charles," she said. "It's up to you now."

"No!" I said. "What do you mean? I can't!"

"You've got to, Charlotte," Cinder said.

I shut Cinder's door carefully behind me and explained to the two men who were sitting comfortably at the table drinking beer that Cinder needed to be left utterly alone. "She says she feels like—like—there's a machete in her head."

"Probably a brain tumor," Mitchell said, taking a sip of his beer.

"Should we call a doctor?" Hector said to me. He looked more solid at close range than he had out in the hall. He must have been twenty or twenty-one. "Or take her to the hospital?"

"No," I said. "I mean, this happens all the time. The only thing to do is let her rest."

"Well, I guess so. Listen—" Hector said. He wrote something on a piece of paper and handed it to me. "Here's my phone number. Could you ask her please to give me a call sometime when she's feeling better?"

Downstairs, Mitchell nodded and walked off, leaving me to go in the opposite direction with Hector. I wanted to say good night to Hector, but we were in the middle of the block, so if I did say good night I would have to continue with him afterward, which would seem peculiar, or else I would have to turn and go back in the direction from which we'd just come, which would seem . . . well, also peculiar. So I decided I would say good night at the corner.

At the corner, Hector turned to me. "Want to get something to eat?"

Something to eat! I was just walking with him to get him out of the apartment! "I guess not," I said. I turned to face him. "Thanks anyway . . . I really am hungry."

"Well," Hector said, "come on, then. There's a good place a couple of blocks away."

What was it that Puerto Ricans ate, I wondered as I walked along beside Hector, but the restaurant we entered was Italian, with pictures of harbors and flowers and entertainers overlapping on the walls, and cloths and glass-stoppered bottles of dark wine on the tables, around which sat large men and handsome, glistening women, all talking and laughing. It seemed, in fact, as if each table were a little boat, bobbing along on the hubbub of pleasure.

Hector and I were seated at our own table, and Hector got us outfitted with glasses for the wine, and a huge platter of vegetables—a whole fried harvest—and I felt that we ourselves had pulled anchor and were setting off like the others into that open expanse.

But then I was staring straight at a gold chain Hector wore. How had I come to be here with this person, I wondered. Yet the links lay flat along his neck, as sleek and secure as a stripe on some strange animal. "I'm sorry about Cinder," I said.

Hector glanced away from me. "Everyone gets headaches at one time or another."

What did he mean? "Actually," I said, "I have a headache myself now. It must be because I got drunk this afternoon."

"This afternoon?" Hector said.

"It was a mistake," I said.

"Oh," he said. "So was that Cinder's boyfriend?"

"Oh, heavens, no," I said. "Mitchell's just a friend. Actually, I never really thought about it before, but I suppose he is really quite attracted to Cinder. But you know what?" The words were forming themselves before I had a chance to think about them. "I don't think he's interested in women. I mean, in being involved with them." Why had I said such a thing? Hector would want to talk about Cinder, not Mitchell.

"I had a cousin like that," Hector said. "He liked girls pretty well, but he didn't want any girl friends. He didn't like other boys, like a lot of boys do. But he wore drag all the time. Pretty dresses, silk underwear, you know? He was very nice. Everybody liked him, but he was about the strangest one in my family."

The waiter moved our vegetables over to make room for vast dishes of spaghetti and sausage.

"What happened to him?" I asked. "Your cousin."

"Oh, he's O.K.," Hector said. "He grew out of it. It was just a teen-age thing for him. But he still doesn't go out much with girls. Hey, this stuff is good, isn't it? He teaches physical education in Pittsburgh now."

We took a long time with our spaghetti, while Hector told me more about his family. It sounded as if they were fond of each other. And he told me about an information-theory class he was taking. "Are you studying?" he asked me.

"I'm finished now. I'm a lot older than you." I looked straight at Hector. I wanted to make sure he understood that I wasn't trying to make him think that I was his age, that the fact that he was a lot younger than I was was of no interest to me. It was Robert, after all, I wasn't good enough for.

"Dessert and coffee?" the waiter asked before Hector could respond. "Or have you lost your appetite?"

"That's right." Hector gestured toward my plate as the waiter cleared it away. "You did pretty good, for a girl."

When we were finished, Hector asked, "So do you like to go dancing?"

For an instant, Robert commandeered the air in front of me. He sat with his feet on his desk, leaning back and smiling. "Flattered?" he asked.

"Oh, no!" I said.

"Too bad," Hector said. "I know a good place uptown."

"No." I got to my feet quickly. "I didn't mean I didn't want to go dancing—I meant I didn't not want to go dancing." I was breathing hard as I looked at him, as if I'd run to catch up with him.

"That's what you meant, huh?" he said. "Far out." But he grinned as he stood, and he stretched, letting one arm fall around me in a comradely manner.

. . .

Oh, it felt good to dance. I hadn't gone dancing since Robert and I had started being unhappy. Hector knew a lot of people in the place we'd come to, and we stopped and talked with them. They spoke to Hector in Spanish, but when Hector put a defending hand on my shoulder and answered in English everyone else switched into English, too, except for a tiny dark star of a girl who continued in Spanish with Hector in a husky baby voice. "Her cousin in Queens has a '62 Corvette that I want," Hector told me. "And she says he's thinking about selling it to me."

He bought us Cokes and finished his own in one motion, while I watched his head tilt back and his throat work. "You don't do drugs?" I said.

"I stay away from that stuff, mostly." He looked very serious. "It seems like you can do a lot of things behind it, but that's an illusion, see. I had a good friend, a heavy user, who died. Everyone thought he was a very happy guy. You see people, you talk to them—their faces say one thing, you never know what's inside." For a moment, he seemed almost incandescent, but then he smiled impatiently toward the room, laying aside his trustful seriousness. "Anyhow," he said, "I like to keep in shape." The gold around his neck winked, and I looked away quickly.

"Excuse me," I said. "I'll be back in a minute." I fought through the dancers and sat down near the wall. When I closed my eyes, I felt private for a moment, but when I opened them I was looking straight into the whole, huge crowd, right to where Hector was standing, listening attentively to the tiny dark girl. He looked dignified and brotherly as she smiled up at him, but then, suddenly, he flared into a laugh of pure appreciation.

In the ladies' room, I held a wet paper towel against my forehead while a herd of girls jostled and giggled around me.

Keep in shape, I thought. What had that meant! Had I been expected to admire him? Who was Hector, anyway? What on earth did he think I was doing there with him? Did he think I was attracted to him? And why had I chattered on with him so during dinner? He was just some kid my roommate had picked up on the street! I was wearing, the mirror reminded me, the same nasty office dress I'd been wearing when I sat next to Mr. Bunder light-years earlier in the day. Hector belonged with that girl who was flirting with him, or with Cinder, not with me, and I knew that just as much as he could ever know that, and if he had wanted to prove something to, or because of, Cinder, he had certainly picked the wrong person to prove it with.

When I got to the exit I glanced back and saw Hector in the throng, struggling toward me. And although because of the music I couldn't hear him, I could see that he was calling my name. I stood in the cool air outside and closed the door slowly against the throbbing room, watching, like a scientist watching the demise of an experiment, as Hector's expression changed from surprise to consternation to . . . what? Was he enraged? Affronted? Relieved?

On the subway, I thought how if Hector had been there with me, if we had been heading downtown together, tired out from dancing, we would have looked aligned. His restful, measuring regard as he leaned back against the wall of the car would have been matched by mine, and our arms would have been close enough so that I could feel the dissipating heat from his against my much paler, thinner one.

There was a group of girls balancing at one of the car's center poles. They were slight and black-haired, like the girl Hector had been talking to, and like her they had long, brilliant nails. Their wrists were marvelously fragile, and their feet, in shiny leather, were like little hooves. I had never asked to compete with such girls, I thought, fuming.

. . .

I wanted to be alone when I got back to the apartment, but Mitchell was in the kitchen, pushing something around on a little hand mirror with a straw, and Cinder was lying on the floor in the peacock-blue dress.

"The dress with the bad seam!" I said.

"Madame wishes another snootful?" Mitchell asked, offering Cinder the mirror.

"Christ, no." Cinder turned over and groaned. "What is that stuff, anyhow?"

"Drug du jour," Mitchell said. "It was on sale."

"Oh, Mitchell, Jesus," she said. Mitchell had been right. She looked even better in that dress than the girl in the store had.

"Charlie," she said, turning to me. I could see that she had been crying. "Listen. Let me ask you something. Do men always tell you that you're really great in bed? That you're the best?"

Only an instant escaped before I knew what to answer. "Always," I said. "They always say that."

"They are so sick," she said. "What a bunch of sickos."

"Guess you had a bad time with John Paul," I said, even though I really didn't want to hear about it.

"That about sums it up," she said. "See that stuff on the floor? That used to be my gorgeous ceramic bowl. I really wish you'd been here, Charlie. I needed you."

"I was needed by you elsewhere," I said. "Remember Hector?"

"Hector?" she said. "What were you doing with Hector?"

"What was I doing with Hector?" I said. "How should I know what I was doing with Hector! I was doing you a favor, that's what I was doing with Hector!"

"Charlie," Cinder said. "What's the matter? Are you mad at me?"

"I'm not mad at you," I said. "Just don't call me that name, please. It's a man's name. My name is Charlotte."

"Come on," Cinder said. "Let's have it. Tell Cinder why you've got a hair across your ass."

"I do not have a hair across my ass," I said. "Whatever that means. I do not have a hair across my ass in any way. It's just that I got Hector out of here so you could see John Paul and then you don't even say, 'Thank you, Charlotte. I really appreciate that.' "

"Thank you, Charlotte. I really appreciate that," Cinder said. "Charlie—Sorry. Charlotte. Listen. You're my best friend. What point would there be in my saying, 'Oh, thank you, Charlotte,' every time you did anything for me? You do thousands of things for me."

"Well," I said.

"Just like I do thousands of things for you. I mean, you know that I do things for you because I care about you and because I want to, not because I feel like I have to or because I want you to owe me anything. So you don't have to say, 'Thank you, Cinder, for letting me come live with you when I had no place else to go. . . . Thank you, Cinder, for dragging me around with you everywhere and introducing me to all your friends.' I know you feel gratitude toward me, just like I feel gratitude toward you. But that's not the point."

"Well, I know," I said. What point? "But still."

"And anyhow," she said, "I did ask you to get that guy out of the apartment, but I didn't ask you to spend the rest of your life with him. What did you do, anyhow?"

"We had dinner," I said.

"Dinner! How hilarious!"

"I don't see why," I said. "People eat dinner every night. Besides, I had to do something with him. And then"—oh, so what, I thought—"we went dancing."

"Oh, unbelievable!" Cinder said. "I can just see it. One of those places full of little Latino girls in pressed jeans and heels, boys covered with jewelry . . ."

"That's—" I said. "That's—" I tried to seize the sensation

that rippled under my hand, of gold against Hector's skin as he drank his Coke and laughed with the girl, but the sensation dried, leaving me with only the empty image.

"One of those places where everyone does this superstructured dancing, one of those places with putrid airwave rock . . ." Cinder said.

"One of those places where everyone's bilingual," I said. "Besides, you were going to go out with him yourself."

"Go out with him, yeah, but not, like, necessarily into public. I mean, God, Charlie—Charlotte—you were so nice to him!"

"Actually," I said, and a thought froze me where I stood, "he was nice to me." I looked at Cinder in horror, seeing the distress on Hector's face as I'd shut the door against him and the roomful of dancers. "He was nice to me, and I just left him there."

"Well," Cinder said. "He'll live."

"I might have hurt his feelings," I said. "It was a mean thing to do."

"Well, it wasn't really mean," Cinder said. "Besides, you're right. It was me he asked out, not you."

My brain started to revolve inside my skull, tumbling its inventory. "I'm going to call him and apologize," I said, rummaging through my pocket for the piece of paper with his number on it.

"God," Cinder said, looking at me. "He gave you his number?"

"To tell you the truth—" I said. And then I couldn't say anything else for several seconds. "He gave me his number for you. He wanted you to call him."

"Charlotte," Cinder said, rolling over. "You liked him."

"He's a perfectly nice man," I snapped. "I neither liked nor disliked him."

"Man?" Cinder said. "He's probably just barely gone

through some puberty rite where he had to spear a sow or something."

"Don't be ridiculous," I said. "He's studying computer engineering. And you know what, Cinder? You're a racist—"

"Racist!" she said. "Now, where is *that* coming from?"

"That's right," I said, "you think you can say these idiotic things about him because he's a Puerto Rican. You don't take him seriously because he's a Puerto Rican—"

"It is not because he's a Puerto Rican!" she said.

"Not because he's a Puerto Rican," Mitchell echoed, and Cinder and I swiveled at the sound of his voice. "Not because he's a Puerto Rican. Because he's *like* a Puerto Rican. He's a Cuban."

"Cuban!" Cinder and I said in unison.

"At least, that's what he told me," Mitchell said. "When we were waiting for Cinder." Mitchell's eyes moved from Cinder to me and back again while we stared at him. His face looked white and slippery, like a bathroom tile. "Hector," he said finally. "You mean the guy who was here before. The Cuban."

"The Cuban!" Cinder whooped. "That's right—the Cuban, Charlie! Who's the racist now, huh?"

"Why don't you get off the floor?" I said. "You're getting stuff all over that dress."

"Come on, Charlotte," Cinder said, but she stood up, and for an instant she looked terribly uncertain. "I really don't see why you're getting so crazy about this. This is just *funny.*"

Funny, I thought. It was funny.

But it wasn't that funny. "There isn't a thing wrong with that dress, is there?" I said. "Besides—" I took a breath. "Hector didn't think I looked like a dinosaur skeleton—"

"Dinosaur skeleton?" Cinder said. "What on earth are you talking about, Charlotte? Why would anybody think you look like a dinosaur skeleton? I really don't know what your problem is. You act like everyone's trying to kill you. You sit there with your mouth open and your finger in your nose like you don't know anything and you can't understand anything and you can't do anything and you want me to tell you what's going on all the time. But that's not what you want at all. You don't really care what I think. You don't care what Mitchell thinks. You just like to make people think you're completely pathetic, and then everyone feels absolutely horrible so you don't really have to pay any attention to anybody. You're like one of those things that hang upside down from trees pretending to be dead so no one will shoot it! You're an awful friend!"

I stared at Cinder.

Good heavens, yes.

But it was too late for me to do anything about being a bad friend. I stared and stared at Cinder's unhappy little face, and then I grabbed my suitcase from the closet and started sweeping things into it from the shelves. Oh, and Mr. Bunder—Hector, Cinder was right. I flooded with shame.

"Charlotte—" Cinder said, but there was nothing else I needed to know, and I scooped my stuff off the shelves and threw it into my suitcase as if I'd been visited by a power. "Charlotte—I'm sorry. I just meant you have a low self-opinion. You should try to be more positive about yourself."

"You'd better see if Mitchell's all right," I said, glancing around to see if there was anything I'd forgotten. "I don't think he is."

"Mitchell," Cinder said, "are you all right?"

"I just don't feel like talking right now," Mitchell said.

"Oh, great," Cinder said. "What a great evening. One friend crashing around like Joan Crawford, and the other fried to a fucking crisp. Come on, Charlotte. Just let's calm down and put your stuff away. John Paul will probably show up any minute to apologize, and he hates a mess."

And, Lord—I'd almost forgotten my photograph of Robert. What was it doing up there anyway—as if he were the president of some company? I yanked it from the wall with both hands, and it tore in half. "Oh, Charlotte," Cinder said. But, to my surprise, I didn't care. Robert had never looked like that picture anyhow. That was how I'd wanted him to look, but he hadn't looked like that.

"O.K., everyone," Cinder said. "Let's just be like normal people now, O.K.? Let's just relax and have a beer or something. Beer, Mitchell?" she asked, holding a bottle out to him, but he seemed to be listening for a distant signal.

"Charlotte," she said. "Beer?" But I, too, was busy elsewhere, and I didn't turn when she said, "Shit. Well, cheers," to see her tilt back the bottle herself, trying to make it look as if everything were completely under control. Well, she could try to make it look like that, she could try to make anything look like anything she wanted, but right then I just wanted everything to look like itself, whatever it might be. And I remember so clearly that moment, standing there astride my suitcase, with part of that photograph of Robert in each hand, my legs trembling and my heart racing with a dark exultation, as if I'd just, in the grace of an instant, been thrown wide of some mortal danger.

What It Was Like, Seeing Chris

While I sit with all the other patients in the waiting room, I always think that I will ask Dr. Wald what exactly is happening to my eyes, but when I go into his examining room alone it is dark, with a circle of light on the wall, and the doctor is standing with his back to me arranging silver instruments on a cloth. The big chair is empty for me to go sit in, and each time then I feel as if I have gone into a dream straight from being awake, the way you do sometimes at night, and I go to the chair without saying anything.

The doctor prepares to look at my eyes through a machine. I put my forehead and chin against the metal bands and look into the tiny ring of blue light while the doctor dabs quickly at my eye with something, but my head starts to feel numb, and I have to lift it back. "Sorry," I say. I shake my head and put it back against the metal. Then I stare into the blue light and try to hold my head still and to convince myself that there is no needle coming toward my eye, that my eye is not anesthetized.

"Breathe," Dr. Wald says. "Breathe." But my head always goes numb again, and I pull away, and Dr. Wald has to wait for me to resettle myself against the machine. "Nervous today, Laurel?" he asks, not interested.

One Saturday after I had started going to Dr. Wald, Maureen and I walked around outside our old school. We dangled on the little swings with our knees bunched while the dry leaves blew around us, and Maureen told me she was sleeping with Kevin. Kevin is a sophomore, and to me he had seemed much older than we were when we'd begun high school in September. "What is it like?" I asked.

"Fine." Maureen shrugged. "Who do you like these days, anyhow? I notice you haven't been talking much about Dougie."

"No one," I said. Maureen stopped her swing and looked at me with one eyebrow raised, so I told her—although I was sorry as soon as I opened my mouth—that I'd met someone in the city.

"In the city?" she said. Naturally she was annoyed. "How did you get to meet someone in the city?"

It was just by accident, I told her, because of going to the eye doctor, and anyway it was not some big thing. That was what I told Maureen, but I remembered the first time I had seen Chris as surely as if it were a stone I could hold in my hand.

It was right after my first appointment with Dr. Wald. I had taken the train into the city after school, and when the doctor was finished with me I was supposed to take a taxi to my sister Penelope's dancing school, which was on the east side of the Park, and do homework there until Penelope's class was over and Mother picked us up. Friends of my parents ask me if I want to be a dancer, too, but they are being polite.

Across the street from the doctor's office, I saw a place called

Jake's. I stared through the window at the long shining bar and mirrors and round tables, and it seemed to me I would never be inside a place like that, but then I thought how much I hated sitting outside Penelope's class and how much I hated the doctor's office, and I opened the door and walked right in.

I sat down at a table near the wall, and I ordered a Coke. I looked around at all the people with their glasses of colored liquids, and I thought how happy they were—vivid and free and sort of the same, as if they were playing.

I watched the bartender as he gestured and talked. He was really putting on a show telling a story to some people I could only see from the back. There was a man with shiny, straight hair that shifted like a curtain when he laughed, and a man with curly blond hair, and between them a girl in a fluffy sweater. The men—or boys (I couldn't tell, and still don't know)—wore shirts with seams on the back that curved up from their belts to their shoulders. I watched their shirts, and I watched in the mirror behind the bar as their beautiful goldish faces settled from laughing. I looked at them in the mirror, and I particularly noticed the one with the shiny hair, and I watched his eyes get like crescents, as if he were listening to another story, but then I saw he was smiling. He was smiling into the mirror in front of him, and in the mirror I was just staring, staring at him, and he was smiling back into the mirror at me.

The next week I went back to Dr. Wald for some tests, and when I was finished, although I'd planned to go do homework at Penelope's dancing school, I went straight to Jake's instead. The same two men were at the bar, but a different girl was with them. I pretended not to notice them as I went to the table I had sat at before.

I had a Coke, and when I went up to the bar to pay, the one with the shiny hair turned right around in front of me. "Clothes-abuse squad," he said, prizing my wadded-up coat out of my arms. He shook it out and smiled at me. "I'm

Chris," he said, "and this is Mark." His friend turned to me like a soldier who has been waiting, but the girl with them only glanced at me and turned to talk to someone else.

Chris helped me into my coat, and then he buttoned it up, as if I were a little child. "Who are you?" he said.

"Laurel," I said.

Chris nodded slowly. "Laurel," he said. And when he said that, I felt a shock on my face and hands and front as if I had pitched against flat water.

"So you are going out with this guy, or what?" Maureen asked me.

"Maureen," I said. "He's just a person I met." Maureen looked at me again, but I just looked back at her. We twisted our swings up and let ourselves twirl out.

"So what's the matter with your eyes?" Maureen said. "Can't you just wear glasses?"

"Well, the doctor said he couldn't tell exactly what was wrong yet," I said. "He says he wants to keep me under observation, because there might be something happening to my retina." But I realized then that I didn't understand what that meant at all, and I also realized that I was really, but really, scared.

Maureen and I wandered over to the school building and looked in the window of the fourth-grade room, and I thought how strange it was that I used to fit in those miniature chairs, and that a few years later Penelope did, and that my little brother, Paul, fit in them now. There was a sickly old turtle in an aquarium on the sill just like the one we'd had. I wondered if it was the same one. I think they're sort of prehistoric, and some of them live to be a hundred or two hundred years old.

"I bet your mother is completely hysterical," Maureen said.

I smiled. Maureen thinks it's hilarious the way my mother

expects everything in her life (*her* life) to be perfect. "I had to bring her with me last week," I said.

"Ick," Maureen said sympathetically, and I remembered how awful it had been, sitting and waiting next to Mother. Whenever Mother moved—to cross her legs or smooth out her skirt or pick up a magazine—the clean smell of her perfume came over to me. Mother's perfume made a nice little space for her there in the stale office. We didn't talk at all, and it seemed like a long time before an Asian woman took me into a small white room and turned off the light. The woman had a serious face, like an angel, and she wore a white hospital coat over her clothes. She didn't seem to speak much English. She sat me down in front of something which looked like a map of planets drawn in white on black, hanging on the wall.

The woman moved a wand across the map, and the end of the wand glimmered. "You say when you see light," she told me. In the silence I made myself say "Now" over and over as I saw the light blinking here and there upon the planet map. Finally the woman turned on the light in the room and smiled at me. She rolled up the map and put it with the wand into a cupboard.

"Where are you from?" I asked her, to shake off the sound of my voice saying "Now."

She hesitated, and I felt sick, because I thought I had said something rude, but finally the meaning of the question seemed to reach her. "Japanese," she said. She put the back of her hand against my hair. "Very pretty," she said. "Very pretty."

Then Dr. Wald looked at my eyes, and after that Mother and I were brought into his consulting room. We waited, facing the huge desk, and eventually the doctor walked in. There was just a tiny moment when he saw Mother, but then he sat right down and explained, in a sincere, televisionish voice I had never heard him use before, that he wanted to see me once a month. He told my mother there might or might not be "cause for concern," and he spoke right to her, with a little frown as she looked down at her clasped hands. Men always get important like that when they're talking to her, and she and the doctor both looked extra serious, as if they were reminding themselves that it was me they were talking about, not each other. While Mother scheduled me for the last week of each month (on Thursday because of Penelope's class), the cross-looking receptionist seemed to be figuring out how much Mother's clothes cost.

When Mother and I parked in front of Penelope's dancing school, Penelope was just coming out with some of the other girls. They were in jeans, but they all had their hair still pulled up tightly on top of their heads, and Penelope had the floaty, peaceful look she gets after class. Mother smiled at her and waved, but then she looked suddenly at me. "Poor Laurel," she said. Tears had come into her eyes, and answering tears sprang into my own, but mine were tears of unexpected rage. I saw how pleased Mother was, thinking that we were having that moment together, but what I was thinking, as we looked at each other, was that even though I hadn't been able to go to Jake's that afternoon because of her, at least now I would be able to go back once a month and see Chris.

"And all week," I told Maureen, "Mother has been saying I got it from my father's family, and my father says it's glaucoma in his family and his genes have nothing to do with retinas."

"Really?" Maureen asked. "Is something wrong with your dad?"

Maureen is always talking about my father and saying how "attractive" he is. If she only knew the way he talks about her! When she comes over, he sits down and tells her jokes. A few weeks ago when she came by for me, he took her outside in back to show her something and I had to wait a long time. But when she isn't at our house, he acts as if she's just some stranger. Once he said to me that she was cheap.

. . .

Of course, there was no reason for me to think that Chris would be at Jake's the next time I went to the doctor's, but he was. He and Mark were at the bar as if they'd never moved. I went to my little table, and while I drank my Coke I wondered whether Chris could have noticed that I was there. Then I realized that he might not remember me at all.

I was stalling with the ice in the bottom of my glass when Chris sat down next to me. I hadn't even seen him leave the bar. He asked me a lot of things—all about my family and where I lived, and how I came to be at Jake's.

"I go to a doctor right near here," I told him.

"Psychiatrist?" he asked.

All I said was no, but I felt my face stain red.

"I'm twenty-seven," he said. "Doesn't that seem strange to you?"

"Well, some people are," I said.

I was hoping Chris would assume I was much older than I was. People usually did, because I was tall. And it was usually a problem, because they were disappointed in me for not acting older (even if they knew exactly how old I was, like my teachers). But what Chris said was, "I'm much, much older than you. Probably almost twice as old." And I understood that he wanted me to see that he knew perfectly well how old I was. He wanted me to see it, and he wanted me to think it was strange.

When I had to leave, Chris walked me to the bar to say hello to Mark, who was talking to a girl.

"Look," the girl said. She held a lock of my hair up to Mark's, and you couldn't tell whose pale curl was whose. Mark's eyes, so close, also looked just like mine, I saw.

"We could be brother and sister," Mark said, but his voice sounded like a recording of a voice, and for a moment I forgot how things are divided up, and I thought Mark must be having trouble with his eyes, too.

From then on, I always went straight to Jake's after leaving the doctor, and when I passed by the bar I could never help glancing into the mirror to see Chris's face. I would just sit at my table and drink my Coke and listen for his laugh, and when I heard it I felt completely still, the way you do when you have a fever and someone puts his hand on your forehead. And sometimes Chris would come sit with me and talk.

At home and at school, I thought about all the different girls who hung around with Chris and Mark. I thought about them one by one, as if they were little figurines I could take down from a glass case to inspect. I thought about how they looked, and I thought about the girls at school and about Penelope, and I looked in the mirror.

I looked in the mirror over at Maureen's house while Maureen put on nail polish, and I tried to make myself see my sister. We are both pale and long, but Penelope is beautiful, as everyone has always pointed out, and I, I saw, just looked unsettled.

"You could use some makeup," Maureen said, shaking her hands dry, "but you look fine. You're lucky that you're tall. It means you'll be able to wear clothes."

I love to go over to Maureen's house. Maureen is an only child, and her father lives in California. Her mother is away a lot, too, and when she is, Carolina, the maid, stays over. Carolina was there that night, and she let us order in pizza for dinner.

"Maureen is my girl. She is my girl," Carolina said after dinner, putting her arms around Maureen. Maureen almost always has some big expression on her face, but when Carolina does that she just goes blank.

Later I asked Maureen about Chris. I was afraid of talking about him because it seemed as if he might dissolve if I did, but I needed Maureen's advice badly. I told her it was just like French class, where there were two words for "you." Sometimes when Chris said "you" to me I would turn red, as if he had used some special word. And I could hardly say "you" to him. It seemed amazing to me sometimes when I was talking to Chris that a person could just walk up to another person and say "you."

"Does that mean something about him?" I asked. "Or is it just about me?"

"It's just you," Maureen said. "It doesn't count. It's just like when you sit down on a bus next to a stranger and you know that your knee is touching his but you pretend it isn't."

Of course Maureen was almost sure to be right. Why wouldn't she be? Still, I kept thinking that it was just possible that she might be wrong, and the next time I saw Chris something happened to make me think she was.

My vision had fuzzed up a lot during that week, and when Dr. Wald looked at my eyes he didn't get up. "Any trouble lately with that sensation of haziness?" he asked.

I got scorching hot when he said that, and I felt like lying. "Not really," I said. "Yes, a bit."

He put some drops in my eyes and sent me to the waiting room, where I looked at bust exercises in *Redbook* till the drops started to work and the print melted on the page. I had never noticed before how practically no one in the waiting room was even pretending to read. One woman had bandages over her eyes, and most people were just staring and blinking. A little boy was halfheartedly moving a stiff plastic horse on the floor in front of him, but he wasn't even looking at it.

The doctor examined my eyes with the light so bright it made the back of my head sting. "Good," he said. "I'll see you in—what is it?—a month."

41

I was out on the street before I realized that I still couldn't see. My vision was like a piece of loosely woven cloth that was pulling apart. In the street everything seemed to be moving off, and all the lights looked like huge haloed globes, bobbing and then dipping suddenly into the pocketed air. The noises were one big pool of sound—horns and brakes and people yelling—and to cross the street I had to plunge into a mob of people and rush along wherever it was they were going.

When I finally got through to Jake's my legs were trembling badly, and I just went right up to Chris at the bar, where he was listening to his friend Sherman tell a story. Without even glancing at me, Chris put his hand around my wrist, and I just stood there next to him, with my wrist in his hand, and I listened, too.

Sherman was telling how he and his band had been playing at some club the night before and during a break, when he'd been sitting with his girlfriend, Candy, a man had come up to their table. "He's completely destroyed," Sherman said, "and Candy and I are not exactly on top of things ourselves. But the guy keeps waving this ring, and the basic idea seems to be that it's his wife's wedding ring. He's come home earlier and his wife isn't there, but the ring is, and he's sure his wife's out screwing around. So the guy keeps telling me about it over and over, and I can't get him to shut up, but finally he notices Candy and he says, 'That your old lady?' 'Yeah,' I tell him. "Good-looking broad,' the guy says, and he hands me the ring. 'Keep it,' the guy says. 'It's for you—not for this bitch with you.' "

One of the girls at the bar reached over and touched the flashing ring that was on a chain around Sherman's neck. "Pretty," she said. "Don't you want it, Candy?" But the girl she had spoken to remained perched on her barstool, with her legs crossed, smiling down at her drink.

"So what did you think of that?" Chris said as he walked

me over to my table and sat down with me. I didn't say anything. "Sherman can be sort of disgusting. But it's not an important thing," Chris said.

The story had made me think about the kids at school—that we don't know yet what our lives are really going to be like. It made me feel that anything might be a thing that's important, and I started to cry, because I had never noticed that I was always lonely in my life until just then, when Chris had understood how much the story had upset me, and had said something to make me feel better.

Chris dipped a napkin into a glass of water and mopped off my face, but I was clutching a pencil in my pocket so hard I broke it, and that started me crying again.

"Hey," Chris said. "Look. It's not dead." He grabbed another napkin and scribbled on it with each half of the pencil. "It's fine, see? Look. That's just how they reproduce. Don't they teach you anything at school? Here," he said. "We'll just tuck them under this, and we'll have two very happy little pencils."

And then, after a while, when I was laughing and talking, all at once he stood up. "I'm sorry to have to leave you like this," he said, "but I promised Mark I'd help him with something." And I saw that Mark and a girl were standing at the bar, looking at us. "Ready," Chris called over to them. "Honey," he said, and a waitress materialized next to him. "Get this lady something to drink and put it on my tab. Thanks," he said. And then he walked out, with Mark and the girl.

But the strange thing was that I don't think Mark had actually been waiting for Chris. I don't think Chris had promised Mark anything. I think Mark and the girl had only been looking at us to look, because I could see that they were surprised when Chris called over to them, and also the three of them stood talking on the sidewalk before they went on together. And right then was when I thought for a minute that Maureen had been wrong about me and Chris. It was not when Chris held my wrist, and not when Chris understood how upset I was, and not when Chris dried off my tears, but it was when Chris left, that I thought Maureen was wrong.

My grades were getting a lot worse, and my father decided to help me with my homework every night after dinner. "All right," he would say, standing behind my chair and leaning over me. "Think. If you want to make an equation out of this question, how do you have to start? We've talked about how to do this, Laurel." But I hated his standing behind me like that so much all I could do was try to send out rays from my back that would make him stand farther away. Too bad I wasn't Maureen. She would have loved it.

For me, every day pointed forward or backward to the last Thursday of each month, but those Thursdays came and went without anything really changing, either at the doctor's or at Jake's, until finally in the spring. Everyone else in my class had spent most of a whole year getting excited or upset about classes and parties and exams and sports, but all those things were one thing to me—a nasty fog that was all around me while I waited.

And then came a Thursday when Chris put his arm around me as soon as I walked into Jake's. "I have to do an errand," he said. "Want a Coke first?"

"I'm supposed to be at my sister's class by six," I said. In case he hadn't been asking me to go with him, I would just seem to be saying something factual.

"I'll get you there," Chris said. He stood in back of me and put both arms around my shoulders, and I could feel exactly where he was touching me. Chris's friends had neutral expressions on their faces as if nothing was happening, and I tried to look as if nothing was happening, too.

As we were going out the door, a girl coming in grabbed Chris. "Are you leaving?" she said.

"Yeh," Chris told her.

"Well, when can I talk to you?" she asked.

"I'll be around later, honey," Chris said, but he just kept walking. "Christ, what a bimbo," he said to me, shaking his head, and I felt ashamed for no reason.

When Chris drove his fast little bright car it seemed like part of him, and there I was, inside it, too. I felt that we were inside a shell together, and we could see everything that was outside it, and we drove and drove and Chris turned the music loud. And suddenly Chris said, "I'd really like to see you a lot more. It's too bad you can't come into the city more often." I didn't know what to say, but I gathered that he didn't expect me to say anything.

We parked in a part of the city where the buildings were huge and squat. Chris rang a bell and we ran up flights of wooden stairs to where a man in white slacks and an unbuttoned shirt was waiting.

"Joel, this is Laurel," Chris said.

"Hello, Laurel," Joel said. He seemed to think there was something funny about my name, and he looked at me the way I've noticed grown men often do, as if I couldn't see them back perfectly well.

Inside, Chris and Joel went through a door, leaving me in an enormous room with white sofas and floating mobiles. The room was immaculate except for a silky purple-and-gold kimono lying on the floor. I picked up the kimono and rubbed it against my cheek and put it on over my clothes. Then I went and looked out the window at the city stretching on and on. In a building across the street, figures moved slowly behind dirty glass. They were making things, I suppose.

After a while Chris and Joel burst back into the room. Chris's eyes were shiny, and he was grinning like crazy.

"Hey," Joel said, grabbing the edges of the kimono I was wearing. "That thing looks better on her than on me."

"What wouldn't?" Chris said. Joel stepped back as Chris put his arms around me from behind again.

"I resent that, I resent that! But I don't deny it!" Joel said. Chris was kissing my neck and my ears, and both he and Joel were giggling.

I wondered what would happen if Chris and I were late and Mother saw me drive up in Chris's car, but we darted around in the traffic and shot along the avenues and pulled up near Penelope's dancing school with ten minutes to spare. Then, instead of saying anything, Chris just sat there with one hand still on the wheel and the other on the shift, and he didn't even look at me. When I just experimentally touched his sleeve and he still didn't move, I more or less flung myself on top of him and started crying into his shirt. I was in his lap, all tangled up, and I was kissing him and kissing him, and my hands were moving by themselves.

Suddenly I thought of all the people outside the car walking their bouncy little dogs, and I thought how my mother might pull up at any second, and I sat up fast and opened my eyes. Everything looked slightly different from the way it had been looking inside my head—a bit smaller and farther away—and I realized that Chris had been sitting absolutely still, and he was staring straight ahead.

"Goodbye," I said, but Chris still didn't move or even look at me. I couldn't understand what had happened to Chris.

"Wait," Chris said, still without looking at me. "Here's my phone number." He shook himself and wrote it out slowly.

At the corner I looked back and saw that Chris was still there, leaning back and staring out the windshield.

. . .

"Why did he give me his phone number, do you think?" I asked Maureen. We were at a party in Peter Klingeman's basement.

"I guess he wants you to call him," Maureen said. I know she didn't really feel like talking. Kevin was standing there, with his hand under her shirt, and she was sort of jumpy. "Frankly, Laurel, he sounds a bit weird to me, if you don't mind my saying," Maureen said. I felt ashamed again. I wanted to talk to Maureen more, but Kevin was pulling her off to the Klingemans' TV room.

Then Dougie Pfeiffer sat down next to me. "I think Maureen and Kevin have a really good relationship," he said.

I was wondering how I ever could have had a crush on him in eighth grade when I realized it was my turn to say something. "Did you ever notice," I said, "how some people say 'in eighth grade' and other people say 'in *the* eighth grade'?"

"Laurel," Dougie said, and he grabbed me, shoving his tongue into my mouth. Then he took his tongue back out and let me go. "God, I'm sorry, Laurel," he said.

I didn't really care what he did with his tongue. I thought how his body, under his clothes, was just sort of an outline, like a kid's drawing, and I thought of the long zipper on Chris's leather jacket, and a little rip I noticed once in his jeans, and the weave of the shirt that I'd cried on.

I carried Chris's phone number around with me everywhere, and finally I asked my mother if I could go into the city after school on Thursday and then meet her at Penelope's class.

"No," Mother said.

"Why not?" I said.

"We needn't discuss this, Laurel," my mother said.

"You let me go in to see Dr. Wald," I said.

"Don't," Mother said. "Anyhow, you can't just . . . wander around in New York."

"I have to do some shopping," I said idiotically.

Mother started to say something, but then she stopped, and she looked at me as if she couldn't quite remember who I was. "Oh, who cares?" she said, not especially to me.

There was a permanent little line between Mother's eyebrows, I noticed, and suddenly I felt I was seeing her through a window. I went up to my room and cried and cried, but later I couldn't get to sleep, thinking about Chris.

I called him Thursday.

"What time is it?" he said with his blistery laugh. "I just woke up." He told me he had gone to a party the night before and when he came out his car had been stolen. He was stoned, and he thought the sensible thing was to walk over to Mark's place, which is miles from his, but on the way he found his car parked out on the street. "I should've reported it, but I figured, hey, what a great opportunity, so I just stole it back."

Chris didn't mention anything about our seeing each other.

"I've got to come into the city today to do some stuff," I said.

"Yeah," Chris said. "I've got a lot to do today myself."

Well, that was that, obviously, unless I did something drastic. "I thought I'd stop in and say hi, if you're going to be around," I said. My heart was jumping so much it almost knocked me down.

"Great," Chris said. "That's really sweet." But his voice sounded muted, and I wasn't at all surprised when I got to Jake's and he wasn't there. I was on my third Coke when Chris walked in, but a girl wearing lots of bracelets waylaid him at the bar, and he sat down with her.

I didn't dare finish my Coke or ask for my check. All I could do was stay put and do whatever Chris made me do. Finally the girl at the bar left, giving Chris a big, meaty kiss, and he wandered over and sat down with me.

"God. Did you see that girl who was sitting with me?" he said. "That girl is so crazy. There's nothing she won't put in her mouth. I was at some party a few weeks ago, and I walk in through this door, 'cause I'm looking for the john, and there's Beverly, lying on the floor stark naked. So you know what she does?"

"No," I said.

"She says, 'Excuse me,' and instead of putting something on she reaches up and turns out the light. Now, that's thinkin', huh?" He laughed. "Have you finished all those things you had to do?" he asked me.

"Yes," I said.

"That's great," Chris said. "I'm really running around like a chicken today. Honey," he said to a waitress, "put that on my tab, will you?" He pointed at my watery Coke.

"Sandra was looking for you," the waitress said. "Did she find you?"

"Yeah, thanks," Chris said. He gave me a kiss on the cheek, which was the first time he had kissed me at all, except at Joel's, and he left.

I knew I had made some kind of mistake, but I couldn't figure out what it was. I would only be able to figure it out from Chris, but it would be two weeks until I saw him again. Every night, I looked out the window at the red glow of the city beyond all the quiet little houses and yards, and every night after I got into bed I felt it draw nearer and nearer, hovering just beyond my closed eyes, with Chris inside it. While I slept, it receded again; but by morning, when I woke up and put on my school clothes, I had come one day closer.

After my next appointment with Dr. Wald, Chris wasn't at Jake's. For the first time since I had gone to Jake's, Chris didn't come at all.

On the way home it was all I could do not to cry in front of Mother and Penelope. And I wondered what I was going to do from that afternoon on.

"And how was Dr. Wald today?" my father said when we sat down for dinner.

"I didn't ask," I said.

My father paused to acknowledge my little joke.

"What I meant," he said, "was how is my lovely daughter?"

I knew he was trying to say something nice, but he could have picked something sincere for once. I hated the way he had taken off his jacket and opened up his collar and rolled up his sleeves, and I thought I would be sick if he stood behind my chair later. "Penelope is your lovely daughter," I said, and threw my silverware onto the table.

From upstairs I listened. I knew that Penelope would have frozen, the way she does when someone says in front of me how pretty she is, but no one said anything about me that I could hear.

Later, Penelope and Paul and I made up a story together, the way we had when we were younger. Paul fell asleep suddenly in the middle with little tears in the corners of his eyes, and I tucked Penelope into bed. When I smoothed out the covers, a shadow of relief crossed her face.

That Saturday, Mother took me shopping in the city without Penelope or Paul. "I thought we should get you a present," Mother said. "Something pretty." She smiled at me in a strange, stiff way.

"Thank you," I said. I felt good that we were driving together, but I was sad, too, that Mother was trying to bring me into the clean, bright, fancy, daytime part of New York that Penelope's dancing school was in, because when would she accept that there was no place there for me? I wondered if Mother wanted to say something to me, but we just drove silently, except for once, when Mother pointed out a lady in a big, white, flossy fur coat.

At Bonwit's, Mother picked out an expensive dress for me. "What do you think?" she said when I tried it on.

I was glad that Mother had chosen it, because it was very

pretty, and it was white, and it was expensive, but in the mirror I just looked skinny and dazed. "I like it," I said. "But don't you think it looks wrong on me?"

"Well, it seems fine to me, but it's up to you," Mother said. "You can have it if you want."

"But look, Mother," I said. "Look. Do you think it's all right?"

"If you don't like it, don't get it," she said. "It's your present."

At home after dinner I tried the white dress on again and stared at myself in the mirror, and I thought maybe it looked a little better.

I went down to the living room, where Mother was stretched out on the sofa with her feet on my father's lap. When I walked in he started to get up, but Mother didn't move. "My God," my father said. "It's Lucia."

My mother giggled. "Wedding scene or mad scene?" she said.

Upstairs I folded the dress back into the box for Bonwit's to pick up. At night I watched bright dancing patterns in the dark and I dreaded going back to Dr. Wald.

The doctor didn't seem to notice anything unusual at my next appointment. I still had to face walking the short distance to Jake's, though. I practically fell over from relief when I saw Chris at the bar, and he reached out as I went by and reeled me in, smiling. He was talking to Mark and some other friends, and he stood me with my back to him and rubbed my shoulders and temples. I tried to smile hello to Mark, who was staring at me with his pale eyes, but he just kept staring, listening to Chris. I closed my eyes and leaned back against Chris, who folded his arms around me. When Chris finished his story, everyone laughed except me. Chris blew a little stream of air into my hair, ruffling it up. "Want to take a ride?" he said.

We drove for a while, fast, circling the city, and Chris slammed tapes into the tape deck. Then we parked and Chris turned and looked at me.

"What do you want to do?" Chris asked me.

"Now?" I said, but he just looked at me, and I didn't know what he meant. "Nothing," I said.

"Have I seemed preoccupied to you lately, honey?" he asked.

"I guess maybe a little," I said, even though I hadn't really ever thought about how he seemed. He just seemed like himself. But he told me that yes, he had been preoccupied. He had borrowed some money to start an audio business, but he had to help out a cousin, too. I couldn't make any sense of what he was talking about, and I didn't really care, either. I was thinking that now he had finally called me "honey." It made me so happy, so happy, even though "honey" was what he called everyone, and I had been the only Laurel.

Chris talked and talked, and I watched his mouth as the words came out. "I know you wonder what's going on with me," he said. "What it is is I worry that you're so young. I'm a difficult person. There are a lot of strange things about me. I'm really crazy about you, you know. I'm really crazy about you, but I can't ask you to see me."

"Why don't I come in and stay over with you a week from Friday," I said. "Can I?"

Chris blinked. "Terrific, honey," he said cautiously. "That's a date."

I arranged it with Maureen that I would say I was staying at her house. "Don't wear underwear," Maureen told me. "That really turns guys on."

Chris and I met at Jake's, but we didn't stay there long. We drove all over the city, stopping at different places. Chris knew people everywhere, and we would sit down at the bar and talk to them. We went to an apartment with some of the people we ran into, where everyone lay around listening to tapes. And once we went to a club and watched crowds of people change like waves with the music, under flashing lights.

Chris didn't touch me, not once, not even accidentally, all during that time.

Sometime between things we stopped for food. I couldn't eat, but Chris seemed starving. He ate his cheeseburger and French fries, and then he ate mine. And then he had a big piece of pecan pie.

Late, very late, we climbed into the car again, but there was nothing left to do. "Home?" Chris said without turning to me.

Chris's apartment seemed so strange, and maybe that was just because it was real. But I had surely never been inside such a small, plain place to live before, and Chris hardly seemed to own anything. There were a few books on a shelf, and a little kitchen off in the corner, with a pot on the stove. It was up several flights of dark stairs, in a brick building, and it must have been on the edge of the city, because I could see water out of the window, and ribbons of highway elevated on huge concrete pillars, and dark piers.

Chris's bed, which was tightly made with the sheet turned back over the blanket, looked very narrow. All the music we had been hearing all night was rocketing around in my brain, and I felt jittery and a bit sick. Chris passed a joint to me, and he lay down with his hands over his eyes. I sat down on the edge of the bed next to him and waited, but he didn't move. "Remember when I asked you a while ago what you wanted to do and you said 'Nothing'?" Chris asked me.

"But that was—" I started to say, and then the funny sound of Chris's voice caught up with me, and all the noise in my head shut off.

"I remember," Chris said. Then a long time went by.

"Why did you come here, Laurel?" Chris said.

When I didn't answer, he said, "Why? Why did you come here? You're old enough now to think about what you're doing." And I remembered I had never been alone with him before, except in his car.

"Yes," I said into the dead air. Whatever I'd been waiting for all that time had vanished. "It's all right."

"It's all right?" Chris said furiously. "Well, good. It's all right, then." He was still lying on his back with his hands over his eyes, and neither of us moved. I thought I might shatter.

Sometime in the night Chris spoke again. "Why are you angry?" he said. His voice was blurred, as if he'd been asleep. I wanted to tell him I wasn't angry, but it seemed wrong, and I was afraid of what would happen if I did. I put my arms around him and started kissing him. He didn't move a muscle, but I kept right on. I knew it was my only chance, and I thought that if I stopped I would have to leave. "Don't be angry," he said.

Sometime in the night I sprang awake. Chris was holding my wrists behind my back with one hand and unbuttoning my shirt with the other, and his body felt very tense. "Don't!" I said, before I understood.

" 'Don't!' " echoed Chris, letting go of me. He said it just the way I had, sounding just as frightened. He fell asleep immediately then, sprawled out, but I couldn't sleep anymore, and later, when Chris spoke suddenly into the dark, I felt I'd been expecting him to. "Your parents are going to worry," he said deliberately, as if he were reading.

"No," I said. I wondered how long he had been awake. "They think I'm at Maureen's." And then I realized how foolish it was for me to have said that.

"They'll worry," he said. "They will worry. They'll be very frightened."

And then I was so frightened myself that the room bulged and there was a sound in my ears like ball bearings rolling around wildly. I put my hands against my hot face, and my skin felt to me as if it belonged to a stranger. It felt like a marvel—brand-new and slightly moist—and I wondered if anyone else would ever touch it and feel what I had felt.

"Look—" Chris said. He sounded blurry again, and helpless and sad. "Look—see how bad I am for you, Laurel? See how I make you cry?" Then he put his arms around me, and we lay there on top of the bed for a long, long time, and sometimes we kissed each other. My shirt sleeve was twisted and it hurt against my arm, but I didn't move.

When the night red began finally to bleach out of the sky, I touched Chris's wrist. "I have to go now," I said. That wasn't true, of course. My parents would expect me to stay at Maureen's till at least noon. "I have to be home when it gets light."

"Do you?" Chris said, but his eyes were closed.

I stood up and buttoned my shirt.

"I'll take you to the train," Chris said.

At first he didn't move, but finally he stood up, too. "I need some coffee," he said. And when he looked at me my heart sank. He was smiling. He looked as if he wanted to start it up—start it all again.

I went into the bathroom, so I wouldn't be looking at Chris. There was a tub and a sink and a toilet. Chris uses them, I thought, as if that would explain something to me, but the thought was like a sealed package. Stuck in the corner of the mirror over the sink was a picture of a man's face torn from a magazine. It was a handsome face, but I didn't like it.

"That's a guy I went to high school with," Chris said from behind me. "He's a very successful actor now."

"That's nice," I said, and waited as long as I could. "Look—it's almost light."

And in the instant that Chris glanced at the window, where

in fact the faintest dawn was showing, I stepped over to the door and opened it.

In the car, Chris seemed the way he usually did. "I'm sorry I'm so tired, honey," he said. "I've been having a rough time lately. We'll get together another time, when I'm not so hassled."

"Yes," I said. "Good." I don't think he really remembered the things we had said in the dark.

When we stopped at the station, Chris put his arm across me, but instead of opening the door he just held the handle. "You think I'm really weird, don't you?" he said, and smiled at me.

"I think you're tired," I said, making myself smile back. And Chris released the handle and let me out.

I took the train through the dawn and walked from the station, pausing carefully if it looked as though someone was awake inside a house I was passing. Once a dog barked, and I stood absolutely still for minutes.

I threw chunks from the lawn at Maureen's window, so Carolina wouldn't wake up, but I was afraid the whole town would be out by the time Maureen heard.

Maureen came down the back way and got me. We each put on one of her bathrobes, and we made a pot of coffee, which is something I'm not allowed to drink.

"What happened?" Maureen asked.

"I don't know," I said.

"What do you mean, you don't know?" Maureen said. "You were there."

Even though my face was in my hands, I could tell Maureen was staring at me. "Well," she said after a while. "Hey. Want to play some Clue?" She got the Clue board down from her room, and we played about ten games.

. . .

The next week I really did stay over at Maureen's.

"Again?" my mother said. "We must do something for Mrs. MacIntyre. She's been so nice to you."

Dougie and Kevin showed up together after Maureen and Carolina and I had eaten a barbecued chicken from the deli and Carolina had gone to her room to watch the little TV that Mrs. MacIntyre had put there. I figured it was no accident that Dougie had shown up with Kevin. It had to be a brainstorm of Maureen's, and I thought, Well, so what. So after Maureen and Kevin went up to Maureen's room I went into the den with Dougie. We pretty much knew from classes and books and stuff what to do, so we did it. The thing that surprised me most was that you always read in books about "stained sheets," "stained sheets," and I never knew what that meant, but I guess I thought it would be pretty interesting. But the little stuff on the sheet just looked completely innocuous, like Elmer's glue, and it seemed that it might even dry clear like Elmer's glue. At any rate, it didn't seem like anything that Carolina would have to absolutely kill herself about when she did the laundry.

We went back into the living room to wait, and I sat while Dougie walked around poking at things on the shelves. "Look," Dougie said, "Clue." But I just shrugged, and after a while Maureen and Kevin came downstairs looking pretty pleased with themselves.

I sat while Dr. Wald finished at the machine, and I waited for him to say something, but he didn't.

"Am I going to go blind?" I asked him finally, after all those months.

"What?" he said. Then he remembered to look at me and smile. "Oh, no, no. We won't let it come to that."

I knew what I would find at Jake's, but I had to go anyway,

just to finish. "Have you seen Chris?" I asked one of the waitresses. "Or Mark?"

"They haven't been around for a while," she said. "Sheila," she called over to another waitress, "where's Chris these days?"

"Don't ask me," Sheila said sourly, and both of them stared at me.

I could feel my blood traveling in its slow loop, carrying a heavy proudness through every part of my body. I had known Chris could injure me, and I had never cared how much he could injure me, but it had never occurred to me until this moment that I could do anything to him.

Outside, it was hot. There were big bins of things for sale on the sidewalk, and horns were honking, and the sun was yellow and syrupy. I noticed two people who must have been mother and daughter, even though you couldn't really tell how old either of them was. One of them was sort of crippled, and the other was very peculiar looking, and they were all dressed up in stiff, cheap party dresses. They looked so pathetic with their sweaty, eager faces and ugly dresses that I felt like crying. But then I thought that they might be happy, much happier than I was, and that I just felt sorry for them because I thought I was better than they were. And I realized that I wasn't really different from them anyhow—that every person just had one body or another, and some of them looked right and worked right and some of them didn't—and I thought maybe it was myself I was feeling sorry for, because of Chris, or maybe because it was obvious even to me, a total stranger, how much that mother loved her homely daughter in that awful dress.

When Mother and Penelope and I got back home, I walked over to Maureen's house, but I decided not to stop. I walked by the playground and looked in at the fourth-grade room and the turtle that was still lumbering around its dingy aquarium, and it came into my mind how even Paul was older now than the kids who would be sitting in those tiny chairs in the fall, and I thought about all the millions and billions of people in the world, all getting older, all trapped in things that had already happened to them.

When I was a kid, I used to wonder (I bet everyone did) whether there was somebody somewhere on the earth, or even in the universe, or ever had been in all of time, who had had exactly the same experience that I was having at that moment, and I hoped so badly that there was. But I realized then that that could never occur, because every moment is all the things that have happened before and all the things that are going to happen, and every moment is just the way all those things look at one point on their way along a line. And I thought how maybe once there was, say, a princess who lost her mother's ring in a forest, and how in some other galaxy a strange creature might fall, screaming, on the shore of a red lake, and how right that second there could be a man standing at a window overlooking a busy street, aiming a loaded revolver, but how it was just me, there, after Chris, staring at that turtle in the fourth-grade room and wondering if it would die before I stopped being able to see it.

Rafe's Coat

One sparkly evening not long after my husband and I had started divorce proceedings, Rafe stopped by for a drink before taking me out to dinner. In his hand was a spray of flowers, and on his face was an expression of inward alertness, and both of these things I suspected to be accoutrements of love.

"Marvelous new coat," I said. "Alpaca, yes?"

"Yup," Rafe said, dropping it onto a chair with an uncharacteristic lack of attention. "England last week. Well, then!" He looked around brightly in the manner of someone who, having discharged some weighty task, is ready to start afresh.

Heavens, he was behaving oddly. I waited for him to say something enlightening, or to say anything at all, for that matter, which he failed to do, so I sat him down and poured him a drink and waited some more.

"Incredibly strange out there" was his eventual contribution. "Dark and crowded."

"England," I said, mystified. "England has become dark and crowded."

"Yes?" Rafe said. "Oh, actually, I'd been thinking of Sixty-seventh Street."

Hmm. Obviously I would have to give Rafe quite a bit of

encouragement if I wanted to hear about the girlfriend whom, by now, I was absolutely certain he'd acquired. And I did want to. I always enjoyed hearing about, and meeting, his woman of the moment. Rafe, like a hawk, swooped down upon the shiniest thing in sight, and his girls were always exotics of one sort or another, if only, as they often were, exotics ordinaire; but whatever their background, race, or interests, they were all amusing, marvelous looking, unpredictable, and none of them seemed ever to require sleep.

Unfortunately, these flashing lights of Rafe's life tended to burn out rather quickly, no matter how in thrall Rafe was initially. And this was the inevitable consequence, I believed, of the discrepancy between his age and theirs. It was not that I necessarily felt that Rafe should be seeing people of our own age (we were both thirty-three, as it happened). In fact, it would have seemed inappropriate. Rafe, at any age, would simply not be suited for the sobriety of adulthood. Still, the years do pass, and there were Rafe's girls, trailing along a decade or so behind him. They could hardly be blamed if they hadn't accrued enough substance (of the sort that only time can provide) to allow Rafe to stretch out his dealings with them beyond a month or two.

"So. I give up, Rafael," I said. "Tell me. Who is the lucky girl you're in love with tonight?"

"Tonight!" he said, and damned if he didn't look wounded.

Now, Rafe was my friend. It was Rafe who had accompanied me to parties and openings and weekends when John, my husband, was too busy (as he usually was) or not interested enough (and he rarely was), and it was Rafe who pulled me out of any mental mud-wallow I might strand myself in, and it was Rafe I was counting on to amuse me now, while John and I parceled out our holdings and made our adieus and slogged through whatever contractual and emotional dreariness was necessitated by going on with life; and if Rafe was going to mature, this was certainly a very poor moment for him to have chosen to do it.

"As it happens," Rafe confessed unnecessarily, "I have started seeing someone."

"Really," I said.

"She's simply wonderful," he said with the fatuous solemnity of a man on the witness stand.

"Good!" I said. I did hope she was wonderful, even though I deplored the dent she seemed to have put in Rafe's sense of humor. "What does she do?"

"Well . . ." Rafe deliberated. "She's an actress."

"Poor thing," I said after some moments had elapsed during which Rafe executed several groupings of resolute nods. "It's such a difficult way to make a living."

Another nod-group. "It is. Yes it is. That's an Ansel Adams, isn't it? Is it new?"

"Darling. I've just moved it from the dining room."

"Oh, yes, of course." Rafe stared at it blankly. "Well, it's sensational in here, isn't it?"

"So, tell me," I said. "Is your friend in some sort of company or repertory situation? Or does she trot about in the summers being Juliet and My Sister Eileen and so on? Or must she spend every minute subjecting herself to scrutiny and rejection?"

"Well, she's done quite a bit of all of those things, yes. Not at the moment, but that's certainly the idea. Yes."

"Oh, dear," I said. "She doesn't have to work in a restaurant, does she? How awful!"

"Oh, not at all," Rafe said. "No. She's doing very well." He scanned the walls for material.

"I'm glad you like the Ansel Adams, Rafe," I said.

"As a matter of fact," he said, "she has a job on a soap opera."

"Well!" I said. "Isn't that splendid! And it will certainly tide her over until she finds something she wants." Oh, why did Rafe always do this? Girl after girl. He was like some noble hound who daily fetched home the *New York Post* instead of the *Times*.

"What's the matter with that?" Rafe said.

"Nothing," I said. "With what?"

"She's just exactly as much an actress as—oh, God, I don't know—Lady Macbeth would be, in one of those new-wave festivals you're so fond of."

"Just exactly," I said.

"It's honest work," he said.

"Heavens, Rafe," I said. "Did I say it wasn't?" These propositions of his were hardly sturdy enough to rebut.

"I'm quite impressed, really," Rafe said. My goodness, Rafe was bristly! Apparently he was quite embarrassed by this girl. "She's very young, for one thing, and she took herself straight to New York from absolutely nowhere, and immediately she got herself a job in a demanding, lucrative, competitive field."

Field! "Well, you won't get me to say I think it isn't impressive," I said, making it clear that this was to be the end of the discussion. "Can I give you another drink?"

"Please," he said. The sound of pouring gave us something sensible to listen to for a moment.

"So, then," I said. "What's the name of this show she's on?"

"Well," Rafe said, "it's called, as I remember, something on the order of, er, 'This Brief Candle.' " He focused furiously over my ear.

Well, stuffiness is often an early adjunct of infatuation, and I was perfectly willing to let Rafe have his say. If he wanted to tell me that this girl should be knighted—or canonized or bronzed—for getting herself a job on a soap opera, that was fine. What was so irritating was that every time Rafe thought I might open my mouth, he leapt to the attack, and by the time we got into a taxi, I would have been happier getting into a bullring with a bunch of picadors.

Fortunately, the restaurant Rafe had chosen turned out to

be wonderfully soothing. It was luxurious and private, and at the sight of the cloakroom, with its rows of expensive, empty coats that called up a world in which generous, broad-shouldered men, and women in marvelous dresses (much like the one I myself happened to be wearing), inclined toward each other on banquettes, I was pierced by a feeling so keen and unalloyed it might have been called—I don't know what it might have been called. It felt like—well, grief . . . actually.

During dinner, Rafe and I stayed on neutral territory—a piece of recent legislation, Marty Harnishveiger's renovations, an exceptionally pointless East Side murder, and my husband and marriage.

"One really oughtn't be able to describe one's marriage as neutral territory, do you think?" I asked Rafe.

"Considering the minefields that most of our friends' marriages are," he said, "neutral territory might be the preferable alternative."

"I suppose," I said. "But 'preferable alternative' hardly seems, in itself, the answer to one's prayers. At least all those minefield marriages around us must have something in them to make them explosive."

"Probably incompatibility," Rafe pointed out. "On the other hand, I never really did understand why you married John."

"He's not so bad," I said. I reminded Rafe that John was in many ways an exemplary husband. "He's highly respected, he has marvelous taste, he's very good looking in a harmless sort of way, he's rich to begin with and makes good money on top of that. . . ."

"No, I know," Rafe said. "I didn't mean to insult him. He's a very nice guy, after all. And I have to say you looked terrific together. It's just that—well, you never seemed to have much fun with him."

"Fun?" I said. "How do you expect the poor guy to be fun? He's not even alive."

Rafe looked suddenly stricken, as if he'd realized he might have left his wallet somewhere. I wondered what he was thinking about, but I didn't want to pry, so I went on. "Have you heard he's been seeing Marcia Meaver? They're probably sitting around together right this minute, wowing each other with forbidden tales of investment banking."

"She's quite nice, though," Rafe said after a moment. "I've met her."

"Oh, I suppose she is," I said. "I didn't mean to be nasty."

"I know," Rafe said. "I know you didn't."

We ordered brandies and leaned back against the leather, considering. I was just getting bored when Rafe hunched forward, peering into his glass.

"What?" I said.

"Nothing," he said. "Ah, well. I guess it just doesn't do, does it, to marry someone on the strength of their credentials."

"Oh, good point, Rafe," I said. "How ever did you think of it?"

"Sorry," he said.

"You're really crazy about this girl, aren't you?" I said.

Then, oddly enough, Rafe just laughed, and his sunny self shone out from behind his strange mood. "I know," he said, "I know. I always say, 'This time it's different, this time it's different,' but you know what? Each time, poor girls, it *is* different." And Rafe looked so pleased with himself and his girls, so confident of my approval—his smile was so heedless, so winning, so *his*—that, well, I was simply forced to smile back.

Smile or no, though, this girl had obviously had an effect on Rafe, and it occurred to me that it would be interesting to tune in on her show to see if I could pick her out from among her fellow soap girls. So the next morning I picked up a *TV Guide* on my way home from exercise class and scanned it for "This Brief Candle." I always did my work in the afternoons (we members of the grants committee of the foundation worked separately until after we had made our initial recommendations to the panel), and I had a lunch date at one, so I was pleased to find that the show aired at eleven.

When I turned on the set, a few cats wavered into view and discussed cat food, and then, after an awe-inspiring chord or two, an hour in the lives of the characters of "This Brief Candle" was revealed to the world. During this hour, a girl I later came to know as Ellie confided to her mother that she suspected her boyfriend of cheating on an exam in order to get into medical school to please his father. Then Colleen, apparently a school counselor of some sort, made a phone call to a person who seemed to be the father—no, the stepfather—of another person, named Stevie. She wished to talk to him, she said, about Stevie's performance. Ominous music suggested that Stevie's performance was either remarkably poor or a mere pretext for Colleen to see Stevie's stepfather. Perhaps Stevie and Ellie's boyfriend were one and the same person! No, surely this Stevie fellow must be far too young. But, on the other hand—

Well, no time to mull that over: two men, Hank and Brent, I gathered, were parking a car outside a house and hoping that they would not arouse the suspicions of Eric, who, it seemed, was someone inside the house; Eric could not be made nervous, they told each other between heavy, charged silences, if they were ever going to get inside and break into his safe for those papers.

Oop! An office materialized, containing a devastatingly attractive silver-haired gentleman. Eric? Ellie's father? Stevie's stepfather? Aha! Not Ellie's father, because Ellie's *mother* walked in and said, "Forgive me for coming here like this, Mr. Armstrong, but I must speak to you right away about the plans for the new power plant." And surely Ellie's mother would not go around calling this man "Mr. Armstrong" if he were Ellie's father. Although she might, come to think of it, under certain circumstances, because, for instance, I couldn't help noticing that Mr. Armstrong's secretary was sitting right there with a very funny look on her face. (But wait: *plans* are something that could fit in a *safe*! And maybe Mr. Armstrong's secretary looked like that because she was in cahoots with Hank or Brent. Or Eric, for that matter.) "Come in here, Cordelia, where we can talk privately," said Mr. Armstrong, escorting Ellie's mother into an interior office. ("Cordelia," when *she* called *him* "Mr. Armstrong"? Oh, *sure.*) "Hold my calls, please, Tracy," he said to his secretary. "Certainly, Mr. Armstrong," Tracy said, the funny look solidifying on her face. No, clearly it was something about Mr. Armstrong, not some old *safe,* that had caused Tracy to look like that.

Here was someone named Carolyn being kissed passionately by a man in a suit. "Oh, Shad, Shad," she said. Shad? Why *Shad*? "Chad, my darling," Carolyn continued, wisely abandoning her attempt to kiss him while saying her lines. "Carolyn, Carolyn," said Chad, I suppose it was (although, come to think of it, I'd never heard of anyone called Chad, either). "Chad," said Carolyn. "Carolyn," said Chad. "Lydia!" said both Chad and Carolyn, breaking apart, as the camera drew back to reveal a woman standing in a doorway. "Well. My dear little sister," said this new woman, coolly. "And good old Chad. Aren't you going to welcome me home, you two? I've come back. And this time I've come back to stay."

"So!" I said when I got through to Rafe at his office. "I just saw 'This Brief Candle'—what's your crush's name?"

"Heather Goldberg," he said.

"What?" I said. "Oh. Her *nom,* not her name."

"How should I know?" Rafe said. "I can't watch that stuff—I'm employed."

"Well, how might I identify her?"

"She's the pretty one," he said.

I snorted. They were all pretty, of course, in a uniform fashion, like an assortment of chocolates whose ornamentations seem meaningless to nonaficionados.

"Why don't you bring her by for a drink this evening?" I said.

"Can't," Rafe said.

"Come on," I said. "I promise to put away the magnifying glass, the scales, the calipers. . . ."

"Not by the hairs on my chinny-chin-chin," Rafe said. "Just kidding, of course—I'd love to. But anyway, you'll meet her at Cookie's next Thursday."

"Cookie's!" I said. "Oh, God, that's right. I'm dreading it." I hate parties. Particularly Cookie's parties, but Louise Dietz had just published a volume of photographs of investigative reporters at home, which was the ostensible raison d'être of this do, so I had to put in an appearance at least.

"Whoop—my other line," Rafe said. "Want to hold?"

"No, darling. I'm frantic. Thursday, then." I hung up and looked around. It had been nice with the TV on. All those other people seeing exactly the same thing as oneself, at the same time—one knew exactly where one was, somehow. It seemed a flawless form of having company. But it was over so suddenly.

I had things to do before lunch, but time was standing completely still, as it does occasionally at that hour. Then one's day will pass unexpectedly into a giant, permeable block of sunshine that converts surfaces into hypnotic sheets of light and drenches one's belongings in a false, puzzling specialness. I hated it—it was terrible. I simply stood in front of the TV, wrenched out of the ordinary smooth flow of entire minutes, and I remembered being home from school as a child, pinioned to my bed by the measles or whatever, while the world blazed beyond me in that noon glare.

When I got to Cookie's on Thursday, Rafe and Heather had not yet arrived. In fact, no one much had yet arrived, so I wandered about the shrubbery in Cookie's living room looking for a hospitable encampment. Eventually I distinguished Marcia

Meaver's name in a stream of syllables that issued from some source not far from me. Naturally, my curiosity was aroused. What was there to be mentioned about Marcia Meaver? Except, of course, that she was going out with my husband. Which, I must admit, did annoy me. It's one thing, after all, when one's husband takes up with a fascinating woman or a woman of great beauty. But Marcia Meaver! I felt I would have to rethink those years of my marriage—John's standards were not, I realized, all that one might have supposed them to be.

I followed the voice I'd overheard, and it led me to a rather clammy blond boy. As I stood at his shoulder, listening, I came to understand that this boy worked under Buddy Katsukoru at the museum, and it was to Buddy that he was now praising himself, fulsomely and with riveting dullness, for having convinced Marcia to make to the museum a tax-deductible gift of some gowns.

"I will remember this," I said. "I've been giving my old clothes to the Salvation Army."

"Schiaparelli," the boy said dimly, without even turning to glance at me.

"Good grief!" Cookie trumpeted from behind us, incidentally saving the boy from the heartbreak of my response. "It's Lydia!"

"Heather, actually," said a girl's voice, and I turned and saw Rafe, and—and—and I couldn't figure out *what* I saw for a moment; but sure enough, if you were to exchange, paper-doll fashion, this girl's dashing suede for one of those demure TV-tart dresses, her calm regard for the shiftings of a tense, hectoring flirt, if you were to paint sharp black lines around this girl's eyes, what I saw, I realized, would in fact be Lydia, the femme fatale, as I'd supposed, of "This Brief Candle."

How interesting. I was eager to take Heather aside and let her share with me her feelings about exploring on a daily basis some dingy side of her personality, but Cookie cut in like a sheep dog and led her off. "Come tell me, dear," Cookie shouted tactlessly, "what it's like to be a bitch!"

"Imagine Cookie needing to ask," I heard the blond boy say as he and Buddy floated toward the bar. Well! Isn't that just absolutely Mr. Guest for you, though! Trashing the hostess the instant she's out of earshot! Cookie might not be the sweetest person in the world, it was true, but she would never do something cheap like that herself!

"So how's the whiz biz?" Rafe asked as he and I settled ourselves into the sofa. "Find any geniuses crawling around under that pile of grant proposals?"

"Not yet," I said. "Oh, it is slow work, no question."

"Oh, by the way," Rafe said, "Heather and I finally got to that performance piece for which you people so thoughtfully provided the funding. The one with the four-hundred-piece glass-harmonica orchestra, where the mechanical whale rolls over for a few hours. *Beached,* isn't it called? It was really great, I have to tell you, we really enjoyed it."

"I'm sorry you didn't care for it, Rafe. And if what you saw had been in fact what you describe, I would hardly blame you. But whether you personally did or did not care for it, the piece you refer to certainly must be considered an important piece. What *are* those—nachos? No thank you, Rafe. Really—a major piece."

"You know," Rafe said. "All these years, I've really wanted to ask you, how do you decide whether something really is a major piece or whether it's a major piece of crap? I mean, seriously, how do you decide whether something is good or not?"

"Well, seriously, Rafe, I decide in the same way that I decide whether Bergdorf's is a good place to shop. I decide in the same way that I decide on which wall to put the Ansel Adams that you so admire. I decide these things by decision-making processes."

"Ah, silly me," Rafe said.

"Really, Rafe. I can't imagine what it is about Cookie's soirée that's inspired you to disburden yourself, finally, of this canker of doubt you say you've harbored for so long. But if you must really hear right now how I can tell whether something is good, I'll explain it to you. The explanation is that I have been trained to do just that. Oh, of course I do have a certain natural eye—and ear—as, obviously, do you. But what you so clearly find to be a sort of sanctified caprice on my part, concerning my funding recommendations, is actually considered, systematic judgment. I'm not saying I could describe its sequence to you, but I have a solid background in the fine arts, as you know. I studied English and art history in school, and I've worked for years in art-related fields. And therefore, I'm qualified to make the judgments I make in the same way that . . . that, well, Mike Dundy over there is qualified to design the cars he designs."

"I take your point," Rafe said.

"Good," I said.

"But it does not suffice to answer my question," he said. "You see, if you were to drive around in a car of Mike's design, and the engine fell out, everyone could agree that there was a flaw in that design."

"Rafe," I said—I simply couldn't believe this! In all the time we'd known each other, Rafe had never indicated any distaste for my profession—"I am not saying that my work is a science. It cannot be. I am not saying that I'm infallible. All I'm saying is this: I'm not a profoundly gifted person myself. I'm a person whose small but very specific gifts and whose very specific training suit me for this task—the task of being able to seek out, with great care and a certain . . . actual precision, and to reward, others who *are* profoundly gifted."

"And here I thought it was all glamour and prestige. There's quite a lot of kicking and biting for those jobs, I understand, among folks who don't rightly appreciate the gravity of the trust, or the backbreaking labor involved in carrying it out."

"Well, I didn't have to kick or bite anyone for my job. I was merely appointed. And you know perfectly well that 'glamorous' is the last thing I find it! Trudging across that great tundra of manuscripts! Of course, you do learn how to, well . . ."

"Skim," Rafe said.

"Certainly not!" I said. "Just to—to read for the worthwhile bits. And I admit that it's very gratifying when you do stumble across something good. And once in a while, you do. You really do. You see, *that's* the thrill of the job for me, when that happens, and you know that *here's* someone who's going to be an important voice. Rafe, I'm sure this sounds pompous to you, but sometimes I'm reading the Arts and Leisure section or whatever, and there will be an article about someone we've encouraged—did you see, by the way, that there were three whole pages on Stanley Zifkin's studio in this issue of *Architectural Digest*?—Anyhow, I see these things, and I feel a sense of, well . . ."

"Ownership," Rafe said. "The sixth sense."

"You're very jolly tonight, aren't you?" I said.

"I'm a jolly good fellow. Ah, there," he said. Heather, having been released at last by Cookie, was coming toward us.

"What's happening in the real world?" Rafe asked her.

"Oh, just taking in the sights. All these people. It's so funny. Parties always make me think how funny it is that everything's all divided up into these different packages. A package of Cookie, a package of you, a package of me. When you see people all together, milling around like this, it seems so, sort of, arbitrary."

"It doesn't seem arbitrary to me at all," I said. "Cookie's Cookie, and I'm not, thank heaven. Anyhow, what do you mean, 'everything'? What's this 'everything' that's divided into me and Cookie?"

Heather shrugged. "Oh, I don't know. Just everything. And what else is funny is that at every single party I've ever been to, every single person I speak to says how much they hate parties."

Rafe nodded. "Hatred of parties. The sentiment that unites all humanity."

"But we're all here," Heather said.

"That's right," Rafe told her. "It's a job that has to be done. Going to parties is the social analogue of carrying out the garbage."

"Well, anyhow," Heather said, "everyone seems to be having fun. Cookie's nice, isn't she?"

"No," I said. "I mean, she is, really, if you look deep enough. She can be very vicious, but underneath she's a fine person, really. She has principles at least, which is more than can be said for a lot of rich people." Something was tugging at my attention. "Jesus," I said. "Look at Geoffrey Berman's jacket! It's *hairy.* One of his research assistants must have grown it for him in a bottle."

"They're certainly crazy about him, aren't they?" Rafe said absently. Obviously, he was paying no attention at all to what I was saying.

"So—um, what does Cookie . . . apply her principles to?" Heather asked.

Rafe laughed.

"Well, I don't know," I said. "They're just something one *has.*"

"Yes?" Heather said. "It sounds so . . . inert, sort of. Like a stack of fish on a plate."

"Fish on a plate!" I said. God, I was hungry. "Do you suppose there's anything edible within reach?"

We threaded our way around a nest of journalists who were disclosing to each other their coastal preferences, and reached the buffet table just in time to catch the gratifying sight of Buddy's friend spilling enchilada sauce on Cookie's Aubusson. Really, Cookie had never served more annoying food. Last year it had been julienned Asiatic unidentifiables; the year before that it was all reheated morels en croute étouffé avec canard au fraise poivré kind of thing; and this year, Spam, it seemed, was more or less our lot. "And with her money," I said. "I really don't know what I'd do if I had Cookie's money."

"You could buy Cookie's sofa," Heather said. "That's what I'd do."

"Really?" I said. "That's odd. I can't really say I'm mad for it."

Heather wasn't listening, though. She and Rafe had become absorbed by the engineering problems of feeding each other tacos. Well, that was certainly something they weren't going to get any help with from me. Besides, there was no point in trying to have a rational conversation with Rafe when he was in one of his playmate-of-the-month moods. I wandered off and eventually found myself talking to Jules Racklin, whom I'd met here and there but never really talked to and who turned out to be a very interesting man. Very intelligent. *Very* interesting.

The day after that party, I happened to turn on the TV at eleven o'clock, and having so recently seen Heather, I do have to say that I was pretty mesmerized by Lydia. The plot of the show didn't seem to have progressed to any great degree since the episode I had seen previously, and at the appearance of each familiar figure, I felt a slight sensation of agreeable reinforcement, of knowing my way around.

I had tuned in while Eric was speaking on the phone. And while I had never actually seen Eric before, I was able to identify him by inference from the conversation I had heard between—um, let's see—Brent and . . . yes, Hank. As he talked, Eric moved a painting on the wall, exposing a safe at which he looked gloatingly for a moment. Then he replaced the painting, hung up the phone, and left his house, never noticing—the foolish fellow—that Brent and Hank were sitting in a car parked right across the street. Carolyn and Chad then drank cocktails and had an agonizing discussion (which I suspected was one of many) about whether they did or did not want to start a family. Carolyn appeared to acquiesce to Chad's insistence that it would be better to wait, but I saw right through her. She felt hurt, I could tell, and disappointed. Then Colleen appeared to be developing, in a supermarket, a rather modern crush on Ellie's mother, who herself, to judge from what followed, was somewhat more interested in Mr. Armstrong. Suddenly there was a woman from another universe holding a box of soap called Vision. What had happened? Ah, one episode of "This Brief Candle" had been concluded, of course. I turned off the set (I had a thousand things to do), and the little light in the center danced furiously, brighter and brighter, into oblivion.

Now. Right. The first thing was to call and thank Cookie. Cookie and I had the requisite little jaw about what a delightful evening, etc. (actually, it had turned out rather nicely, due to that nice Jules Racklin), and when I'd heaped upon Cookie what I hoped were sufficient thanks, I felt I might as well hit her up for a couple of grand for the foundation. Not that it would do any good, but you never knew. She might have some good ideas for sources, anyhow. Cookie always had on hand the scrap of information one needed, if one could bear to pick through the refuse to get it.

"Heavens, dear," she said, when I suggested a donation. "I'd be thrilled to, as you know or you wouldn't have asked, but I just don't have that sort of money lying around at the moment." My God. Poor Cookie had probably spent her last pesos on taco chips for the party. "Why don't you call Nina Morisette? That dame is absolutely loaded, I'm telling you, darling. To her, that kind of money is like two cents. And I mean *two cents*."

"Nina's such a tightwad, though," I said. "When you talk to her you'd think she was starving."

"Oh, I know, dear," Cookie said. "She is a witch, isn't she? But her familiar—what's his name? Garvin Something, Something Garvin—is the one to talk to. He's a complete fool, I promise you, and he can get her to give to any ridiculous thing."

"By the way," I said, feeling that the time had come to change the subject, "wasn't it nice to meet Rafe's girlfriend?"

"Wasn't it," Cookie agreed. "Such a sweet child. They all are, though, aren't they? I do wonder how he can tell all those sweet children apart. Ah, me. Then again, I suppose one might as well ask how anyone can tell us sour wrecks apart!"

"Ahaha," I agreed politely while Cookie ratified her little witticism with raucous baying.

"I talked to her for some time," Cookie continued when she'd recovered, "and she really did seem sweet, you know. It's amazing how evil she is on that TV show of hers."

"Yes, what is that girl up to?" I asked. "Lydia—isn't that her name?"

"Oh, well!" Cookie said. "It's quite exciting, really, because the girl who used to play Lydia got fired, so right before she left, the writers or producers or whoever had her seduce her sister Carolyn's fiancée, Jad, and then go off somewhere to make unseen trouble for a while, while the audience could forget what she looked like. In the meantime, Carolyn and Jad got married, and then Lydia (who's Heather now, of course) came back and started vamping Jad again like crazy. And that's just what she's doing for fun! She's also gotten herself involved with a fellow named Brent, just to spite Brent's girlfriend Colleen, who really is a bit lame, when you get right down to it, and as a favor to Brent (at least that's what Brent thinks—it's really so she'll have power over him) Lydia's seducing this man Eric to get some blueprints from him that Brent can use to blackmail Mr. Armstrong!"

"Oh, no!" I said. "Is *that* who Eric was talking to on the phone just now? *Lydia?*" A silence descended on the other end of the phone like a gavel.

"I can't imagine," Cookie said.

"But weren't you watching?" I asked foolishly.

"Dear, that show is just something I stumble upon once a century or so," Cookie said, gingerly depositing my question in the toilet.

Damn. Cookie was actually embarrassed. And I would have to pay, for sure. "Well, anyway, dear," she said, "I'm glad you enjoyed yourself last night. I thought you must be enjoying yourself when I saw you there with Jules. He really is a scorcher, isn't he? Best-looking man I ever saw."

"Very pleasant," I said thinly. "Anyway, Cookie dear . . ."

"Oh, he's a dish, all right. I just knew how much you'd enjoy him. When he walked in alone, I got down on my knees and I thanked God that Pia Dougherty hadn't been able to make it. Naturally, I'd had to invite her, too, but, fortunately, it seems she's out getting photographed with some goats in Kashmir for somebody's spring collection. Oh, I don't know—I really just don't. Everyone talks about how gorgeous she is, but I really don't see it, do you? I mean, it's really *him,* isn't it? He's the really stunning one."

"Oh, the time!" I said. "Just look! I must hang up and run." I hung up and sat. Pia Dougherty, huh. Maybe Buddy would give me a good write-off if I donated my phone to the museum.

I must admit I wasn't having just the greatest time with men. I was finding that you have to get to know someone a bit in order to become interested in getting to know him at all, and that was such a bore! The same questions, the same little conversations, over and over: Were you close to your father? Just think—so, you, too, as a child, were afraid of getting hit by the baseball! Tell me, do you really believe that it's possible to rid oneself of unconscious concerns over fuel costs when discussing our Middle-Eastern policies? And so on and so forth—just like having to slog through those statistics courses in college before being allowed to register for Abnormal Personality. I did go out now and again, of course, but in a perfunctory, frog-kissing sort of spirit, and a frog, in my experience, is a frog to the finish.

My own love life, at that time, then, provided me with no information to sort through—nothing to think about or try to get in order. It was as useful to the production of conversation as disappearing ink is to the production of literature, and so I began to tap, for all it was worth, that skill which one develops during adolescence, of turning to account the love lives of one's friends. And since among my friends Rafe had always tended to have the most multiform and highly colored love life, I looked forward most to seeing him.

Sadly, though, he had become quite uncooperative since he'd taken up with Heather. He rarely put in an appearance, and when he did, he just sat around lumpishly and quaffed down great quantities of my expensive scotch.

"How are you these days, Rafe?" I would say.

"Fine," he would say, with a remote, childish formality. "Just fine."

"Yes? How's everything going?" I would say.

"Oh, fine, thanks. Very well."

"Good . . . and how's Heather?"

"Oh, she's quite well. Just fine. Say, you don't have any more of that scotch, do you? It's awfully good."

One evening he came over in a state of overt grumpiness. It seemed that he and Heather had had tickets to something, but Heather had been required on the spur of the moment to learn a huge new set of lines. "One of the guys in the show was in an accident today," Rafe said, "so they have to do something about it."

"What can they do?" I said. "Either he was in an accident or he wasn't, I'd think."

"What I mean," Rafe said, "is that they'll have to write him out of the story for a week or so. And then they'll have to think of some reason why he's in a cast from head to toe. It's going to be pretty conspicuous, after all."

"Oh.—Yes.—I see. How awful. And rather eerie, for that matter. Will they think up some accident for him to have had in the script, do you suppose?"

"I don't know," Rafe said. "It seems logical."

"You know," I said, "a few weeks ago I happened to see the show, and this man whose name is Mr. Armstrong had this terrible cold. And somebody else said he'd gotten it from kissing his secretary, Tracy. And, you know, maybe the week before the actress that plays Tracy really had had a cold, come to think of it. But in any case the writers couldn't have manufactured that guy's runny nose."

"Yup. Part of the credit for that cold just has to go to the ultimate scriptwriter, doesn't it?" Rafe yawned, bored by his own cliché. "Hey, speaking of the determining hand, you're just about winding up this year's work, right?"

"Yes," I said. The panel was reviewing each other's recommendations all that month. "We don't start up again for a while. But to tell you the truth," I confessed, "I've been thinking about getting into publishing instead of going on with the foundation."

"Oh," Rafe said.

" 'Oh'? Is that all? I thought you'd be pleased."

"Why?" Rafe said. "That is, I have no objection, but why did you think I'd be pleased, particularly?"

"I thought you disapproved of what I do."

"I don't," Rafe said. "I don't think I disapprove of it."

"I'm glad to hear that," I said. "In any case, I feel I've done my turn for society. I feel that now it's time for me to become involved in something for myself. I want to get somewhere—to use my abilities to . . . to . . . *build,* in some way. Don't you think that's important?"

"Well," Rafe said. "It seems to me that what's important is how you feel about your work while you're doing it."

"What?" I said. "I feel fine about my work while I'm doing it, whatever that means. And while I'm not doing it."

"That's good," Rafe said, without conviction.

"I feel just fine about my work," I said. "I really don't know what we're talking about."

"I'm not sure myself," he said. "But there's something about the way Heather . . . I mean, I've noticed, watching Heather, that, well, what she does doesn't make her feel important."

"I should think not," I said.

"No, but I mean, it doesn't make her feel *un*important either. I mean, I've noticed, watching Heather, that because she distinguishes between herself and her work, in some way, that—"

"Really?" I said. I really couldn't take one more instant of this. "Do tell me. How interesting. Let's see. You've noticed, you've noticed—that it's better to be on a soap opera than to subsidize art. No—you've noticed that it doesn't matter whether you're Eva Braun or Florence Nightingale as long as you *feel good about it.*"

"You will be astonished to learn," Rafe said, "that that is not what I mean. I don't really mean that *you're* important, at all, in your work. I mean that it's the work itself that—oh, obviously, of course . . . I don't know. I've just been watching how, if it's really your work that's important to you, rather than some idea of yourself doing the work—that is, if your approach to your work is one of genuine interest in the work rather than yourself—then it will necessarily follow that the work will itself respond somehow, with a genuine—"

"Genuine!" I said. "Genuine! That's a pretty loaded word you're tossing around there! Look, Rafael, *everything* is genuine, if you're going to start giving me this kind of stuff! I've already told you that my work is important to me. I don't know why you insist on thinking it isn't. See, that's genuine Glenlivet you're drinking out of genuine Baccarat. You're sitting in a genuine Eames genuine chair. I don't know what you're talking about! Do you think I should go out and get myself killed in some war to prove I'm serious? Do you think I should get a job on a soap opera? What do you think? The Spanish Civil War is over! The entire Abraham Lincoln Brigade is dead! I really don't know what we're talking about! That's a genuine TV set over there on which a genuine simulacrum of a genuine version of your girlfriend is genuinely conjured up—and furthermore, my genuine body has the same damn genuine molecular structure as her body's damn genuine molecular structure!"

Heavens! What had gotten into me? What had the Abraham Lincoln Brigade or Heather's molecular structure to do with publishing? It was just that Rafe's murky attitudinizing really had gotten to me. It really had. He had really changed since he'd started seeing that girl.

"I'm sorry," I said. "I'm very sorry to say these things to you, but, really, Rafe, you used to be so charming."

"It seems so long ago, now, doesn't it?" he said sadly, swirling the ice cubes around in his drink.

It was a long, long time before I saw Rafe again. Several months, probably, elapsed before, one afternoon, he called.

"Can I take you to dinner?" he said.

"What, tonight?"

"Well, are you free?"

I was delighted he had called, actually. I was sorry I'd jumped on him that evening when he'd obviously just been confused and troubled; and when we met, at a very pretty Italian restaurant in my neighborhood, neither of us mentioned how long it had been since we'd seen each other.

Rafe ordered a bottle of Cliquot. "To the free peoples of the world," he said, lifting his glass.

"What's the matter?" I said. "Is Heather giving you a hard time?"

"Oh, we just haven't seen too much of each other for a while."

"You finally got tired of each other, huh?" I said.

"No. We just don't like each other. Jesus, that's not true." He raked his hands through his hair, which, in view of the horror he had of disarranging it, indicated profound anguish.

"Poor Rafe," I said, but with measured commiseration. I was waiting to hear more before deciding whether it was sympathy that was required or (had I been that sort of person) an "I told you so."

"She wanted to get married, you see. Have children." My God, what a thought. Rafe surrounded by weensy Rafe replicas. "In fact, she gave me something like an ultimatum. Oh, God. I'm too old to settle down. I've really got to start running around again."

"It does seem to suit you, Rafe."

"I just couldn't. She's a wonderful girl, but I couldn't. Particularly the children part, you know? I do want children of course, eventually, but just not right now. And just the fact that she says to me, 'Look, I really want children, I want them now, I think that if we're to continue we should get married,' and I don't have any response at all, except sheer terror—well, that indicates to me that it's wrong, you know? No matter how I think I feel about her, that proves that it's just wrong." How glossy his hair looked in the candlelight while he shoved it around like that! "Don't you think that's true?" he said.

"Well," I said slowly—I felt I was looking at us both from a great height—"I suppose it must be."

"See, that's what I mean," he said. "Here, have some of my zucchini. How do *you* feel about children, anyway? I've always wondered whether you were disappointed about not having any."

"I might still have some one of these days. I'm only your age, remember?"

"Sure," he said. "Of course. But how do you feel about them now?"

"Oh, I don't know, really," I said. "They are dear, but to tell you the truth, Rafe, I sometimes find them—I don't know—off-putting. I mean, those tiny faces all lit up with some entirely groundless joy, and then something happens and they just crumple all up like old Christmas wrappings. All that anguish, all that drama! I mean, it's quite cute and whatnot, but who can understand it? Of course, they're so sweet—absolutely adorable—and yet I can't help feeling that they're, well . . . *oddities*. Almost a bit creepy, somehow."

"I know," Rafe said, sounding faintly surprised. "That's sort of how I feel, really."

I looked across at him, sitting there lost in his fleecy sadness, and I wondered if Heather knew what she'd given away. Perhaps she really was looking for something more ordinary than life with Rafe, or perhaps, having been dazzled by him, as doubtless she had been, she feared that there was nothing to rely on beneath his sophistication and glamour. But that was the thing about Rafe, I knew. Underneath the alpaca and wool, underneath the—well, no matter—*fundamentally,* I mean, he was as good a man as you could ever hope to find.

"She really is a marvelous girl," Rafe said, as if in verification of his own opinion (although by then, of course, it didn't really matter if his opinion was correct or not). "She has a quality I've never really encountered in anyone else. A sort of directness, or clarity, that gives her courage. Like some magic sword."

It occurred to me that this quality Rafe so touchingly considered her to have was perhaps her quality (and it truly was a very attractive one) of youthful, vigorous ignorance concerning life's more serious sides. "Poor Rafe," I said. Poor Rafe.

"So. I've missed you," he said. "Tell me what you've been up to. Any luck with the job hunting?"

"To tell you the truth," I said, "I've decided to do some

traveling before I tie myself down again. Some friends have asked me to come visit them on Patmos for a while, and I thought, oh, why not? I've been dying to get out of my place, anyway, so I'm packing everything up and I'm getting a subtenant."

"You're leaving?" Rafe said, looking up, and we looked right smack into each other's face.

I was just getting to sleep that night when the phone rang. It was Rafe. "Hello there," I said. "What's on your mind?"

"I was wrong," he said. "I had to call you. I misinterpreted the meaning of my own feelings." Had I been asleep, perhaps, when the phone rang? "I realized after we talked tonight," he said, "that I was wrong. If I turn away from this, I'm turning away from . . . from everything. I know that, and I'm going to ask Heather to marry me."

"I see," I said. I had a headache. I must have been asleep when the phone rang.

"That fear that I mentioned to you—it's just nothing, do you see? It's just something like—like that law in physics—you know?—that the strength of the reaction is equal to the . . . to the . . . the whatever. Remember that law? Isn't there some kind of law like that?"

"I don't know." My *head.* "I got a C in physics."

"Whatever," he said. "What I mean is that the reason I've been so frightened is because it's so important to me, the possibility of a life with Heather—a real life. It's a gift, I've realized. No, not a gift—an invitation, a test. If I'm able to accept it, do you see, for that reason alone I'm good enough to be given it."

"I see," I said. He sounded actually feverish.

"And, really, I actually do love her," he said.

"Well, then," I said. "That's what counts."

"I wanted to call you right away," he said. "Because we were talking. You know."

"I'm glad," I said.

"So," he said.

"So," I said. "Well, good night, Rafe, dear. Thank you for calling."

God damn it. I hated being awakened at night. I could never get back to sleep. Maybe I'd go make myself some warm milk. No one else was going to do it, anyhow, that was for sure.

I took out the milk, and my one pot and one cup that weren't packed yet, and very sensibly I poured, instead of milk into the pot, scotch into the cup, thereby saving myself some dishwashing, and wandered into the living room, which was piled high with cartons prepared for storage.

A gift, huh? An invitation, a test? What on earth had happened to Rafe's brains in the few hours since I'd seen him? Jesus, I felt terrible, though. And if the truth be told, in fact, the shaming truth, another thing that I actually seemed to feel was (oh, God!) *lonely*! As if I were being excluded from this "real life," this . . . this "everything" that Rafe imagined he was being invited to share in! How amazing! I'm really not the sort of person who feels jealous of someone else's happiness (even supposing this folly of Rafe's were to be considered happiness). I'm not the sort of person who feels that one loses by another's gain. I'm the sort of person who takes pleasure in a friend's pleasure. Oh, I know there are people who believe the realm of human activity to be an exchange, as it were, where for every good thing acquired, some good thing has to be given back. "Here are my teeth," for instance, such people believe you would say when they fell out. "Now may I have that harvest table that's in the window of Pierre Deux?" These people believe that there is some system that ensures that you cannot have yards of eyelashes in addition to a talent for entertaining, unless the news vendor on the corner falls down a flight of steps and has to be hospitalized. And people of this opinion, naturally enough, quail when another person, even a friend as close as Rafe, threatens to bite into the world's short supply of happiness. But I am not of this opinion; I do not believe these things, and even if I did, I would be prepared nonetheless to be happy for Rafe. Even if he was making an awful mistake.

But then, the problem remained of why people did lose their teeth. Why didn't I have yards of eyelashes? Why would a news vendor have to fall down a flight of steps? Why would anyone have to be a news vendor at all? Obviously, if one were to understand all this, one would have to read some horrible math text about the laws of chance and probability. Anyhow, my head was still killing me.

How inhospitable my own living room seemed! Just all those cartons, and a huge, gilt, good-for-nothing mirror, exactly as empty as the room, and a few oddments I was leaving for the comfort of my subtenant, including a hideous Bristol vase that John had given to me early on in our marriage. He'd said the color reminded him of his childhood. Yuck. I'd offered it back to him, naturally, when he moved out, but he'd wanted it to stay with me. John was a loyal old boy, no doubt about that—loyal to the vase, loyal to his childhood—and now, from what I heard, he was being loyal to Marcia Meaver.

I slept, finally, for a few hours, after it had already become light, and got up just in time to catch the final segment of that day's "This Brief Candle." I turned on the set, and there was Heather (well, Lydia) right in my living room with her sister Carolyn and Carolyn's husband, Jad.

"Chad, darling," Carolyn said. (So it *was* Chad! I *swear* it was Chad.) "That was Hank on the phone. Something peculiar has happened at Mr. Armstrong's office. I must go right away."

"Well," Chad said to Lydia after the door slammed. He cleared his throat. "Guess I'll just go into my workroom and try to get a few things done." He smiled in a sickened, hopeless attempt at heartiness.

"Why don't you?" Lydia said, never taking her eyes off him for a second. "Why don't you, Chad? But first, my darling brother-in-law, I'd like you to sit down. Because you and

I have a little matter to discuss. One that isn't going to be getting any littler, if you see what I mean. So we can't put it off much longer." Close-up of Lydia's face, inscrutably triumphant.

I stared and stared at the screen, but all there was to see, suddenly, was a batch of brats hell-bent on wrecking their clothes. I turned off the TV and sat, exhausted, while the little white light in the center boiled brighter and brighter until it was gone, and then, on some overpowering and incomprehensible impulse, I went to the phone and I called Cookie. Her line was busy, and even though it stayed busy for a good half an hour, I just kept standing there, for some reason, dialing her number.

"Hello, dear!" she said, when I finally got through. "How marvelous to hear your voice! It's been weeks!"

"Hasn't it," I agreed. "Well, except for the Schillers' the other night."

"But that hardly counts, does it, dear?" Cookie said. "One feels one must creep about in disguise there, doesn't one, like an Arab."

"One does indeed," I said. Did Arabs creep about in disguise?

"It's torture, isn't it, how one daren't say a word at the Schillers', or one is sure to read some horrible twisted version of it in some publication the next morning. But on the other hand, of course, one must keep one's own ears open because of all that information flying around. I suppose it's rather what the agora must have been."

"I suppose so," I said. The agora? Arabs? Was Cookie taking some sort of course? An alphabetical survey of everything? I myself couldn't remember for the life of me what the agora had been.

"Each time I go to the Schillers' I come home utterly destroyed," she said. "And each time, I swear I'm never going to go again. But how can one turn one's back on such a spectacle?"

"This one looked relatively sedate to me," I said.

"Sedate!" Cookie roared. "Oh. You missed the bit when Marjorie went to get her coat and found Rupert Fallodin making *advances* to Alison."

"So what?" I said. "Some married people find each other attractive."

"I know that, dear," Cookie said with dignity. "But Rupert has been seeing Marjorie for months, you know, and it was quite a shock to her. And when she came downstairs she made a few remarks about him. At the top of her lungs, to be precise. It was extraordinary! Some very unusual habits Rupert has, it seems. Of course, Marjorie had polished off about a quart of scotch by that time. I mean, so had I, naturally, but so had she." Cookie barked happily. "Oh, it was a very steamy evening. Did you see Melissa Hober? She was tagging along behind Constance Ripp like an anthropologist tags along behind his Indian. Once, Constance stopped short, and Melissa almost broke that incredible chin of hers against Constance's skull!"

"It's hard to imagine Melissa tagging along behind anyone," I said.

"Oh, she can accommodate just about any degree of self-abasement if she thinks it'll get her published, you know. Constance is taking over as the poetry editor of *Life and Times,* you see, and evidently Melissa knows that Constance has an unfailing weakness for a pretty face, which is something Melissa obviously imagines herself to be in possession of."

"Constance?" I asked, amazed. "Is Constance gay?" How could Constance be gay? I was the sort of person who was usually very perceptive about other people, and it had never occurred to me that Constance was gay!

"Is Constance gay!"Cookie hooted. "Does a pope shit in the woods? Oh, dear! I never would have said a thing if I'd thought for a moment that there was one living soul who didn't know. Well, I'm sure it isn't really a secret, even though Constance does put on that ridiculous act. But what did you think Honoria della Playa was—the au pair girl?"

"Constance had an affair with Honoria della Playa?" I said.

"Oh! My mouth!" Cookie said. "But naturally I assumed you knew all about that."

Oh, Cookie was having a splendid day with me. But I really didn't have time for it. What was I doing on the phone, anyhow?! Here I was, participating in Cookie's juvenile, pointless gossip, when I had to get all this stuff into storage! I really had to hang up immediately. Immediately. "Well, darling—" I said.

"Oh! By the way," Cookie interrupted, "how's Rafe these days? I haven't seen him for absolutely ages."

"I haven't seen much of him myself, actually," I said. "I don't suppose you happen to have heard anything about him, have you?"

"Well, strange that you ask," Cookie said. "Isn't that strange. Amanda Krotnick called just now—right before you did, as it happens—and she was saying that she hasn't seen Rafe in a blue moon, either."

Amanda Krotnick. Amanda Krotnick. Oh, yes—her husband used to play squash with John.

"And Amanda told me that she's been following Rafe's girlfriend on TV, just out of a friendly interest in Rafe." (What? Oh, yes, I suppose Rafe had mentioned her to me. I think she used to go to gallery openings with him and that sort of thing once in a while, when I didn't feel like it or was tied up with John or something.) "And Amanda said that she thinks Heather's TV alter ego, Lydia, you know, is pregnant by her sister's husband, Jad. Isn't that something? You see (this is according to Amanda, of course) it really puts Jad in a very peculiar position, because apparently Lydia plans to go ahead and have the baby, and sooner or later, naturally, she's going to begin to show."

I sat down right on a carton. "The things they do on those soap operas!" I said. "Imagine, if that's what people did with their time!"

"Well, *I* certainly don't have the time for them," Cookie said. "And I don't know how Amanda finds the time, either."

I hadn't meant that watching soap operas was an astonishing thing to do with one's time, although, of course, it was. I had meant that it would be astonishing if people spent their time the way people on the soap operas spend their time. But I didn't give a damn what I'd meant.

"So, what brings you to the phone, dear? What can I do for you?" Cookie said.

"Oh—" I said. "I was just calling. To say goodbye, really. I'm leaving soon, you know."

"Heavens! That's right!" she said. "We must get together before. Lunch next week?"

"Perfect," I said. "Lunch."

"Marvelous," Cookie said. "We'll call each other. Goodbye, dear."

Oh, God. How awful, that mirrored view of cardboard cartons. The reflection of pure desolation. At least I wasn't looking too awfully terrible myself, I noticed. Not too horrible, considering life and so forth. Somehow I'd managed to change remarkably little over the years.

All right—on with all the things to be done. What were they? Maybe I'd call Rafe.

"Hello," said a voice that belonged to Rafe himself, and I didn't have time to remember why I'd called. I'd been expecting a secretary to answer.

"Oh, Rafe," I said. "I just called to say . . . to say that I hope you got some sleep last night."

"I didn't," he said. My God, he sounded awful.

"That's too bad," I said, and neither of us seemed to have anything else to say. "Anyway."

"I'm going straight home when I finish up here today to get some sleep," he said. "But if you're not all booked up tomorrow evening, why don't I come by? I'll bring a picnic."

Rafe arrived the next night laden down with paper bags. "Assiette de eats," he said. He put the bags in the kitchen and hung up his coat. "What sensational flowers!"

"Aren't they," I said. "Oh, Rafe—squab! And grapes—and—good heavens!—*mauve* paper plates!"

"I had my reasons," he said. "I calculated that they would be an excellent foil for the—yes, *perfect*—pesto."

"Oh, and radicchio-and-fennel salad! My absolute favorite. You always find such good things, Rafe."

"It's my flair for life," he said with an odd look on his face.

"It's true, Rafe. That's one of the things I've always loved about you," I said, but the odd look hovered for a moment.

I opened a bottle of nice wine that I'd picked up and poured us paper cupfuls of it, and we made ourselves at home with our picnic, among the cartons.

"I got a new secretary today," Rafe said. "I found her in a rock club the other night. She's a cute kid, but the trouble with interviewing someone in a rock club is that you can't hear what they're saying to you. I guess I'll have to spend this week showing her how to answer the phone."

"Rafe," I said. How good it was to be sitting around together.

"What is this?" he said, reaching over. "China silk?" I sat very still while he rubbed my collar.

"Nice," he said, but by the time he sat back, I could see his thoughts were on something else.

"What is it, Rafe?" I asked.

"Nothing," he said. "Not a thing, not a thing."

"You know," he said after a moment. "I never meant you to think, that time, that I was saying that you were self-absorbed, or something of that sort."

"Oh, I know," I said. When had he said I was self-absorbed? "I don't think of myself as a particularly self-absorbed person, so it wouldn't really have struck home in any case." How strange. So Rafe had accused me of being self-absorbed.

"Anyhow," Rafe said, "I wanted to make sure you knew I never meant anything like that."

"Rafe, darling," I said, "would you mind getting me a glass of water?" I seemed to have gone through quite a bit of wine without really noticing. "Thanks."

"It's strange, you know," Rafe said. "I always thought Heather and I were having these conversations. And that I was listening to her. And even learning things from her. But I don't think she was ever actually saying anything in particular, or even *being* anything in particular. I just sort of concocted it all by myself. I was really just staring at her, because she's so pretty."

I went to the kitchen and got us a bottle of cognac. "No sense wasting this on the subtenant."

"I'm sorry about calling so late the other night," Rafe said.

"Why not?" I said. "We're friends." I certainly wished he'd get around to telling me what was going on between him and Heather. "Anyhow, I guess everything's resolved itself, in one way or another."

"Oh, yes," he said. "It was just one of those night things that happen when you're by yourself sometimes. And it just evaporated."

"Yes," I said. I poured us both some more cognac. "I guess you just figured it out on your own."

"Well, actually," he said, "I did call her. And we talked. We had a nice talk. We agreed that we were just never suited to each other, but that we'd always consider each other friends. Anyhow, she's gotten all mixed up with some guy. Evidently she thinks it's serious."

We drank and sat in the dim light and talked, and then it was very late, somehow, and Rafe was getting his coat. Rafe was putting on his lovely, soft coat, and he was going to go.

"Well, good night," he said. "Thanks again."

"Rafe," I said suddenly, to my own astonishment, "why do you suppose you and I never had an affair?" Oh, was I going to be hung over in the morning!

"Well," he said, pausing at the door, "for one thing, you were a married lady."

"I know," I said. "But for another thing?"

"Oh, I just don't think it would have worked, do you?" he said. "We're too much alike, really, aren't we? We'd climb into bed and I'd say, 'Great sheets—where'd you get them?' Or I'd take off my clothes and you'd say, 'Oh, fabulous—underwear with bison.' That sort of thing. We just wouldn't really have been able to concentrate."

"Underwear with bison?" I said. "Really?" Rafe smiled. "Rafe," I said. "We're actually not alike anymore, though, are we? You've changed."

"Now, now," he said. "Don't do that." He licked a little tear from my cheek. "Yum. I'll bet *that's* the drink of the gods." And he gave me a little kiss on the forehead.

I leaned against the door as it closed behind him. Oh, Jesus. I was actually dizzy! I must really have gotten myself loaded. In any case, it was truly late, and sooner or later I was going to have to stand myself upright without benefit of the door and take myself off to bed. Which would entail turning around. Turning around to the sight of those cartons, that vase, the empty mirror, the nothing, nothing, nothing at all that had come of my life in New York. And what was it I was planning to get for myself on Patmos, then? What? Rocks, sheep, a stack of fish on a plate, that's what! And I turned, and stood, and looked, supporting myself against the door, for what felt like hours.

At least, that was what I remembered, in a bunched-up sort of way, when I woke up the next morning, somehow not hung over at all.

Rafe and I never managed to get in touch with each other before I left—I suppose I was just too busy getting ready. Oddly enough, though, I did run into Heather just about the day before I left, when the sort of impulse that later compels one not to jeer at people who turn to their horoscopes in the paper led me to Saks. It was she who recognized me first, even though I had been staring straight at the beautiful face I should have known so well.

"I hear you're going off on adventures," she said, taking my hand in a way that made me feel strangely at ease. "Are you excited?"

"I suppose so," I said. "Yes." I felt a bit dazed looking at her. She really was lovely. Very . . . vivid, in some way. "How did you hear I was leaving? From Rafe?"

"Yes," she said. "He called a week or so ago. I was glad. We'd just let things get bad, and I hate to leave things bad, or even just unresolved, with someone I've cared about. Don't you?"

"Well, yes," I said. "I suppose I must."

"So he came over and we talked. Really conversed, I mean, for a change. Instead of just fighting, or falling into bed, or any of those things you do with people when you're breaking up with them. It was nice. I was really glad he called. I couldn't have just called him, you know, even though I wanted to give him my news. It would have sounded like I was giving him a last chance, almost—that sort of thing, don't you think? But it really was all over between us quite a while ago."

"News?" I said. "Last chance?"

"Oh," she said, and stopped. "That is, I'm going to get married, you see."

"Really," I said. "How wonderful."

"Yes," she said. "In fact, Neil's supposed to meet me here any minute. You know, I feel I know you so well, even though we only met once. Rafe talked about you so often, though, I almost feel that we've . . . shared something."

"I feel the same way," I said.

"Oh, look," she said. "There's Neil now. I can introduce you."

It took me a moment to place the man who had walked up to us and was putting his arm around Heather. He certainly didn't look much like Brent, that drip in the car that Lydia was doing something or other with, although that, I saw, was who (in a manner of speaking, of course) he was. In person he seemed like a nice young man, and he was obviously very much in love, as, obviously, was Heather herself.

"Well, I've got to get myself upstairs and look for some new clothes," she said.

"Yes," I said faintly. She would be needing some.

"Nice to meet you," Neil said, as he and Heather washed away from me in the crowd.

What a marvelous-looking baby it was going to be, with parents like Heather and Brent—Neil, rather. Or Lydia, to think of it another way, and Neil, or Brent. Or Rafe. As a matter of fact. Come to think of it.

So many faces, so many faces. People were pouring in and out of the doors, swarming between the counters, rising in swatches on the escalators. So many faces just right there, and any face possible from all the branchings of history for that baby. The faces around me swam and blended, and for an instant I was almost too dizzy to stand, but then I saw Heather's face, quite, of course, itself, and all the other faces consolidated properly again upon their discrete owners, as Heather waved back to me from the escalator and smiled. And even though I had dozens of things to do, *dozens* of things, I stopped to wave back and watch as, brighter and brighter, a dwindling dot in the stream of shoppers, Heather was borne away to some other floor.

A Lesson in Traveling Light

During the best time, when it was still warm in the afternoons and the sky was especially blue and the smell of spoiling apples rose up from the ground, Lee and I drove down from the high meadows with our stuff in the van, looking for someplace to live.

The night before we left, we went down the road to say goodbye to Tom and Johanna. Johanna looked like glass, but Tom was flushed and in a violent good humor. He passed the bottle of Jack Daniel's back and forth to Lee and slapped him on the back and talked a mile a minute about different places he had lived and people he had met and bets he had won and whatnot, so I figured he and Johanna had been fighting before we got there.

"Done a lot of traveling?" Tom asked me.

"No," I said. He knew I hadn't.

"Well, you'll enjoy it," he said. "You'll enjoy it."

Tom was making an effort, I suppose, because I was leaving.

"Hey," he said to Lee, having completed his effort, "are you going to see Miles?"

"I guess we might," Lee said. "Yeah, actually, we could."

"Who's Miles?" I said.

"Is he still with that girl?" Tom said. "The one who—"

"No," Lee interrupted, laughing. "He's back with Natalie."

"Really?" said Johanna. "Listen, if you do see him, tell him I still wear the parka he left at our place that day." Tom stared at her, but she smiled.

"Who's Miles?" I said.

"Someone who used to live around here. Before I brought you back up the mountain with me," Lee said, turning to face me. His eyes, when he's been thinking about something else, are like a blaze in an empty warehouse, and I caught my breath.

After dinner Lee and I walked back to our place, and as the house came into view I tried to fix it in my memory. It already looked skeletal, though, like something dead on a beach.

"That's what it is," Lee said. "Old bones. A carapace. You're creating pain for yourself by trying to make it something more."

I looked again, letting it be bones, and felt light. I wanted to leave behind with the house the old bones of my needs and opinions. I wanted to be unencumbered, a warrior like Lee. When we'd met, Lee had said to me, "I feel like I have to take care of you."

"That's good," I had said.

"No it isn't," he had said.

I wondered if he ever thought about places he had lived, other faces, old girlfriends. Once in a while he seemed bowed down with a weight of shelved memories. Having freight in storage, though, is what you trade to travel light, I sometimes thought, and at those moments I thought it was as much for him as for me that I wanted Lee so badly to stay with me.

The first night of driving we stopped in Pennsylvania.

"We're very close to Miles and Natalie's," Lee said. "It would be logical to stop by there tomorrow."

"Where do they live?" I said.

Lee took out a big U.S. road map. "They're over here, in Baltimore."

"That's so far," I said, following his finger.

"In a sense," he said. "But on the other hand, look at, say, Pittsburgh." His finger alighted inches from where we were. "Or Columbus."

"Or Louisville!" I said. "Look how far that is—to Louisville!"

"You think that's far?" Lee said. "Well, listen to this—ready? Poplar Bluff!"

"Tulsa!" I said. "Wait—Oklahoma City!"

We both started to shout.

"Cheyenne!"

"Flagstaff!"

"Needles, Barstow, Bishop!"

"Eureka!" we both yelled at once.

We sat back and eyed the map. "That was some trip," Lee said.

"Are we going to do that?" I said.

Lee shrugged. "We'll go as far as we want," he said.

After all that, it looked on the map like practically no distance to Baltimore, but by the time we reached it I was sick of sitting in the van, and I hoped Natalie and Miles were the sort of people who would think of making us something to eat.

"What if they don't like me?" I said when we parked.

"Why wouldn't they like you?" Lee said.

I didn't know. I didn't know them.

"They'll like you," Lee said. "They're friends of mine."

Their place turned out to be a whole floor of a building divided up by curves of glass bricks. Darkness eddied around us and compressed the light near its sources, and the sounds our shoes made on the wood floor came back to us from a distance.

Natalie must have been just about my age, but there might be an infinite number of ways to be twenty, I saw, shocked. She sat us down on leather sofas the size of whales and brought us things to drink on a little tray, and she wore a single, huge red earring. It was clear that she and Miles and Lee had talked together a lot before. There were dense, equidistant silences, and when one of them said something, it was like a stone landing in a still pond. I watched Natalie's earring while a comma of her black hair sliced it into changing shapes. After a while Miles and Lee stood up. They were going to see some building in another part of the city. "Anything we need, babe?" Miles asked Natalie.

"Pick up a couple of bottles of wine," she said. "Oh, yeah, and some glue for this." She opened her fist to disclose a second red earring in pieces in her palm.

"What's the matter?" I heard Lee say, and he was speaking to me.

Natalie and I moved over to the kitchen to make dinner, and she asked me how long Lee and I had been together.

"He's so fabulous," she said. "Are you thinking of getting married?"

"Not really," I said. We'd discussed it once when we'd gotten together. "It seems fairly pointless. Is there anything I can do?"

"Here," she said, handing me a knife and an onion. "Miles and I got married. His parents made us. They said they'd cut Miles off if we didn't."

"Is it different?" I said.

"Sort of," she said. "It's turned out to be an O.K. thing, actually. We used to, when we had a problem or something, just talk about it to the point where we didn't have to deal with it anymore. But now I guess we try to fix it. Does Lee still hate watercress?"

"No," I said. Watercress? I thought.

"It's very good," Natalie said, "but I still wouldn't be surprised if it ended tomorrow."

"Natalie," I said, "would you pierce my ears?"

"Sure," she said. "Just let me finish this stuff first." She took back from me the knife and the onion, which was still whole because I hadn't known what to do with it.

When Lee and Miles got back, I put the ice cube I was holding against my earlobe into the sink, and we all sat down for dinner.

"Nice," Lee said, holding his glass. Lee and I had always drunk wine out of the same glasses we drank everything else out of, and it was not the kind of wine you'd have anything to say about, so Lee with his graceful raised glass was an odd sight. So odd a sight, in fact, that it seemed to lift the table slightly, causing it to hover in the vibrating dimness.

"It is odd, isn't it," I said, feeling oddness billow, "that this is the way we make our bodies live."

Miles lifted his eyebrows.

"I mean," I said, forgetting what I did mean as I noticed that Lee had picked the watercress out of his salad, "I mean that it's odd to sit like this, in body holders around a disk, and move little heaps of matter from smaller disks to our mouths on little metal shovels. It seems like an odd way to make our bodies live."

I looked around at the others.

"Seems odd to me," Miles said. "I usually lie on the floor. With my chin in a trough. Sucking rocks."

"*Miles,*" Natalie said, and giggled.

That night the clean, clean sheets wouldn't get warm, so I climbed out of bed and put on Lee's jacket and sat down to watch Lee sleep. He shifted pleasurably, and in the moonlight he looked as comfortable and dangerous as a lion. I watched him and waited for day, when he would get up, and I would give him back his jacket, and we could leave this place where he drank wine from a wine glass and strangers knew him so well.

In the morning Natalie and Miles asked if we wanted to stay, but Lee said we couldn't. We had planned to start out by the end of summer, he told them, and we were late.

Outside we saw how the light was already thin and banded across the highway, and we drove fast into sunset and winter. We were quiet mostly, and when we spoke, it was softly, like TV cowboys expecting an ambush.

That evening we bought some medicine at a drugstore because my ear had swollen up and I had a fever. I lay my head back into sliding dreams and woke into free-fall.

"Hey," Lee said, smoothing my hair back from my face. "You're asleep. You know that?" He scooped me over into his lap, and I nuzzled into his foggy grey T-shirt. "So look, killer," he said. "You want to stay here or you want to come in back with me?"

The next day my fever was gone and my ear was better.

For a while we were still where the expressways are thick coils and headlights and brake lights interweave at night in splendor. In the dark we would pull off to sleep in the corner of a truck stop or in a lot by a small highway, and in the morning, heat or cold, intensified by our metal shell, would wake us tangled in our blankets, and we would make love while fuel trucks roared past, rattling the van. Then we would look out the window to see where we were and drive off to find a diner or a Howard Johnson's.

We were spending more money than we had expected to, and Lee said that his friend Carlos, who lived in St. Louis, might be able to find him a few days' work. Lee looked through some scraps of paper and found Carlos's address, but when we got there, a group of people standing on the front steps told us that Carlos had moved. The group looked like a legation, with representatives of the different sizes and ages of humans, that was waiting to impart some terrible piece of information to a certain traveler. One of them gave us a new address for Carlos, which was near Nashville. Lee had never mentioned Carlos, so I assumed they weren't very close friends; but expectation had whetted Lee's appetite to see him, it seemed, because we left the group waiting on the steps and turned south.

Lee and Carlos were all smiles to see each other.

"What kind of money are you looking to make?" Carlos asked when we had settled ourselves in the living room.

"Nothing much," Lee said. "Just a little contingency fund. I'm clean these days."

"Well, listen," Carlos said. "Why don't you take the store for a week or two. I had to fire the guy I had managing it, and I've been dealing with it myself, but this would be an opportunity for me to look into some other stuff I've had my eye on." Carlos opened beers for himself and Lee. "Could I get you something?" he asked me, frowning.

"I'd like some beer, too," I said.

"Here," he said. "Wait. I'll get you a glass."

"Get back to Miami much?" Lee said.

"Too crowded these days, if you know what I mean," Carlos said. "Besides, I've pretty much stopped doing anything I can't handle locally. This is just where I live now, for whatever reason. And I've got my business. I don't know. It's a basis, you know? Something to continue from." He looked away from Lee and sighed.

During the days, when Lee and Carlos were out, I sat in back watching the sooty light travel from one side of the yard to the other. Sometimes a little boy played in an adjoining yard, jabbing with a stick at the clumps of grass there, which were stiff and grey with dirt. He was grey with dirt himself, and grey under the dirt. His nose ran, and the blue appliqué bear on the front of his overalls looked stunned.

I wondered what that boy had in mind for himself—whether his attack on the grass was some sort of self-devised preparation for an adulthood of authority and usefulness or whether he pictured himself forever on that bit of dirt, heading toward death in bear overalls of graduated size. I took to going in when I saw him and watching TV.

The night before we left Carlos's, Lee and I were awake late. We didn't have much to say, and after a while I noticed I was hungry.

"What? After that meal I made?" Lee said. "All right, let's go out."

Carlos was still awake, too, sitting in the living room with headphones on.

"Great," he said. "There's an all-night diner with sensational burgers."

"Burgers," Lee said. "You still eat that shit?"

Going into the diner, Lee and Carlos were a phalanx in themselves with their jackets and jeans and boots and belts, and I was proud to have been hungry. I ordered warrior food, and soon the waitress rendered up to me a plate of lacy-edged eggs with a hummock of potatoes and butter-stained toast, and to Lee and Carlos, huge, aromatic burgers.

"Are you going to see Kathryn?" Carlos asked.

"I don't know," Lee said. "It depends."

"I'd like to see her myself, come to think of it. She's a fantastic woman," Carlos said, balancing a French-fry beam on a French-fry house he was making. "She always was the best. You know, it's been great having you guys stay, but it makes me realize how much I miss other people around here. Maybe I should go out to the coast or something. Or at least establish some sort of nonridiculous romance."

"What about Sarah?" Lee said.

"Sarah," Carlos said. "Jesus." He turned to me. "Has Lee told you all about this marvel of technology?"

"No," I said.

"Well, I mean, listen, man," Carlos said, shaking his head. "She's a hot-looking lady, no question about it, but when I said 'nonridiculous' I had in mind someone you wouldn't be afraid to run into in the living room." He shook his head again and started drumming his knife on the table. "She sure is one hot-looking lady, though. Well, you know her."

"We have to get up really early," I said.

"That's okay," Lee said, but Carlos stood up. He looked exhausted.

"Yeah, sorry," he said. "Let's pull the plug on it."

Over the next few days I thought of Carlos often. His face had been shadowed when we said goodbye, so I couldn't recall it, and I thought how if I had been his girlfriend instead of Lee's I would have stayed there with him in that living room that seemed to just suck up light and would have heard from the inside the door slam and the van's motor start.

Lee and I drove back east a bit, to have a look at the Smokies. We parked the van in a campground under a bruise-colored sunset and set off on foot to pick up some food to cook outside on a fire. There were bugs, though, even though it was chilly, and the rutted clay road slipped and smacked underfoot, so we stopped at a Bar-B-Que place, where doughy families shouted at each other under throbbing fluorescent lights.

I had a headache. "It's incredible," I said, "how fast every place you go gets to be home. We've only just parked at that campground, but it's already home. And yesterday Carlos's place seemed like home. Now that seems like years ago."

"That's why it's good to travel," Lee said. "It reminds you what life really is. Finished?" he said. "Let's go."

"Let's," I said. "Let's go home." I inserted my finger under the canopy of his T-shirt sleeve, but he didn't notice particularly.

In time we came to a part of the country where mounds of what Lee said were uranium tailings winked in the sunlight, and moonlight made grand the barbed-wire lace around testing sites, Lee said they were, and subterranean missiles. It was quite flat, but I felt that we were crossing it vertically instead of horizontally. I felt I was on ropes behind Lee, struggling up a sheer rock face, my footing too unsure to allow me to look anywhere except at the cliff I clung to.

"What is it you're afraid of?" Lee said.

I told him I didn't know.

"Think about it," he said. "There's nothing in your mind that isn't yours."

I wondered if I should go back. I could call Tom and Johanna, I thought, but at the same instant I realized that they weren't really friends of mine. I didn't know Johanna very well, actually, and Tom and I, in fact, disliked each other. I had gone to bed with him one day months earlier when I went over to borrow a vice grip. He had seemed to want to, and I suppose I thought I would be less uncomfortable around him if I did. That was a mistake, as it turned out. I stayed at least as uncomfortable as before, and the only thing he said afterward was that I had a better body than he'd expected. It was a long time before I realized that what he'd wanted was to have slept with Lee's girlfriend.

When I'd returned home that afternoon carrying the vice grip that Tom remembered to hand to me when I left, I felt as if it had been Lee who had spent the afternoon rolling around with Johanna, not me with Tom, and my chest was splitting from jealousy. I couldn't keep my hands off Lee, which annoyed him—he was trying to do something to an old motorcycle that had been sitting around in the yard.

"Lee," I said, "are you attracted to Johanna?"

"What kind of question is that?" he said, sorting through the parts spread out on the dirt.

"A question question," I said.

"Everyone's attracted to everyone else," he said.

I wasn't. I wasn't attracted to Tom, for instance.

"Why do you think she stays with Tom?" I said.

"He's all right," Lee said.

"He's horrible, Lee," I said. "And he's mean. He's vain."

"You're too hard on people," Lee said. "Tom's all tied up, that's all. He's frightened."

"It's usual to be frightened," I said.

"Well, Tom can't handle it," Lee said. "He's afraid he has no resources to fall back on."

"Poor guy," I said. "He can fall back on mine. So are you attracted to Johanna?"

"Don't," Lee said, standing up and wiping his hands on an oily cloth. "Okay? Don't get shabby, please." He had gone inside then, without looking at me.

Now home was wherever Lee and I were, and I had to control my fear by climbing toward that moment when Lee would haul me up to level ground and we would slip off our ropes and stare around us at whatever was the terrain on which we found ourselves.

We started to have trouble with the van and decided to stop, because Lee knew someone we could stay with near Denver while he fixed it. We pulled up outside a small apartment building and rang a bell marked Dr. Peel Prayerwheel.

"What's his real name?" I asked Lee.

"That is," Lee said.

"Parents had some unusual opinions, huh?" I said.

"He found it for himself," Lee said.

Peel had a nervous voice that rushed in a fluty stream from his large body. His hair was long except on the top of his head, where there was none, and elaborate shaded tattoos covered his arms and neck and probably everything under his T-shirt.

We stood in the middle of the kitchen. "We'll put your things in the other room," Peel said, "and I'll bring my cot in here. That's best, that's best."

"We don't want to inconvenience you, Peel," Lee said.

"No, no," he said. "I'm only too happy to see you and your old lady in my house. All the times I came to you. When I was in the hospital. Anything I can do for you. I really mean it. You know that, buddy."

"He took me in," Peel said, turning to me. "He was like family." Peel kept standing there, blinking at the floor, but he couldn't seem to decide what else to say.

While Lee looked around town for parts or worked on the van, Peel and I mostly sat at the kitchen table and drank huge amounts of tea.

"Maybe you'd like a beer," he said one afternoon.

"Sure," I said.

"Right away. Right away," he said, pulling on his jacket.

"Oh—not if we have to go out," I said.

"You're sure?" he said. "Really? Because we can, if you want."

"Not unless you want one," I said.

"No, no," he said. "Never drink alcohol. Uncontrolled substance. Jumps right out of the bottle, whoomp! . . . Well, no real harm done, just an ugly moment . . ." He blushed then, for some reason, very dark.

When Lee came home, Peel and I would open up cans of soup and packages of saltines. "Used to cook like a bastard," Peel said. "But that's behind me now. Behind me."

One morning when we got up, Peel was standing in the middle of the kitchen.

"Good morning, Peel," I said.

"Good morning," he said. "Good morning." He stood there, looking at the floor.

"Do you want some tea?" I said.

"No, thank you," he said. Then he looked at Lee.

"Well, buddy," he said. "I got a check from my mother this morning."

"Was that good or bad?" I asked Lee later. Lee shrugged. "How does he usually live?" I said.

"Disability," Lee said. "He was in the army."

At night I felt so lonely I woke Lee up, but when we made love I kept thinking of Peel standing in the kitchen looking at the floor.

One morning I had a final cup of tea with Peel while Lee went to get gas.

"Thank you, Peel," I said. "You've been very kind."

"Not kind," Peel said. "It doesn't bear scrutiny. I had some problems, see, and your old man looked out for me. He and Annie, they used to take me in. He's a fine man. And he's lucky to have you. I can see that, little buddy. He's very lucky in that."

I reached over and touched one of Peel's tattoos, a naked girl with devil horns and huge angel wings.

"That's my lady," Peel said. "Do you like her? That's the lady that flies on my arm."

A day or two later Lee and I parked and sat in back eating sandwiches. Then Lee studied maps while I experimented along his spine, making my mouth into a shape that could be placed over each vertebra in turn.

"Cut that out," Lee said. "Unless you want to lose an hour or two."

"I don't mind," I said.

"Oh, there," Lee said. "We're just outside of Cedar City."

I looked over Lee's shoulder. "Hey, Las Vegas," I said. "I had a friend in school who got married and moved there."

"Do you want to visit her?" Lee said.

"Not really," I said.

"It isn't too far," he said. "And we can always use a shower and a bit of floor space."

"No," I said.

"Why not?" Lee said. "If she was your friend."

I didn't say anything.

Lee sighed. "What's the matter?" He turned and put his arms around me. "Speak to me."

"We'll never be alone," I said into his T-shirt.

"We're alone right now," Lee said.

"No," I said. "We're always going to stay with your friends."

"It's just temporary," Lee said. "Until we find a place we

want to be for ourselves. Anyhow, she isn't *my* friend—she's *your* friend."

"Used to be," I said. Then I said, "Besides, if we stayed with her she'd be your friend."

"Sure," Lee said. "My friend and your friend. The people we've stayed with are your friends now, too."

"Not," I said, letting slow tears soak into his T-shirt.

"Well, they would be if you wanted to think of them as friends," Lee said. His voice was tense with the effort of patience. "You're the one who's shutting them out."

"Someone isn't your friend just because they happen to be standing next to you," I said.

Lee lifted his arms from around me. He sighed and leaned his head back, putting his hands against his eyes.

"I'm sorry you're so unhappy," he said.

"You're sorry I'm a problem," I said.

"You're not a problem," he said.

"Well, then I should be," I said. "You don't even care enough about me for me to be a problem."

"You know," Lee said, "sometimes I think I care about you more than you care about me."

"Sure," I said. "If caring about someone means you don't want anything from them. In fact, you know what?" I said, but I had no idea myself what I was going to say next, so it was just whatever came out with the torrent of sobs I'd unstoppered. "We've called all your friends because you don't want to be with me, and you want people I know to help you not be with me, too, but we won't even call my parents and they're only less than a day away because then I might turn out to be real and then you'd have to figure out what to do with me instead of waiting for me to evaporate because you're tired of me and we're going to keep going from one friend of yours to another and making other people into friends of yours and then they'll all help you think of some way to leave me so you can go back to Annie whoever she is or grind me into a paste just like come to think of it you probably did to Annie anyhow."

"Oh, Jesus," Lee said. "What is going on?"

I leaned my head against his arm and let myself cry loudly and wetly.

"All right," Lee said, folding his arms around me again. "O.K."

"Come on," Lee said after a while. "We'll find a phone and call your parents."

I was still blinking tears when we pulled into an immense parking lot at the horizon of which was a supermarket, also immense, that served no visible town. It had become evening, and the supermarket and the smaller stores attached to it were all closed, even though there were lights inside them.

"There," Lee said. "There's a phone, way over there." He reached for the shift, but I jumped out.

"I'll walk," I said.

There was a shallow ring of mountains all around, dark against the greenish sky, and night was filling up the basin we were in. The glass phone booth, so solitary in the parking lot, looked like a tiny, primitive spaceship.

I rarely spoke to my parents, and I had never seen the mobile home where they'd now lived for years. It couldn't be possible, I thought, that I had only to dial this phone to speak to them. Why would the people who were my parents be living at the other end of that phone call?

When I sat down inside the phone booth and closed the door, a light went on. Perhaps when I lifted the receiver instructions would issue from it. How surprised Lee would be to see the little glass compartment tremble, then lift from the ground and arc above the mountains. I picked up the receiver, unleashing only the dial tone, and dialed my parents' number.

My mother was out playing cards, my father told me.

"Why aren't you with her?" I said. "I thought you liked to play, too."

"You thought wrong," my father said. "And anyway," he said, "I can't stand the scum she's scooped up in this place."

"Well," I said, "I guess you've probably found friends of your own there."

"Friends," my father said. "Poor SOBs could only make it as far as a trailer park, you'd think they were living in Rolls-Royces."

"Well," I said.

"They're nosy, too," my father said. "These people are so nosy it isn't funny."

"Sorry to hear it," I said.

"It's nothing to me," my father said. "I don't go out, anyhow. My leg's too bad."

A tide shrank in my chest.

"Hear anything from Mike and Philly?" I said.

"Yeah—Philly's doing quite well, as a matter of fact," my father said. "Quite well. Spoke to him just the other week. He's managing some kind of club, apparently."

"Probably a whorehouse," I said, not into the phone.

"What?" my father said.

I didn't say anything.

"What?" he said again.

"That's great," I said. "What about Mike?"

"Mike," my father said. "He left Sharon again. That clown. Sharon called and said would we take the kids for a while. Of course we would have if we could. I don't think she's too great for those kids, anyhow."

A Greyhound bus had appeared in the parking lot, and a man carrying a small suitcase climbed out. I wondered where he could possibly be going. He walked into the darkness, and then the bus was gone in darkness, too.

"What about you?" my father said. "What're you up to? Still got that boyfriend?"

"Yes," I said. I glanced over at the van. It looked miniature in front of the vast supermarket window, itself miniature against the line of mountains in the sky. "In fact," I said, "we were thinking of coming to visit you."

"Jesus," said my father. "Don't tell me this one's going to marry you. Hey," he said suspiciously, "where're you calling from?"

It was almost totally dark, and cold lights were scattered in the hills. People probably lived up there, I thought, in little ranch-style houses where tricycles, wheels in the air, and broken toys lay on frail patches of lawn like weapons on a deserted battlefield.

"I said, where are you calling from?" my father said again.

"Home," I said. "I have to get off now, though."

As soon as I hung up, the phone started to ring. It would be the operator asking for more money. It was still ringing when I climbed into the van, but I could hardly hear it from there.

Lee and I sat side by side for a moment. "It's peaceful here," I said.

"Yeah," Lee said.

"No one was home," I said.

"All right," Lee said—there were different reasons he might have let me say that, I thought—"let's go on."

That night I apologized.

"It's all right," Lee said.

"No," I said. "And I really do like your friends. I liked staying with them."

"We won't do it anymore," Lee said.

"We can't stay at motels," I said. "And it's nice to get out of the van every once in a while."

Lee didn't say anything.

"Besides," I said. "We don't even know where we're going."

I wondered if Lee had fallen asleep. "What about your friend Kathryn"—I said it softly, in case he had—"that Carlos mentioned? Would you like to see her?"

"Well," Lee said finally, "she doesn't live that far from here."

As soon as we climbed out of the van in front of Kathryn's house, a girl flew out of the door, landing in Lee's arms. They laughed and kissed each other and laughed again.

"Maggie," Lee said, "what are you doing here?"

"Fact is, Lee," she said, "Buzzy's partner got sent up, so I'm staying here awhile case anybody's looking for anybody."

"Yeah?" Lee said. "Is Buzzy here?"

"He's up in Portland," she said. "He said it would be better if we went in different directions just till this cools off. I guess he's got a honey up there."

Lee shook his head, looking at her.

"Never mind, baby," she said. "I'll win, you know that. I always win." Lee laughed again.

Inside, Kathryn put out her hands and Lee held them. Then she looked at me. "You're cold," she said. "Stand by the fire, and I'll get you something to put on."

"I'm O.K.," I said. "Anyhow, I've got things in the van." But she took a huge, flossy blanket from the back of the sofa and wound it slowly around and around me.

"You look like a princess!" Maggie said. "Doesn't she? Look, Lee—she looks like a princess that's—what are those stories?—under a dark enchantment." Kathryn stood back and looked.

We drank big hot glasses of applejack and cinnamon, and the firelight splashed shadows across us. Kathryn and Maggie and Lee talked, their words scattering and shifting with the fire.

Numbness inched into my body, and my mind struggled to make sense of what my ears heard. Maggie had left the room—I grasped that—and Lee and Kathryn were talking about Carlos.

"I miss him. You know that, Lee?" Kathryn was saying. "I think about a lot of people, but I miss Carlos."

"You should call him," I tried to say, but my sleeping voice couldn't.

"Well," Lee said.

"Wait," I wanted my voice to say. I knew I wouldn't be able to listen much longer. "He talked about you. . . ."

"I don't know," Lee said. "I found myself feeling sorry for him. It was pretty bad. I hated to feel that way, but it seems like he hasn't grown. He just hasn't grown, and the thing is, he's lost his nerve."

"Kathryn," I wanted to say, and couldn't, and couldn't, "Carlos wants to see you."

I slid helplessly into sleep, and it must have taken me some time to struggle back to the surface, because when I'd managed to, Lee was saying, "Yeah, she is. She's very nice. We're having some problems now, though. And I don't know if I can help her anymore."

I heard it as a large globe floating near me, just out of reach. I tried to hold it, to turn it this way and that, but it bobbed away on the surface as I slipped under again.

I woke in a bed in another room, bound and sweating in the blanket, and I could hear Lee's and Kathryn's voices as a murmur. I flung the blanket away and pushed myself out of my clothes as sleep swallowed me once more.

In the morning I awoke puffed and gluey from unshed tears. I wrapped the blanket around myself and followed voices and the smell of coffee into the kitchen where Maggie and Kathryn and Lee were eating pancakes.

"That's one sensational blanket," Maggie said. "This morning it makes you look like Cinderella."

I dropped the blanket. "Now it makes me look like Lady Godiva," I said, not smiling. Kathryn's laugh flashed in the room like jewelry.

When I came back to the kitchen, dressed, the others were having seconds. "Oh, God," Maggie said. "Remember those apple pancakes you used to make, Lee? Those were the best."

"I haven't made those in a long time," Lee said. "Maybe I'll do that one of these mornings."

"If we're going to be staying for a while, I want to go get some things from town," I said, standing back up.

"Relax," Lee said. "We'll drive in later."

Kathryn and Maggie gave us a list of stuff they needed, and we set out.

"Kathryn's very beautiful," I said. "Maggie is too."

"Yeah," Lee said.

"You and Kathryn seem like good friends," I said.

"We're old friends," Lee said. "Your feelings never change about old friends."

"Like Carlos," I said. "Hey, why is Maggie's boyfriend giving her a hard time?"

"He's an asshole," Lee said.

"Kathryn doesn't have a boyfriend," I said.

"No," Lee said.

"She must get lonely up there," I said.

"I don't think so," Lee said. "Besides, people come to her a lot."

"Yes," I said.

"Like Maggie," he said. "People who need something."

We parked in the shopping center lot and went to the supermarket and the hardware store and the drugstore, and Lee climbed back into the van.

"You go on ahead," I said. "There's some other stuff I need to do."

"It's a long walk back," Lee said.

"I know," I said.

"You're sure you know the way?" he said.

"Yes," I said.

"It's cold," he said.

"I know," I said.

"All right," he said, "if that's what you want."

I felt a lot better. I felt pretty good. I looked around the parking lot and saw people whose arms were full of packages or who held children by the hand. I watched the van glide out onto the road, and I saw it accelerate up along the curve of the days ahead. Soon, I saw, Lee would pull up in front of Kathryn's house; soon he would step through the door and she would turn; and soon—not that afternoon, of course, but soon enough—I would be standing again in this parking lot, ticket in hand, waiting to board the bus that would appear so startlingly in front of me, as if from nowhere.

Days

I had never known what I was like until I stopped smoking, by which time there was hell to pay for it. When the haze cleared over the charred landscape, the person I had always assumed to be behind the smoke was revealed to be a tinny weights-and-balances apparatus, rapidly disassembling on contact with oxygen.

The First Two Weeks I lie on the floor and howl with grief. A friend tells me, "During the third week it will occur to you that you're insane, and you'll think, Well, now I'm insane. What difference does it make whether I smoke or not? This is a trick to get you to smoke."

The Third Week I am insane, but I am determined to wait it out.

Today I bump into someone crossing the street. I begin an apology, but when he tells me to watch where I am going in a tone I consider unnecessarily condemning, I seize him by the lapels. For an instant we look at each other. Then I release him back into the surge of pedestrians and continue on, stiff with fear.

I have gained twenty pounds. I weep unstintingly for the victims of tragedy I see around me on subways, in restaurants, and on the street, but the victims look at me oddly and move away. I find that I have elaborate opinions about things I have never previously given a thought to, and that it is imperative that everyone within earshot understand exactly what I mean, and why, in detail, I mean it.

Everything makes me angry, unless it makes me sad. I cannot tell how long anything takes.

Spring   The smoke-free air is a flat, abrasive surface that I must inch my way along, but I am subject to sudden seizures of pellucid hatred which impel me out the door during dinner or in the early hours of the morning, or, when I am too helpless to move, into weak, furious storms of tears. Although I am demanding and insatiable, everything I want is sucked dry of flavor and color and warmth by the time I get it, like packaged foods in an employee cafeteria. When I wake up in the morning, my jaws ache.

Friends   My attachments to people are chaotic and unreliable. I can't tell whether I am behaving oddly or not. Sometimes I feel that people think I am but don't mention it, and this makes me angry when I think they're right. I am angrier, however, when I think they're wrong.

Sometimes I explode at a surprised acquaintance. I am afraid that I may say the final thing to someone, but these episodes occur so quickly that no one seems to comprehend what has happened. There is a feeling only of a slight break in continuity, as if a roomful of people had received an extraterrestrial visit that was posthypnotically expunged.

Summer

I have always not been able to do things, but I can't rely on this as a principle now. Unfortunately, it is now possible to find out what I am not able to do only by observing myself in action. If I start to shake or fume, whatever it is that I'm doing is something I don't do. I feel that I am a zoologist trying to discover the natural environment of an unknown animal found in a pet store. I wish this were the task of someone else, but the biological setup of our planet requires a rather strict one-to-one relationship between each corporeal entity and the consciousness with which it is accustomed to associate, and it seems that I am stuck. I will just have to keep trying various things, according to no principles whatsoever.

I Take a Vacation

I go spend several weeks in a huge house with many people where I seem unable to go outside into the sunlight. Instead I lie in bed in my dark, chilly room, drinking glass after glass of vodka. Once in a while I break an emptied bottle on the wall or the floor.

Occasionally I feel called upon to say something. "Well, I don't know," I say when I encounter someone in the kitchen, where I sit for hours late at night staring and crying. "I'm feeling a little weird lately." This seems to take care of the matter.

One day someone takes me to swim, which is something I have not done voluntarily for as long as I can remember, in the warm, curving pool of a nearby motel, which hums with fluorescent light.

I was once told that catatonics seem to enjoy swimming and I can see why. The water registers one's presence and confers meaning to one's motor impulses, yet there is no threat in water, as there always is in air, of sudden, shattering injuries, inflicted or received.

I think I might like to try going swimming again, if I can find someplace to do it in the city.

Kathy tells me that she goes swimming at the YMCA, and she points out that there's no reason I shouldn't try it. She is an extremely judicious person. If she doesn't see any reason not to try it, I probably don't have to think through the whole thing to see if I do. Next Tuesday she will bring me as her guest.

I find that often between opening my eyes in the morning and putting on my final piece of clothing, three or four hours will elapse. Sometimes I am on my way out the door when something happens—the phone rings, or I notice that there are dishes in the sink, or I remember that I should get a load of laundry together, or I catch an unnerving glimpse of myself in the mirror, or I realize that I have errands that lie in opposite directions and that none of them is really important enough to take precedence over the others, or important enough to do at all, when it comes down to it, and that I don't have enough money to do all, or maybe even any, of them, and I probably never will, and even if I should, so what—and there I am for the rest of the day.

People quite often ask me what I do with my time. I don't know what to tell them. Actually, I don't know what they are getting at. What it really is that I don't know is why they want to make me feel the way they are obviously going to make me feel when they ask me this.

Wednesday Kathy took me to swim at the Y with her yesterday.

In the Y The Y is this whole thing. In it there are floors and floors and floors, all equipped for different kinds of amusements. On the third floor alone, besides the locker room for women and the showers and the sauna, and the clothes dryer, and the lounge with a TV, there is a meeting room, the Mini-Gym, and the Martial Arts Room.

The Roof On top of the Y there is a roof with brightly colored plastic chairs shaped like long, narrow hands, which hold people tenderly under the sun.

The Track There is a track on the eighth floor—a thin band around the edge of a room on which people in sneakers run slowly around to music that sounds like it is coming from a cranked-up toy.

The Basketball Court There is nothing in the middle of the track—just a huge hole bounded by a railing, under which there is the seventh-floor basketball court. From the side of the track, Kathy and I watch long lines of people doing sloppy-looking exercises on the court below.

The Pool The tiny, cold pool is on another floor altogether, which seems mostly to have something to do with men

The pool has its own showers, and it has a man, too, who sits in a little glass booth. The pool feels unbearably cold, but Kathy convinces me that it's necessary to suspend one's evaluation of the temperature until after half a length.

Kathy I ask Kathy how she can remember where everything is. She says, "Well, someone once asked my mother how she remembered all of our names, and I mean, that really just wasn't one of her problems with us."

But in fact Kathy can also, when the elevator stops in front of us, tell whether it's on its way up or down.

The Locker Room The best thing, I think, is the locker room. At its portals is Bess, who lights up in a smile upon seeing Kathy. Dusty sunlight streams down on her through the wire meshing on the windows.

In the locker room itself, everything is very quiet, and the lockers are arranged in rows, like a cornfield, so you don't have to stand in the middle of a bare room, all fat. There are large lockers to use while you're in the building and small lockers, not big enough for real clothes, to use when you're not. This is to save space (and it really does; I figured it out).

There are women combing their hair by dryers on the wall and talking quietly by their lockers. Somewhere a voice says, "Well, the trouble with anesthesiology is, everyone you work with is asleep."

The Sauna The sauna is like a little tropical hut.

Monday Kathy calls to ask if I want to go to the Y tomorrow. I'd like to, and probably I'll be able to, especially because she wants to meet there, so I won't be able to call her at the last minute and cancel.

Smoking It used to be that I never got angry. That is, I would start to feel angry, but the moment I opened my mouth to voice my feelings a cigarette would be inserted into it, and instead of expelling a stream of words I would inhale a stream of smoke. Only then would I exhale, casting a velvety mist over everything in the vicinity. How I long to do that again!

Tuesday We do get to the Y today, just as planned.

In the lobby we decide we are going to swim, sauna, and exercise. Many showers and changes of costume are entailed by this program, and when we try to determine the most expeditious way to proceed, I feel helpless and defeated. Kathy suggests we take each thing as we come to it, and I feel much better.

We hang our jeans and T-shirts on hooks in the large locker. We put our shoes on the bottom and line up the soap, shampoo, and our pocketbooks on the top shelf. The locker is like a small apartment, and we are keeping it nice. We have both more or less mooshed our underwear into our jeans, but everything is still at a manageable stage. It takes a lot of concentration to remember, between taking things off and putting things on, and putting in the large locker and on oneself the things that one has brought, and putting in the large locker and on oneself the things that have been in the small locker, exactly where each thing should go. But when we are finally ready to go up to the pool, I feel that I have a solid foundation on which to build.

Upstairs, without seeming to notice us particularly, the swimmers adjust their lines more narrowly, and we climb in. I swim back and forth, twice on my side, and twice with a kickboard.

It takes a lot of effort to keep your head from getting wet when you swim, so that in itself is probably very good exercise.

Downstairs, I can't help noticing that people shower at dramatically different tempi. No one in the shower seems disturbed by this, however, so I assume there is no normative manner in which to shower, and proceed in my own way. No one says anything about it, either encouraging or derogatory.

Spending Time

I like the women who are here in the locker room in this long afternoon, and I wonder about their lives. A picture comes into my mind and grows. In this picture I am still here in the locker room, but it is winter now, and the light is falling. I have a career, in this picture. I am a banker, or an account executive, whatever that is, or I work for a foundation. Every day after work, I go to the Y and I swim back and forth in the pool or stretch and bend in the tiny, dark gym. There are other women in the locker room, these women perhaps, and others. Their lives are less substantial than mine, and they dress quickly and simply, leaving before I do, to go home to small apartments. I shower and dry myself and take from my locker a long silk slip and a gown. I put on a necklace and earrings of dark pearls, fine pale stockings, and shiny shoes with very high heels. I take from my locker a long fur stole and wrap myself up in it. I walk down the stairs—moonlight throws the shadow of the wire cage across my gloved hand on the railing, and my shiny shoes resonate on the linoleum. As I leave the building, the last few others are hurrying off along the slushy sidewalk or unchaining bicycles from the rack in front of the building. I am left alone now on the wide front steps where I am waiting.

I wish it were winter now.

Ellen calls and asks what I'm doing with myself. When I say I don't really know, she says, "Well, I mean, you get up, and then what do you do?"

Sometimes it seems to me that there is a growing number of women, and that I am not among them.

I joined the Y today. It will turn out to be a big, horrible waste of money, but I just wanted to be at the Y, which is cool and dim and echoing. It is automatically reassuring to be in that building filled with people of different colors and backgrounds and ages. The web of commonality is a safety net, in case anybody might be falling. Falling . . .

For days I have not been able to get out of the apartment. About the point at which it is borne in on me that it is going to be impossible to leave, I begin to get angry. I feel as if years of rage have condensed around the sides of my brain and are dripping down into it, forming pools in which all its other contents are becoming sodden and useless.

Today I go to the Y and I change and shower and swim and shower and ride a bicycle that doesn't move in the Mini-Gym, and shower and sauna and shower and change, and now I have done all these things alone.

Oh, I see how Kathy can tell whether the elevator is going up or down. There is a little arrow that lights up when the door opens, either red, pointing down, or green, pointing up.

Today was my sixth time at the Y. I know Kathy so well, but I didn't know this about her: she has a whole life at the Y that she shares with scores and scores of people who don't know her at all. I like to come to the Y with Kathy and be part of things, but I like to come alone, too. I feel that I am cultivating a silent area of my life.

I think I'm swimming a bit better. I can do five lengths now, and I can swim on my back and on each of my sides. I still can't quite put my head in the water, though. The water is always cold at first, but I think about how short half a length is, and then I can do it.

Ellen calls again, to see if I am feeling O.K., which I am until she calls. I tell her that I'm swimming a lot these days. She says, "I didn't know you could swim. How much do you do?"

People will go so far to make each other feel bad. But I don't feel bad. After all, I do go swimming.

The Y is a secret that everybody knows! I see people there that I know from all sorts of other places, and I see people from the Y all over the neighborhood. Sometimes in a store I will see that a person behind the counter or one shopping in the next aisle is really a pleasant seal from the pool.

In the locker room today I run into Jennifer, a woman I know a bit from somewhere else. She tells me that swimming is the best exercise there is! What a nice person.

The pool is so cold today I can't even do my half a length to get warm. I stand there and stand there in the shallow end, but I just can't do it.

Downstairs I tell Bess, "Just couldn't swim today. Just too cold."

"Ummmm hmmmm," she says equably.

I get to the Y again today, but I just can't face the idea of getting into, or failing to get into, the pool. I can't face going back home, though, either, so I settle on the Mini-Gym, which is very soothing. It has the ghostly atmosphere of a schoolroom during vacation.

Today a man does sit-ups facing the windows. A woman, also facing the windows, bends in half exactly as the man's fingers reach his toes. Another woman opposite the first stretches her arms in an arc above her head. I choose a central latitude, perpendicular to the others. I lie on my side and begin to raise a leg to the silent count.

I have just realized something really terrifying—*I don't swim!* I feel sick. What did I think I was doing, going swimming? I wasn't going swimming! I can't swim! I can't even put my head in the water!

This can't go on, my just coming to the Y to do exercises. It is a *known fact* that no one can do exercises regularly. Every single magazine article about it says they're just too boring to do regularly. Also, it only takes half an hour. One change of clothes, one shower, and then I have to go home.

Late at night I think of the terrible things I've put my friends through in the past months. I begin to think of the things I've always put my parents through, and I know this means big trouble. I get out of bed in a sweat of fear and call my friends, crying stormily, and cry more because I've awakened them.

Thursday At the Y today, chunks of a conversation that had been going on around me in the shower suddenly reassemble—feet, minutes, miles, and pacing—to reveal, whole in my auditory memory, a conversation about running.

Also Thursday THAT I CANNOT SWIM DOES NOT NECESSARILY MEAN I CANNOT RUN. This thought breaks over me with repeating fresh force, like peals of hallucinatorily echoing thunder.

Friday Now that I have been sensitized, I realize that for months I have been surrounded by a continuous susurrus about running.

Saturday Not only is running not cold, but I won't drown if I should stop suddenly. I think on Monday I'll just give it a whirl.

Monday I can't get out of the apartment. The hours stretch and telescope. I find myself standing over the kitchen table, which I had approached for some reason earlier. I break out of position only to find that some minutes have elapsed during which I have been staring into the mirror. At what, I wonder. I remember that I had meant to get something from the table, but I seem to be sitting in the other room, where a dull awareness of things to be done impinges on me. Outside the window, the day, in nervous jumps, dies.

Tuesday This morning I am propelled to the Y. I don't know exactly how I am going to pitch into my goal of running once I get there, but it can't be all that impossible. I clearly remember the track that Kathy showed me the first day she brought me, and what it was was a track, is all, with people running around it.

Besides, I could always sound out the friendly guard, whose name, I have learned, is Surf—or Serf, it could be. Oh—it could be Cerf, come to think of it. I change into my gym clothes and a pair of socks borrowed from a sock-wearing friend and my old but unloved blue sneakers and wander out into the hall, where I do in fact find Surf.

Am I going to grab him by the shoulders, cover his hands with kisses, and implore him to tell me what I should do? No. I casually mention that I am going to do some running today.

"Have you ever run before?" he asks. I look at him closely, but the face that looks back is a neutral one. I tell him that I haven't. "Well, don't do too much," he says. "About four laps today. You've got to go easy at first."

Good. Without having aroused his suspicion (what do I mean? suspicion of what?) I have gotten the information I need, which is that, despite the supercharged atmosphere of conversations about it, there is no particular trick to running, unless, of course, there is something so obvious that Surf wouldn't have thought to tell me, or so embarrassing that he couldn't bring himself to tell me, or so ineffable that he wasn't able to tell me.

I take the elevator to the eighth floor, which is where the track is, I know, even though I haven't seen it since my first day.

The Track Now that I am about to set foot on it, I find the track a great deal more interesting than I did when I last saw it. There is a tiny, enticing stairway on the far side of the track. A sign pointing down to it says, TO THE PHYSICAL OFFICE. What sort of office could that be?

On the track are some people I have seen in the locker room, the pool, or the Mini-Gym, and some entirely new people, including a few leathery men who look too old even to walk. All of these people are running slowly around the track, and I study them to see if there's anything I can pick up about what they're doing, but the basic move seems to be just what one would think—one foot down, then the other in front of it, the first again in front, and so on.

Then suddenly I myself step out onto the track, easing myself into the light traffic. It becomes almost instantly clear that the slowness with which the others had appeared to run is illusory. They are running fast, very fast indeed. My legs are moving as fast as I can move them, I lean out ahead of my feet, my mind empty of everything except the sounds of feet and breath, but everyone on the track is streaking by me. The track itself, which only minutes earlier appeared to be a tiny oval, now seems immense. It takes a long, long time to round the ends, and the straight goes on forever. I notice also that there is a bunchy, horizonal cast to my forward progress in comparison to that of my trackmates.

It occurs to me that the four laps suggested by Surf are an unrealistic goal, and I downward revise to three.

Downstairs Jennifer is at her locker, and while I'm working up the energy to open my locker, I tell her that I'm running now, instead of swimming.

"Terrific," she says warmly. "How much do you do?"

"Three laps," I tell her. We look at each other in consternation. Then I think to add that today was my first day, and we are less embarrassed.

Wednesday My legs hurt incredibly. I lie in bed while the hours parade by me, icy and knowing, like competitors in a beauty contest.

Thursday At the Y I run three laps, I walk five laps, and then I run two more laps!

On the way home, I treat myself, on impulse, to a pair of socks, all my own, and appropriate in appearance. I just go into a store and ask for tube socks.

I have always wondered, up until this moment, whenever I have heard them mentioned, what tube socks are. Now I realize that not only do I, like everyone else, know exactly what tube socks are but also that they are exactly what I want. (How could I ever have pretended to myself that I don't know what tube socks are?! Nobody can't know what tube socks are! They're SOCK TUBES, and they are the only sort of socks that make any sense, because you just stick your foot into one any old way and leave it there, and the sock, not your foot, has to adjust. The feelings of confusion produced by the term "tube sock" are not, I realize, due to the nature of the tube sock itself but rather to the term's implication that all socks are not tube socks and the attendant question of why they are not.) The pair I pick out has elegant bands of navy and dark red near the tops.

It seems that my commitment to my socks was warranted. It is now several weeks since I bought them, and I have still been going to the track. Not every day, of course, but what I would call several times a week. I only fear that my impulses to run are a mistake, like my impulses, for instance, to sew, which, upon examination, invariably turn out to be impulses of some other kind—impulses, perhaps, to own a certain garment, or impulses to be *able* to sew, or impulses to be the sort of person who likes to sew, or whatever, but not primary sewing impulses.

In an attempt to eliminate possible hypocrisy from my approach, I have taken to testing myself as I stand at the edge of the track. I say to myself in a voice of profound compassion, a voice that it would be rude to ignore and one that it is difficult not to answer in the way it obviously hopes to be answered, "Well. That certainly does look difficult. If we don't want to do it today, we truly needn't. We can just come back tomorrow! We don't always have to feel like running—sometimes we're just too tired, or too busy, or too weak. It doesn't mean we won't run again ever; it just means we won't run today." But I recognize behind the seductive insinuations a familiar enemy who wishes to swindle me out of my little bit of fun.

On the track my mind fills to the top with running.

Fall Today I walk into the Y shivering. The guards at the elevator, who always greet me now, say, "What'sa matter? You cold?" I nod yes. They look at each other and giggle. "You need a man," one of them ventures. "That's right!" the other chimes in. "You need a man!" They roar with laughter and punch each other on the arm. "You need—" they lean on each other, weak with hilarity—"you need a man like *us*!" they shout as the elevator door closes, shutting me in with five men whose grim gazes never waver from the truncated scene.

People have stopped giving me advice right on the track, so I must look more comfortable. People often ask me how long I've been running and how far I can run and tell me that the first two miles are the hardest, but that's different. I can run fifteen laps now, sometimes, which is a far cry from three, and I can almost keep up with the slowest of the tiny, ancient men who scuttle along the inside railing of the track.

What hasn't stopped is something far more humiliating than unsolicited advice. When I finish my exercises, I walk, instead of taking the elevator, up the many flights to the track. This is seriously difficult, and I do it largely for the beneficial effect it must therefore have on my willpower. Almost every third time I make this journey (thus, about once a week) some huge bozo thunders by and says something like: "Think you're going to make it? Haw, haw" or, "What have *you* been up to? Haw, haw." I used to just nod and smile weakly. "Haw, haw," I would agree as each bozo would thud off, but now I feel that I have matured beyond this exchange.

Today as I am clambering up the stairs an immense pink man in tiny white shorts careens up behind me. "You sure look beat!" he roars happily. I am ready to enter into a discussion of *his* looks, but he is gone. I feel the familiar sensation of burning rubber right below my follicles, indicating that quite soon I will be overwhelmed by fury or sorrow and the rest of my day will be spent in raging immobility. I sit down on the steps. I won't be able to run now, but I don't dare go home, either. This man has just happened by, and I am about to have been *upset* by him.

Life's blows are so swift. One is just living along (walking up some stairs, for example), and at just any moment one could contract a viral inflammation of the brain, or a loved one could be getting squashed by a car, or a carton of lead statuettes could fall on one's foot. Had I done one more round of exercises, I never even would have encountered this man who has revealed, with one careless stroke, the ruin that is my life.

A Strange Lack of Consequences It turns out that I was all right after I met that man yesterday. Something was his fault (at least, nothing was my fault). But it didn't turn out to be his fault that I couldn't run, because I *could* run. I ran, I saunaed, I showered, I got dressed, and I went home.

One thing that's quite nice about this running is that you just keep doing what you have just been doing, without having to stop to think about it.

I Risk Conscious Feelings of Desire I can no longer deny myself awareness of the fact that while I wear plain navy-blue sneakers—carried over, probably, from my horrible camp days, which, like everything else, scarred me for life—everyone else has highly evolved, stripy, elegant sneakers in the colors of toys designed in Italy for rich kids.

In the sauna today someone tells me that you begin to lose weight after you begin to run two miles a day. "Of course," she adds, "you have to stop eating, too."

Well, I'll cross that bridge when I come to it. Not that I'm running every day, either.

I Converse Like Others I am beginning to have conversations about running, just as other people do. But I can't quite get the hang of it. When people say to me, smiling, "You don't mean *you* run," I think it must be true that in some real sense I don't. It angers me that I must be so assertive on such shaky grounds to make people believe that I run, and that then when they believe me, they don't care.

I Am a Self-Reliant Person I develop a routine of stopping about halfway through my run and either walking around the track or shaking myself up on a shake-up machine I've watched other people use. I can run more this way, and the second stint is easier.

Kathy says she would like to use the machine, too, but she thinks it may be embarrassing. I am immediately embarrassed, but then I remember that it cannot precisely be said to be myself who is embarrassed. I go and use the machine.

Today I overhear a conversation between a man and a woman I know. "Oh, hey," she says. "I got those Adidas you told me to."

"The green ones?" he asks. "Fantastic."

My God. For years I have understood Adidas to be an airline. I undergo a sudden perceptual intensification, as if I were a special instrument being trained onto its proper task by expert operators. I pull up a chair and sit down. My acquaintances smile and sparkle and toss their beautiful hair. The woman is saying, "You're right about running outside. It's a whole other thing, really fantastic." Their eyes shine, their teeth flash.

"I run too!" I say suddenly.

"You?" They turn and gaze at me. "In those?" They point at my black boots with their high, spiky heels, and they laugh. I pull my feet under me and look at the floor.

Something like a pain is accruing around my left heel. If it keeps up, I may go see if the PHYSICAL OFFICE might pertain to it.

. . .

My pain is still there. If it is there again the next time I run, I'll go to the PHYSICAL OFFICE.

Sure enough, my pain is there again. I'll go to the PHYSICAL OFFICE the next time I run, if I still have it.

Today my heel hurts so much that after a few laps I have to stop. After standing at the edge of the track for a bit, I bolster myself up and follow the arrow to the PHYSICAL OFFICE.

Breakthrough The PHYSICAL OFFICE turns out to be a small, greenish room. A grinning man welcomes me, and we nod to each other many times, and then I explain that I've done something to my heel. The man prods it. "I don't know," he ventures. "Seems like you've done something to your heel."

I agree this must be it. "What should I do?" I ask. "I really can't run."

"It's probably a good idea not to run for a few days," the man tells me.

"Do you think I should get running shoes?" I ask.

The man looks reflectively off into the distance. "You know," he says, "you could probably use a pair of running shoes."

"Well, thanks a lot, then," I tell him airily. We nod and smile and wave.

Suddenly I know just what I want, what to do about it, and where to go to do it. I have sometimes passed a place, it suddenly occurs to me, called Runners World, which has in its window a line of glowing shoes.

I Get Help   I go looking for Runners World, and there it is, to my surprise, right where I expect it to be. Several people are in the store, all talking about running, and I sit and listen to them with interest for some time until a man leaning on the counter asks if I would like some help. He seems to be the ideal man, intelligent, handsome, and concerned, so I tell him yes, I would. I explain that I think I may need shoes. He asks me where I run and how much.

"Then this is the shoe for you," he says. "The SL 72." He hands me a pair of boxy, royal blue shoes with white stripes and deeply ridged soles. I had hoped for something more streamlined, with slanting, aerodynamic stripes rather than these neat, horizontal ones, in a less wholesome color; but if this is the shoe for me, this is the shoe for me.

And when I put them on, my feet are more comfortable than they have ever been before. The man who has selected these shoes for me alone tells me that he is a running coach at the Y.

"Do you run in the morning?" he asks. "Lots of girls run in the morning."

I feel that there is nothing I can't say to this man. I lean up to him and ask softly, "What's the difference between running inside and running outside?"

"Colder outside," he says, and hands me my shoes, all tucked up into their box.

My shoes live in my locker along with my tank suit, goggles, and swimming cap (which, who knows, I might want to use sometime), my yoga pants, my T-shirt, my soap and shampoo and skin cream, and several pairs of tube socks.

I can run more easily and quickly, and my feet don't hurt.

. . .

Jennifer is in the locker room today when I go in, and I show her my shoes. "Hey, wow," she says. She reaches into her locker. "Look!" she says, holding out to me an identical pair.

Winter I see Ellen today, and before she gets a chance to ask what I'm up to, I tell her that I'm running a lot lately. She is delighted to hear it. It seems that she, too, after getting home from the office, reading to the kids, clearing up after the dinner guests, studying for her orals, and knocking off an article or two for some little journal, likes to get in a few miles.

Yesterday I asked the woman in the laundry around the corner why I always get less underwear back than I put in. It has taken me years to ask this question. The woman tells me that naturally I always get the same amount of underwear back that I put in and turns back to her work, looking both insulted and smug. I stand and stare at her, unable to think of anything to say, while tears of hatred run off my face.

I spend the rest of the day walking in short bursts and stopping in phone booths, where I stand for five or ten minutes. There is no one I can bear to call. I think the woman in the laundry may be right. Even if she is wrong, it is unlikely to be her fault, really, that my underwear is disappearing. Even if she takes pleasure in depleting my raggy stock of underwear for some reason, it hardly matters. But then, why am I so angry?

In the locker room I overhear a woman telling some friends that she has picked a fight with her boyfriend this morning, saying brutal and humiliating things to him and getting him to say brutal and humiliating things to her. After she throws him out of the apartment, she slashes every one of her paintings.

At this her friends gasp. "Oh, no!" they say, with a horror that to me is obviously utterly formal and hollow. "How terrible!"

"No it isn't," the woman says. "They were bad paintings. They were all shallow and vain and cowardly."

Oh, how I wish I could paint! My paintings, too, would be shallow and vain and cowardly, and I would go home right now and slash them to ribbons.

The locker room is full of ex-smokers, doing prodigious amounts of exercise, talking torrentially at uncontrolled volume, gaining weight at a fantastic clip, lying in the sauna till they're faint, crying, drinking quantities of carrot juice, and bearing in, over the weeks, a bright rainbow of shoes.

Kathy is back in town after months away, and I get to take her to the Y on my guest pass, and we use my locker. "Hi," "Hi, Kath," "Howrya doin'?" people say, glad to see her but not at all surprised, because everyone comes and goes. Kathy has returned to find me a good person to go running with.

Running

Sometimes it's quite easy to run. I step out on the track, and I run around and around and around, and once in a while, a spring is released in my body after a mile or so, and I am flooded with power. Sweat springs to my surface, and I speed along with no effort, as in a dream of flying. I try to forget these episodes as soon as they're over; I feel that running on the basis of hoping for another one would be like believing in God in order to pray for a Mercedes.

Sometimes it's very difficult to run, and boring, too. Each lap seems endless, and my legs feel stiff and weighted. It's even difficult on these days to remember how many laps I've done. On these bad days, I sometimes feel so tired that just going home is a major endeavor. People in the street seem to sense my fatigue and say wounding things about me. These people should be more careful. People look so solid, I look so solid, walking along; but hit suddenly with something heavy, people could just topple over or gust into the air like old, empty cardboard boxes.

On extremely good days, I step smartly out of the door to go home, and people in the street move over to include me in their numbers, or even nod approvingly as I walk along exhibiting human health. On such days the winter seems mild and pleasant.

An Unpleasant Encounter

Today I get to the Y much later than I've ever been there, and everything is completely different. The basketball court below the track is thronging with tiny little girls in bright leotards shimmering on balance beams and bouncing into the air on trampolines, like bright kernels of popcorn. The track is very crowded, and the people on it look serious and fast. A lawyer I know is among those running, and I feel self-conscious. There is an implicit pressure in the growing dark at the windows, so unlike the pale, tranquil wash I am used to there.

After I run a mile, I take a breather by the side of the track, and a man standing near me says, "You weren't out there very long." I can't tell what this man is up to, but I can tell it's not right. "How much did you do?" he asks.

" 'Bout a mile," I tell him.

"That's not very much," he says, in the whining, punitive tone of an adult bent on forcing a child to admit to a wrongdoing. "How long have you been running?"

When I was about thirteen, a man sitting next to me on a train put his hand more or less up my skirt. He just sat there then, perfectly happy, and I just sat there, afraid of hurting his feelings in case he hadn't noticed where his hand was, or had a good reason for having put it there, or something, until the stop before mine, when I said, "Oh, I'm sorry, I have to get out soon." Ever since then I have made an effort to evaluate dispassionately my rights and needs against those of others; but it's not so easy, as we all know, and I often err to the advantage of one party or the other.

I decide to give the man next to me the benefit of the doubt, and I tell him how long I've been running. "Oh?" he says. "That's funny. You should be used to it by now." And he steps out on the track again.

I step out, too, to run, but I find that I can't, and lock into a standstill at the inside of the track, although stopping on the track is, for good reason, absolutely forbidden. My visual field—a wheel of thundering men encircling a space through which little red and blue and green girls are flying—tilts and spins, as in a film.

The man passes me once, twice, three times. He knows that I am there, but he won't look at me. The fourth time he goes by, my hand shoots out and grabs his arm. I glimpse the lawyer I know looking surprised, but not surprised enough for me. "What did you mean, I should be used to it?" I ask the man in my grasp. My hands are shaking. "Oh, not really anything," he says. His tone is careful. "You must have meant something"—I speak slowly, with admirable self-control—"and I wonder what it was you did mean."

"I'll tell you," he says. "I want to finish running first, and then I'll talk to you." He breaks away. I wait. I keep waiting, and the man keeps running. He's obviously quite tired, but he's too alarmed to stop. When he gets a bit blue around the edges, I thread my way off the track, stand for a minute out of sight on the stairwell, and then peek back out, catching the eye of my man, who is now walking, to show him that he need not think I'm gone. He starts to run again. Satisfied, I go down to the locker room.

At a locker near mine, a blond woman with a nice atmosphere whom I have often seen on the track is changing her clothes. I tell her what has just happened to me.

"What a drip," she says. "Most people here aren't like that at all. I bet you felt like picking him up by his feet and smashing his head on the track," she says in her pleasant voice, pulling up her socks.

"Gee, I feel awful," I say, and sniffle.

"Me too," she says. "I think I'm coming down with a cold." We go downstairs together and out into the benign evening.

My Dream This is a dream I frequently have: I glance down at my hand. The posture I have denied it for so long, the gesture it has so often hopelessly initiated, is suddenly deliciously completed. I am holding a lit cigarette! I am now able, I reason in my dream, to display the scope of my will. I can either inhale from this cigarette in my hand or not, as I freely choose. I freely choose to inhale, and the fantasy instantly collapses; the entire mendacious simulacrum shivers and falls at my feet, leaving me—a slave who will have to smoke now, forever—in the barren waking world where it is easy to recognize the dreadful thing I had briefly mistaken for choice. Then I wake truly, empty-handed in the merciful morning.

Spring I do three miles! At the end of my second mile, and then at the end of my second and a half, rather than feeling I am at the end of my capacity, I feel as though I have established a new relationship with my legs, and I don't want to stop, ever. But I do at the end of three miles, anyhow, because

I don't want to hurt myself or to become a different sort of person without giving the matter proper thought.

I call up Kathy and tell her. "Hey, Kath, I ran three miles!" "Hey, wow, that's really great!" she tells me. I try to describe the sensation I had of sudden ease and endless availability of energy. "I think that's what they mean by a second wind," Kathy says. "That's why it's possible for a person like you or me to run three or six or twenty-six miles, because you can get it over and over again."

"Sometime I'd like to try for five miles," I tell Kathy. "Why not?" she says, excited by the idea. "They say the first three miles are the hardest."

The days are becoming brighter and longer. The air and the city have expanded in the warmth, and there is room to walk around. In different parts of the city, clusters of silvery buildings gleam, their surfaces reflecting clear sky and sailing clouds, and men and women stride among them, their clothing billowing like pennants. In the bright sunshine, stores spring up, windows full of gaudy running shoes. What a bore.

Tuesday On my way to the Y I notice how hot it is. Far too hot to run. I turn around and go home, where I have things to do.

Wednesday It is even hotter today.

Thursday I run today, but after a mile I am ready to die of boredom and exhaustion.

. . .

During the past few weeks I've felt so impatient at the Y. I find that somehow I can hardly run, it is too hot to sauna, the conversations I overhear are dull and trivial, and the exercise apparatuses look dingy and foolish.

The man who gave me a hard time on the track has established residency in my mind. I discover that just as he exercises power over me, I can exercise power over him. This man in my mind may have a low opinion of me, but I can have a low opinion of him, too, if I so choose. I can have a low opinion of his low opinion of me as well. Also, I notice, I can have a high opinion of his low opinion of me, an opinion that according to this very schema is worthless. I amuse myself by raising and lowering him in my estimation and by combining in various ways, and then distinguishing between, him, his opinion of me, me, and my opinion of him.

It seems that an opinion of someone is not a serious matter.

The sun penetrates through the sky to my skin, and I blink in the light like a bear coming out of hibernation. I feel that I have been dreaming watchfully in this hibernation, my sleeping brain accounting for many passing years, and that I have awakened suddenly, shedding the strain of my dreams, to find that less time has elapsed than has been mourned in my sleep.

Years have passed, it is true, but not many, many years.

Halfway to the Y I remember that I haven't brought my towel. I turn around and go back to the apartment. After I lock the door again, go downstairs, and proceed three or four blocks toward the Y, I remember that once again I have forgotten my towel. I can rent one at the Y, but the one I rent would not be *my* towel, which had figured (in its own small way, to be sure) in my plans for the day. I turn around, go home, hang up some clothes I had left on a chair, make the bed so I won't get in it, and leave, locking the door and heading for the Y, forgetting, it occurs to me some few blocks later, my towel.

Clearly I am not supposed to go to the Y today. But then, what am I supposed to do? I stop to think, causing a pileup on the corner.

Back at home I sit down on the neatly made bed. I put my hands over my ears and shut my eyes to clear my mental field. A little directive asserts itself. It is appearing as neatly as if it were being typed out on a fortune-cookie slip. I AM HUNGRY, it tells me, and, by gum, I *am* hungry. Today, instead of going to the Y, I will take myself out to lunch.

I allow my new skills to lead me to a restaurant. I notice with some surprise that the restaurant I have chosen is a pretentious vegetarian restaurant, crowded and uncomfortable. I consult myself and reveal that I would like soup du jour and a house salad. The soup, which I already know to be overpriced, turns out to be terrible as well. I eat it with great relish. My salad arrives, a wilting pile of vegetable parings garnished with American cheese.

"Chopsticks?" asks the waitress. I do a quick internal scan. "Yes, please." I top off my lunch with a cup of lukewarm coffee, pay the shocking check, and ease myself out of my small torture chair, sighing with satisfaction.

At home I again ask myself what I would like to do, and again my answer arrives. I want, it appears, to write letters. Perhaps there's been some mistake, I think. But I decide to try, and I find it is true: I do want to write letters.

It is amazing to be able to find out what I want to do at any given moment, out of what seems to be nothing, out of not knowing at all. It is secretly and individually thrilling, like being able to open my fist and release into the air a flock of white doves.

My new insight has stood the test of time. Three days have passed, and it has not faded. I call Kathy and tell her that I've discovered the point of life.

"Gosh!" she says. "What is it?" Kathy is always up for something new.

I tell Kathy about the point of life being to have a good time. "Gee," says Kathy, rolling this around on her brain. "That's very interesting. But you know," she adds gently, "I'm not really sure that I really like having a good time, exactly."

Naturally I have anticipated this objection. No one likes to have a good time, but this is due to a misconception as to what a good time is, or faux fun, I explain grandly. "The thing is," I tell Kathy, "you're the only person who can tell what it is to have a good time, and since you're the only person who can have your own good time, whatever it is that a good time is, is what a good time is! So you can just know what it is and have it!"

"Gosh," says Kathy. "Maybe so. I'm going to think about that." She is feeling pretty good herself, having landed a terrific new job, which she tells me all about.

I keep expecting to wear out my new divinatory gift with gluttony, like someone who catches an enchanted fish and makes more than the allotted number of wishes, winding up with a pudding on his or her nose, or living in the pigsty, or whatnot; but it seems, on the contrary, to grow more and more reliable, and with ever-increasing frequency and rapidity I think of what I would like to do and I do it.

. . .

The days just clutter up with things I feel like doing and then do. One after another, I fill up and dispatch dayfuls of things.

Summer I haven't been to the Y for months, and I almost forgot about it, but this evening I pass it by on my way to dinner. It is fairly late, and many people are leaving the building, walking down the front steps alone or in twos and threes, unchaining their bicycles from the racks in front, and dispersing into the evening. I am quite a distance away, but I feel as though I can see them clearly. Their faces are calm, and they seem invigorated, as if they have been running. The evening sky is domed above the large, lit building, and more and more men and women stream out of the doors, radiating outward toward the next thing they are to do, each headed, it looks from where I stand, dead on target.

Transactions in a Foreign Currency

I had lit a fire in my fireplace, and I'd poured out two coffees and two brandies, and I was settling down on the sofa next to a man who had taken me out to dinner when Ivan called after more than six months. I turned with the receiver to the wall as I absorbed the fact of Ivan's voice, and when I glanced back at the man on my sofa, he seemed like a scrap of paper, or the handle from a broken cup, or a single rubber band—a thing that has become dislodged from its rightful place and intrudes on one's consciousness two or three or many times before one understands that it is just a thing best thrown away.

"Still in Montreal?" I said into the phone.

"Yeah," Ivan said. "I'm going to stay for a while."

"What's it like?" I said.

"Cold," he said.

"It's cold in New York, too," I was able to answer.

"Well, when can you get here?" he said. "We'll warm each other up."

I'd begun to think that this time there would be no end to the waiting, but here he was, here was Ivan, dropping down into my life again and severing the fine threads I'd spun out toward the rest of the world.

"I can't just leave," I said. "I have a job, you know."

"They'll give you a few weeks, won't they?" he said. "Over Christmas?"

"A few weeks," I said, but when he was silent I was sorry I'd said it.

"We'll talk it all over when you get up here," he said finally. "I know it's hard. It's hard for me, too."

I turned slightly, to face the window. The little plant that sat on the sill was almost leafless, I noticed, and paint was peeling slightly from the ceiling above it. How had I made myself believe this apartment was my home? This apartment was nothing.

"O.K.," I said. "I'll come."

I replaced the receiver, but the man on the sofa just sat and moved his spoon back and forth in his cup of coffee with a little chiming sound.

"An old friend," I said.

"So I assumed," he said.

"Well," I said, but then I couldn't even remember why that man was there. "I think I'd better say good night."

The man stood. "Going on a trip?"

"Soon," I said.

"Well, give me a call when you get back," he said. "If you want to."

"I'm not sure that I'll be coming back," I said.

"Uh-huh, uh-huh," he said, nodding, as if I were telling him a long story. "Well, then, good luck."

I flew up early one morning, leaving my apartment while it was still dark outside. I had packed, and flooded my plant with water in a hypocritical gesture that would delay, but not prevent, its death, and then I'd sat waiting for the clock face to arrive at the configuration that meant it was time I could reasonably go.

. . .

The airport was shaded and still in the pause before dawn, and the scattering of people there seemed to have lived for days in flight's distended light or dark; for them, this stop was no more situated in space than a dream is.

How many planes and buses and trains I had taken, over the years, to see Ivan! And how inevitable it always felt, as if I were being conveyed to him by some law of the universe made physical.

We'd met when I was nineteen, in Atlanta, where I was working for a photographic agency. He lived with his wife, Linda, who had grown up there, and their one-year-old, Gary. But he traveled frequently, and when he would call and ask me to go with him or meet him for a weekend somewhere—well, Ivan was one of those men, and just standing next to him I felt as if I were standing in the sun, and it never occurred to me to hesitate or to ask any questions.

And Ivan warmed with me. After their early marriage, Linda had grown increasingly fearful and demanding, he told me, and years of trying to work things out with her had imposed on him the cautious reserve of an unwilling guardian. It was a habit he seemed eager to discard.

After a time, there was a divorce, and Ivan moved about from place to place, visiting and taking photographs, and I got a job in New York. But he would call, and I would lock the door of whatever apartment I was living in and go to him in strange cities, leaving each before I could break through the transparent covering behind which it lay, mysterious and inert. And I always felt the same when I saw Ivan—like an animal raised in captivity that, after years of caged, puzzled solitude, is instantly recalled by the touch of a similar creature to the natural blazing consciousness of its species.

The last time we were together, though, we had lain on a slope overlooking a sunny lake, and a stem trembled in my hand while I explained, slowly and quietly, that it would not do any longer. I was twenty-eight now, I said, and he would have to make some sort of decision about me.

"Are you talking about a decision that can be made honestly?" He held my chin up and looked into my eyes.

"That is what a decision is," I said. "If the next step is self-evident, we don't call it a decision."

"I don't want to be unfair," he said, finally. And I came to assume, because I hadn't heard from him since, that the decision had been made.

Soft winter light was rolling up onto the earth as the plane landed, and the long corridors of the airport reflected a mild, dark glow.

An official opened my suitcase and turned over a stack of my underpants. SOMETHING TO DECLARE . . . NOTHING TO DECLARE, I saw on signs overhead, and strange words below each message. Oh, yes—part of this city was English-speaking, part French-speaking. A sorry-looking Christmas wreath hung over the lobby, and I thought of something Ivan had said after one of his frequent trips to see Gary and Linda in Atlanta: "I can't really have much sympathy for her. When she senses I'm not as worried about her as she'd like me to be, she takes a slight, semiaccidental overdose of something or gets herself into a little car crash."

"She loves you that much?" I asked.

"It isn't love," he said. "For all her dependence, she doesn't love me."

"But," I said, "is that what she thinks? Does she think she loves you that much?"

He stood up and stretched, and for a moment I thought that he hadn't registered my question. "Yeah," he said. "That's what she thinks."

Near the airport exit, there was a currency-exchange bureau, and I understood that I would need new money. The man behind the cage counted out the variegated, colorful Canadian bills in front of me. "Ah," he said, noticing my expression—he spoke with a faint but unfamiliar accent—"an unaccustomed medium of exchange, yes?"

I was directed by strangers to a little bus that took me across a plain to the city, a stony outcropping perched at the cold top of the world. There were solitary houses, heavy in the shallow film of light, and rows of low buildings, and many churches. I found a taxi and circumvented the question of language by handing the driver a piece of paper with Ivan's address on it, and I was brought in silence to a dark, muscular Victorian house that loomed from a brick street in a close row with others of its kind.

Ivan came downstairs bringing the morning gold with him and let me in. His skin and hair were wheat and honey colors, and he smelled as if he had been sleeping in a sunny field. "Ivan," I said, taking pleasure in speaking his name. As he held me, I felt ebbing from me a terrible pain that I had been unaware of until that moment. "I'm so tired."

"Want to wake up, or want to go to sleep?" he said.

"Sleep," I said, but for whole minutes I couldn't bring myself to move.

Upstairs, the morning light, gathering strength, made the melting frost on the bedroom window glow. I slept as if I hadn't slept for a week, and then awoke, groping hurriedly through my life to place myself. Understanding, I looked out the window through the city night shine of frost: I was in Montreal with Ivan, and I had missed the day.

I stood in the doorway of the living room for a moment, looking. Ivan was there, sharing a bottle of wine with two women. One of them was striking and willowy, with a spill of light curls, and the other was small and dark and fragile-looking. When had Ivan become so much older?

The small woman was studying a photograph, and her shiny hair fell across her pretty little pointy face. "No, it is wonderful, Ivan," she was saying. She spoke precisely, as if picking her way through the words, with the same accent I had heard at the airport. "It is a portrait of an entire class. A class that votes against its own interests. It is . . . a *photograph* of false consciousness."

"Well, it's a damn good print, anyway," the other woman said. "Lovely work, Ivan."

"We're playing Thematic Apperception Test," Ivan said, and the dark girl blushed and primly lowered her eyes. "We've had responses from Quebec and England. Let's hear from our U.S. representative." He handed me the photograph. "What do you see?"

Two women who, to judge from this view, were middle-aged, overweight, and poor stood gazing into a shop window at a display of tawdry lingerie. High up in the window was a reflection of mounded clouds and trees in full leaf. I did not feel like discussing the picture.

"Hello," the small girl said, intercepting my gaze as I looked up. "I am Micheline, and this is my friend Fiona."

Fiona reached lazily over to shake hands. "Hello," I said, allowing our attention to flow away from the photograph. "Do you live here, Fiona, or in England?"

"Oh, let's see," she said. "Where do I live? Well, it's been quite some time since I've even seen England. I've been in Montreal for a while, and before that I was in L.A."

"Really," I said. "What were you doing there?"

"What one does," she said. "I was working in film."

"The industry!" Micheline said. A hectic flush beat momentarily under her white skin, as if she'd been startled by her own exclamation. "There is much money to be made there, but at what personal expense!"

"Fiona has a gallery here," Ivan said.

"No money, no personal expense." Fiona smiled.

"It is excellent," Micheline said. "Fiona exhibits the most important new photographs in Canada. Soon she will have a show of Ivan's work."

"Wonderful," I said, but none of the others added anything. "We're rather on display here, Ivan," I said. "Are you planning to do something about curtains?"

Ivan smiled. "No." Ivan's rare smile always stopped me cold, and I smiled back as we looked at each other.

"It is not important," Micheline said, reclaiming the conversation. "The whole world is a window."

"Horse shit," Fiona said good-naturedly, and yawned.

"Yes, but that is true, Fiona," Micheline said. "Privacy is a—what is that?—*debased* form of dignity. It is dignity's . . . atrophied corpse."

"How good your English has become," Fiona said, smiling, but Ivan had nodded approvingly.

"The rigorous Northern temperament," Fiona said to me. "Sometimes I long for just a weekend in Los Angeles again."

"Not me!" Micheline said. She kicked her feet impatiently.

"Have you lived there as well?" I asked.

"No," she said. "But I am sure. Beaches, hotels, drinks with little hats—"

"That's Hawaii, I think," I said.

"Perhaps," Micheline said, looking sideways at me out of her doll's face.

"So what about it?" Ivan said. "Have you two decided to stay for dinner?"

"No," Micheline said, jumping to her feet. "Come, Fiona." She held out her hand to Fiona, blushing deeply. "We must go."

"All right." Fiona yawned and stood. "But let's have a rain check, Ivan. Micheline raves about your cooking. Maybe we'll come back over the weekend for Micheline's things. Sorry to have left them so long. We've been a while sorting things out."

"No problem," Ivan said. "Plenty of closet space."

At the door, Micheline was piling on layers and layers of clothing and stamping like a little pony in anticipation of the snow.

"Tell me about them," I said to Ivan after dinner, as we lay on the sofa, our feet touching. "Who are they?"

"What do you mean, 'who'?" he said. "You met them."

"Come on, Ivan," I said. "All I meant was that I'd like to know more about your friends. How did you meet them? That sort of thing."

"Actually," he said, "I hardly know Fiona. Micheline just brought her over once before."

"Micheline's so extreme," I said, smiling.

"She's very young," Ivan said.

"I used to be young," I said. "But I was never that extreme, was I?"

"She's a purist," Ivan said. "She's a very serious person."

"She seemed a bit of a silly person to me," I said. "Have she and Fiona been together long?"

"Just a month or so," he said.

"Micheline doesn't seem as if she's really used to being with another woman, somehow," I said. Ivan glanced at a page of newspaper lying on the floor below him. Some headline had caught his eye, apparently. "She was sort of defiant," I said. "Or nervous. As if she were making a statement about being gay."

"On the contrary," Ivan said. "She considers that to be an absolutely fraudulent opposition of categories—gay, straight. Utterly fraudulent."

"Do you?" I said.

"What is this?" Ivan said. "Are you preparing your case against me? Yes, *The People of the United States of America versus Ivan Augustine Olmstead.* I know."

"How long did she live here?" I said.

"Three months," he said, and then neither of us said anything or moved for about fifteen minutes.

"Ivan," I said. "I didn't call you. You wanted me to come up here."

He looked at me. "I'm sorry," he said. "But we're both very tense."

"Of course I'm tense," I said. "I don't hear from you for six months, then out of the blue you summon me for some kind of audience, and I don't know what you're going to say. I don't know whether you want some kind of future with me, or whether we're having our last encounter, or what."

"Look," he said. He sat upright on the sofa. "I don't know how to say this to you. Because, for some reason, it seems very foreign to you, to your way of thinking. But it's not out of the blue for me at all, you see. Because you're always with me. But you seem to want to feel rejected."

"I don't want to feel rejected," I said. "But if I've been rejected I'd just as soon know it."

"You haven't been rejected," he said. "You can't be rejected. You're a part of me. But instead of enjoying what happens between us, you always worry about what *has* happened between us, or what *will* happen between us."

"Yes," I said. "Because there is no such thing as an independent present. How can I not worry each time I see you that it will be the last?"

"You act as if I had all the power between us," he said. "You have just as much power as I do. But I can't give it to you. You have to claim it."

"If that were true," I said, "we'd be living together at least half the time."

"And if we were living together," he said, "would you feel that you had to go to work with me or stay with me in the darkroom to see whether my feelings about you changed minute by minute? It's not the quantity of time we spend together that makes us more close or less close. People are to each other what they are."

"But that can change," I said. "People's interests are at odds sometimes."

"Not really," he said. "Not fundamentally. And you would understand that if you weren't so interested in defending your isolating, competitive view of things."

"What on earth are you talking about, Ivan? Are you really saying that there's no conflict between people?"

"What I'm saying is that it's absurd for people to be obsessed with their own little roles. People's situations are just a fraction of their existence—the difference between those situations is superficial, it's arbitrary. In actuality, we're all part of one giant human organism, and one part can't survive at the expense of another part. Would you take off your sock and put it on your hand because you were cold? Look—does the universe care whether it's you or Louis Pasteur that's Louis Pasteur? No. From that point of view, we're all the same."

"Well, Ivan," I said, "if we're all the same, why drag me up here? Why not just keep Micheline around? Or call in a neighbor?"

He looked at me, and he sighed. "Maybe you're right," he said. "Maybe I just don't care about you in the way that you need. I just don't know. I don't want to falsify my feelings."

But when I saw how exhausted he looked, and miserable, loneliness froze my anger, and I was ashamed that I'd allowed myself to become childish. "Never mind," I said. I wished that he would touch me. "Never mind. We'll figure it out."

It was not until the second week that I regained my balance and Ivan let down his guard, and we were able to talk without hidden purposes and we remembered how it felt to be happy together. Still, it seemed to me as if I were remembering every moment of happiness even as it occurred, and, remembering, mourning its death.

One day, Ivan was already dressed and sitting in the kitchen by the time I woke up. "Linda called this morning," he said. "She let the phone ring about a hundred times before I got it. I'm amazed you slept through it."

I poured myself a cup of coffee and sat down.

"I wonder why people do that," he said. "It's annoying, and it's pointless."

"It wasn't pointless in this case," I said. "You woke up."

"Want some toast?" Ivan asked. "Eggs?"

"No, thanks," I said. I hardly ever ate breakfast. "So, is she all right?"

"Fine," he said. "I guess."

"Well, that's good," I said.

"Remember that apartment I had in Washington?" he said. "I loved that place. It was the only place I ever lived where I could get the paper delivered."

"How's Gary?" I said.

"Well, I don't know," Ivan said. "According to Linda, he's got some kind of flu or something. She's gotten it into her head that it's psychosomatic, because this is the first time since he was born that I haven't come home for Christmas."

"Home," I said.

"Well," Ivan said. "Gary's home."

"Maybe you should go," I said.

"He'll have to adjust sometime," Ivan said. "This is just Linda's way of manipulating the situation."

I shrugged. "It's up to you." I wondered, really for the first time, what Ivan's son looked like. "Do you have a picture of Gary?"

"Somewhere, I think," Ivan said.

"I'd like to see one," I said.

"Sure," he said. "You mean now?"

"Well, I'd like to," I said.

Steam rose from my coffee and faded into the bright room. Outside the window, light snow began to fall. In a few minutes Ivan came back with a wallet-sized snapshot.

"How did you get into this picture?" I said.

He took it from me and peered at it. "Oh. Some friends of Linda's were over that day. They took it."

"So that's Linda," I said. For nine years I'd been imagining the wrong woman—someone tired and aggrieved—but the woman in the photograph was finely chiseled, like Ivan. Even in her jeans she appeared aristocratic, and her expression was somewhat set, as if she had just disposed of some slight inconvenience. She and Ivan could have been brother and sister. The little boy between them, however, looked clumsy and bereft. His head was large and round and wobbly-looking, and the camera had caught him turning, his mouth open in alarm, as if he had fallen through space into the photograph. A current of fury flowed through me, leaving me as depleted as the child in the picture looked. "What if he *is* sick?" I said.

"Kids get sick all the time," Ivan said.

"You could fly down Christmas Eve and come back the twenty-sixth or twenty-seventh."

"Flying on Christmas Eve's impossible anyhow," he said.

"Well, you could go down tomorrow."

"What about you?" he said.

"What about me?" I said.

"If I can even still get reservations," he said.

"Call and see," I said. "I'll call." Linda had probably never, in awe of Ivan's honey-colored elegance that was so like her own, hesitated to touch him as I sometimes did. As I did right now.

The next day, Ivan bought some toys, much more cheerful and robust than the child they were for, and then I watched him pack. And then we went out to the airport together.

I took the little airport bus back alone, and I felt I had been equipped by a mysterious agency: I knew without asking how to transport myself into a foreign city, my pockets were filled with its money, and in my hand I had a set of keys to an apartment there. The snow still fell lightly, detaching itself piece by piece from the white sky, absorbing all the sound. And the figures past which we rode looked almost immobile in their heavy clothing, and not quite formed, as if they were bodies waiting to be inhabited by displaced souls. In the dark quiet of the bus, I let myself drift. Cities, the cities where I visited Ivan, were repositories of these bodies waiting to be animated, I thought sleepily, but how did a soul manage to incarnate itself in one?

All night long I slept easily, borne away on the movements of my new, unfettered life, but I awoke to a jarring silence. Ivan had taken the clock.

I looked around. It was probably quite late. The sun was already high, and the frost patterns, which seemed always on the verge of meaning, were being sucked back to the edges of the window as I stared. In the kitchen I sat and watched the light pooling in rich winter tints across the linoleum, and eventually the pink-and-pewter evening came, and frost patterns encroached on the windows again. How quickly the day had disappeared. The day had sat at the kitchen window, but the earth had simply rolled away from under it.

It was light again when I woke. I thought suddenly of the little plant on my windowsill in New York. It would be dead by now. I felt nauseated, but then I remembered I hadn't eaten the day before.

There was nothing in the refrigerator, but in the freezer compartment I found a roll of chocolate-chip-cookie dough. How unlike Ivan to have such a thing—what circumstances had prompted him to buy it? Ah—I saw Micheline and Ivan with a shopping cart, laughing: the purists' night off.

I searched through the pots and pans—what a lot of clatter—but there was a cookie sheet. Good. I turned on the oven and sawed through the frozen dough. Soon the kitchen was filling with warmth. But an assaultive odor underlay it, and when I opened the oven door, I found the remains of a leg of lamb from earlier in the week that we'd forgotten to put away. The bone stood out, almost translucent, and the porous sheared face of meat was still red in the center. "Get rid of all this old stuff," I heard myself say out loud in a strange, cheerful voice, and I jabbed a large fork into it. But I had to sit for several minutes breathing deeply with my head lowered before I managed to dump the lamb into the garbage can along with the tray of dough bits and get myself back into bed, where I stayed for the rest of the day.

The next afternoon, it seemed to me that I was ready to go out of the apartment. I took a hot bath, cleansing myself carefully. Then I looked through my clothing, taking it out and putting it away, piece by piece. None of the things I'd brought with me seemed right. Steam poured from the radiators, but the veil of warmth hardly softened the little pointed particles of cold in the room.

The hall closet was full of women's clothes, and there I found everything I needed. I supposed it all belonged to Micheline, but everything felt roomy enough, even though she looked so small. I selected a voluminous skirt, a turtleneck jersey, and a long, heavy sweater. There was a pair of boots as well—beautiful boots, fine-grained and sleek. If they belonged to Micheline, they must have been a gift. Surely she never would have chosen them for herself.

The woman who stood in the mirror was well assembled, but the face, above the heavy, dark clothing, was indistinct in the brilliant sunlight. I made up my eyes heavily, and then my mouth with a red lipstick that was sitting on Ivan's bureau, and checked back with the mirror. Much better. Then I found a jacket that probably belonged to Ivan, and a large shawl, which I arranged around my head and shoulders.

Outside, everything was outlined in a fluid brilliance, and underfoot the snow emitted an occasional dry shriek. The air was as thin as if it might break, fracturing the landscape along which I walked: broad, flat-roofed buildings with blind windows, low upon the endless sky. There were other figures against the landscape, all bundled up like myself against the cold, and although the city was still unfathomable, I could recall no other place, and the rudiments of a past seemed to be hidden here for me somewhere, beyond my memory.

I entered a door and was plunged into noise and activity. I was in a supermarket arranged like a hallucination, with aisles shooting out in unexpected directions, and familiar and unfamiliar items perched side by side. If only I had made a list! I held my cart tightly, trusting the bright packages to draw me along correctly and guide me in my selections.

The checkout girl rang up my purchases: eggs (oh, I'd forgotten butter; well, no matter, the eggs could always be boiled, or used in something); a replacement roll of frozen cookie dough; a box of spaghetti; a jar of pickled okra from Texas; a package of mint tea; foil; soap powder; cleanser; violet toilet paper (an item I'd never seen before); and a bottle of aspirin. The girl took my money, glancing at me.

Several doors along, I stopped at a little shop filled with pastries. There were trays of jam tarts and buns, and plates piled up with little chocolate diamond shapes, and pyramids of caramelized spheres, and shelves of croissants and tortes and cookies, and the most wonderful aroma surged around me. "Madame?" said a woman in white behind the counter.

I looked up at her, over a shelf of frosted cakes that held messages coded in French. On one of them a tiny bride and groom were borne down upon by shining sugar swans, and my heart fluttered high up against my chest like a routed moth. I spoke, though, resolutely in English: "Everything looks so good." Surely that was an appropriate thing to say—surely people said that. "Wait." I pointed at a tray of evergreen-shaped cookies covered with green sugar crystals. Tiny bright candies had been placed on them at intervals to simulate ornaments. "There."

"Very good," the woman said. "The children like these very much."

"Good," I said. What had she meant? "I'll take a dozen."

"Did you have a pleasant Christmas?" she asked me, nestling my cookies into a box.

"Yes," I said, perhaps too loudly, but she didn't seem to notice the fire that roared over me. "And you?"

"Very good," she said. "I was with my sister. All the children were home. But now today it feels so quiet." She smiled, and I understood that her communication had been completed, and we both inclined our heads slightly as I left.

"Hello," I said uncertainly to the butcher in the meat market next door. It occurred to me that I ought to stop and get something nourishing.

"What can I do for you?" the butcher asked in easy English.

"Actually," I said dodging a swift memory of the leg of lamb in Ivan's garbage can, "I'd like something for supper." Ah! I had to smile—what the woman in the bakery had been telling me was how it felt to be a person when one's sister and some children were around.

"Something in particular?" the butcher asked. "If I'm not being too nosy?"

"Please," I said across a wall of nausea. "Sausages." That had been good thinking—at least they would be in casings.

"Sausages," he said. "How many sausages?"

"Not so many," I said, trying not to think too concretely about the iridescent hunks of meat all around me.

"Let's see," he said. "Should we say . . . for two?"

"Good," I said. Fortunately there was a chair to wait in. "Did you have a pleasant Christmas?" I asked.

"Excellent," the butcher said. "Goose. And yours?"

"Oh, excellent," I said. I supposed from his silence that that had been insufficient, so I continued. "It feels so quiet today, though. All the children have gone back."

"Oh, I know that quiet," the butcher said. "When they go."

"They're not exactly my children, of course," I said. "They're my sister's. Stepsister's, I mean. My sister would be too young a person to have children old enough to go back anywhere. You know," I said, "I have a friend who believes that in a sense it doesn't matter whether I'm a person with a stepsister who has children or whether someone else is."

The butcher looked at me. "Interesting point," he said. "That's five seventy-eight with tax."

"I know it sounds peculiar," I said, counting out the price. "But this friend really believes that, assuming there's a person with a stepsister, it just doesn't ultimately matter—to the universe, for instance—whether that person happens to be me or whether that person happens to be someone else. And I was thinking—does it actually matter to you whether that person is me or that person is someone else?"

"To me . . . does it matter to me . . ." The butcher handed me my package. "Well, to me, sweetheart, you *are* someone else."

"Well." I laughed uneasily. "No. But do you mean—wait—I'm not sure I understand. That is, did you mean that I might as well be the person with the stepsister? That it's an error to identify oneself as the occupant of a specific situation?" The butcher looked at me again. "I mean, how would you describe the difference between the place you occupy in the world and the place I occupy?"

"Well"—his eyes narrowed thoughtfully—"I'm standing over here, I see you standing over there, like that."

"Oh—" I said.

"So," he said. "Got everything? Know where you are?"

"Thanks," I said. "Yes."

"You're all set, then," he said. "Enjoy the sausages."

Back at the apartment, I unpacked my purchases and put them away. Strange, that I missed Ivan so much more when we were together than when we were apart.

I was dozing when I heard noises in the kitchen. I went to investigate and found a man with black hair and pale, pale skin standing near the table and holding the bakery box to his ear as if it were a seashell.

"Sorry," he said, putting it down. "The door was open. Where's Ivan?"

"Gone," I said.

"Oh," he said. "Be back soon?"

"No," I said. Well, I was up. I put on the kettle.

"Sit down," he said. "Relax. I don't bite." He laughed—the sound of breaking dishes. "Name's Eugene." He held out a hand to me. "Mind if I sit for a minute, too? Foot's killing me."

He pulled up a chair across from me and sat, his long-lashed eyes cast down.

"What's the matter with your foot?" I said after a while.

"Well, I'm not exactly sure. Doctor told me it was a calcium spur. Doesn't bother me much, except just occasionally." He fell silent for a minute. "Maybe I should see the guy again, though. Sometimes things . . . become *exacerbated,* I guess is how you'd put it. Turn into other things, almost."

I nodded, willing him toward the door. I wanted to sleep. I wanted to have a meal.

"I was walking around, though," he said, "and I thought I'd drop in to see Ivan."

"I'm going to have a cup of tea," I said. "Do you want one?"

"He doesn't have any herb tea, does he?" Eugene said. "It's good for the nerves. Soothing." He was wearing heavy motorcycle boots, I saw, that were soaking wet. No wonder his feet hurt. "Yeah, Ivan owes me some money," he said. "Thought I'd drop by and see if he had it on him by some chance."

I put the teapot and cups on the table. I wondered how soon I could get Eugene to go.

"Where're you from?" Eugene said. "You're not from here, are you?"

"New York," I said. I also wanted to get out of these clothes. They were becoming terribly uncomfortable.

"Yeah, that's what I thought. I thought so." He laughed miserably again. "Good old rotten apple."

"Don't like it much, huh?" I said.

"Oh, I like it all right," Eugene said. "I love it. I was born and raised there. Whole family's there. Yeah, I miss it a lot. From time to time." He sipped delicately at his tea, still looking down. Then he tossed his thick black hair back from his face, as if he were aware of my stare.

"Aren't you cold?" I asked suddenly. "Walking around like that?" I reached over to his leather jacket.

"Oh, I'm fine, thank you, dear," he said. "I enjoy this. Of course I've got a scarf on, too. Neck's a very sensitive part of the body. Courting disaster to expose the neck to the elements. But this is my kind of weather. I'd live outside if I could." He lifted his eyes to me. They were pale and shallow, and they caught the light strangely, like pieces of bottle glass under water. "Candy?" he said, taking a little vial from his pocket and shaking some of its powdery contents out onto the table.

"No, thanks," I said.

"Mind if I do?" He drew a wad of currency from another pocket and peeled off a large bill.

"That's pretty," I said, watching him roll it into a tight brown tube stippled with green and red. "I've never seen that one before."

"Pretty," he said. "You bet it's pretty. It's a cento. Still play money to me, though. A lot better than that stingy little monochrome crap back home, huh?"

Eugene tipped some more from the vial onto the table.

"So why don't you go back?" I said. "If you like it so much."

"Go back." He sniffed loudly, eyes closed. "You know, I don't feel this stuff the way a woman does. They say it's a woman's drug. I don't get that feeling at the back of my head, like you can." His light eyes rested on my face. "Well, I can't go back. Not unless they extradite me."

"For what?" Maybe I could just ask Eugene to go. Or maybe I could grab his teacup and smash it on the floor.

"Shot a guy," he said.

"Yes?" I tucked my feet under me. This annoying skirt! I hated the feeling of wool next to my skin.

"Now, don't get all nervous," Eugene said. "It was completely justified. Guy tried to hurt me. I'd do it again, too. Fact, I said so to the judge. My lawyer kept telling me, 'Shut up, maniac, shut up.' And he told the judge, 'Your Honor, you can see yourself my client's as crazy as a lab rat.' How do you like that? So I said, 'Listen, Judge. What would you do if some cocksucker pulled a knife on you? I may be crazy, but I'm no fool.' " Eugene leaned back and put his hands against his eyes.

I poured myself some more tea. It felt thick going down. I hadn't even had water, I remembered, for some time. "Would you like another cup?" I asked.

"Yeah," Eugene said. "Thanks."

"You know Ivan a long time?" he asked.

"Nine years," I said.

"Nine years. A lot of bonds can be forged in nine years. So how come I never met you? Ivan and I hang out."

"Oh, God, I don't know," I said. "It's an on-and-off type of thing. We're thrashing it out together now."

"You're thrashing it out together," he said. "You're thrashing it out together, but I only see one of you."

"Right," I said. "So how did you get to Canada, anyhow?"

"Oh. They put me in the hospital," he said. "But I've got

friends. Here," he said. "Look." He emptied a pocket onto the table. There was a key chain, and an earring, and something that I presumed was a switchblade, and a bundle of papers—business cards and phone numbers and all sorts of miscellany—that he started to read out to me. "Jesus," he said, noticing me inspecting his knife. "You'll take your whole arm off that way. Do it like this." He demonstrated, flashing the blade out, then he folded it up and put it back in his pocket. "Here—look at this one." He handed me a card covered with a meaningless mass of dots. "Now hold it up to the light." He grabbed it back and placed it over a lamp near me. The dots became a couple engaged in fellatio. "Isn't that something?"

"Yes," I said. "I think you should go now, though. I have to do some things." His face was changing and changing in front of me. He receded, rippling.

"Wait—" he said. "You don't look good. Have you been eating right?"

"I'm all right," I said. "I don't care. Please leave."

"You're in bad shape, lady," he said. "You're not well. Sure you don't want any of this?" He offered me the vial. "Pick you right up. Then we'll fix you some more tea or something. Get some vitamins into you."

"No, no. It's just these clothes," I said, plucking at them. "I've got to get out of these clothes." He was beautiful, I saw. He was beautiful. He sparkled with beauty; it streamed from him in glistening sheets, as if he were emerging from a lake of it. I kicked at Micheline's boots, but Eugene was already kneeling, and he drew them off, and the thick stockings, too, and my legs appeared, very long, almost shining in the growing dark, from beneath them.

"Got 'em," he said, standing.

"Yes," I said, holding my arms up. "Now get this one," and he pulled the sweater over my head.

"Sh-h-h," he said, folding the sweater neatly. "It's O.K." But I was rattling inside my body like a Halloween skeleton as he carried me to Ivan's bed and wrapped a blanket around me.

"Look how white," I said. "Look how white your skin is."

"When I was in the jungle it was like leather," he said. "Year and a half, shoe leather. Sh-h-h," he said again, as I flinched at a noise. "It's just this." And I understood that it was just his knife, inside his pocket, that had made the noise when he'd dropped his clothes on the floor. "You like that, huh?" he said, holding the knife out for me.

Again and again and again I made the blade flash out, severing air from air, while Eugene waited. "That's enough now," he said. "First things first. You can play with that later."

When we finished making love, the moon was a perfect circle high in the black window. "How about that?" Eugene said. "Nature." We leaned against each other and looked at it. "You got any food here, by the way?" he asked. "I'm famished."

By the time I'd located a robe—a warm, stripy thing in Ivan's closet—Eugene was rummaging through the icebox. "You got special plans for this?" he said, holding up the violet toilet paper that apparently I'd refrigerated.

"Let's see . . ." I said. "There're some sausages."

"Sausages," he said. "Suckers are delicious, but they'll kill you. Preservatives, saturated fats. Loaded with PCBs, too."

"Really?" I said.

"Don't you know that?" he said. "What are you smiling about? You think I'm kidding? Listen, Americans eat too much animal protein anyhow. Fiber's where it's at." He nodded at me, his eyebrows raised. "What else you got?"

"There's some pickled okra," I said.

"Ivan's into some heavy shit here, huh?" he said.

"Well . . ." It was true that I hadn't shopped very efficiently. "Oh, there are these." I undid the bakery box.

"Holy Christ," Eugene said. "How do you like that—little

Christmas trees. Isn't that something!" He arranged them into a forest on the table and walked his fingers among them. "Here we come a-wassailing among the leaves so green," he sang, and it sounded like something he didn't often do.

> Here we come awandering
> so fair to be seen.
> Love and joy come to you,
> and to you your wassail too,
> And God bless you and send you
> a happy New Year,
> And God send you a happy New Year.

"What's the matter?" he said. "You don't like Christmas carols?" So I did harmony as he sang another verse:

> We are not daily beggars
> that beg from door to door,
> But we are neighbors' children
> whom you have seen before.
> Love and joy come to you,
> and to you your wassail too,
> And God bless you and send you
> a happy New Year,
> And God send you a happy New Year.

Eugene clapped. Then he made an obscene face and stuck a cookie into his mouth. "Oh, lady," he said, holding the cookie out for me to finish. "These are fuckin' *scrumptious.*"

That was true. They were awfully good, and we munched on them quietly in the moonlit kitchen.

"So what about you and Ivan?" Eugene asked.

"I don't know," I said. "I'm starving with Ivan, but my life away from him—my own life—I've just let it dry up. Turn into old bits and pieces."

"Well, honey," Eugene said, "that's not right. It's your life."

"But nothing changes or develops," I said. "Ivan just can't seem to decide what he wants."

"No?" Eugene looked away tactfully, and I laughed out loud in surprise.

"That's true," I said. "I guess he decided a long time ago." I stared down at the table, into our diminished cookie forest, and I felt Eugene staring at me. "Well, I didn't want to be the one to end it, you know?" I said. "But time does change things, even if you can't see it happen, and eventually someone has to be the one to say, 'Well, now things have changed.' Anyhow, it's not his fault. He's given me what he could."

Eugene nodded. "Ivan's a solitary kind of guy. I respect him."

"Yes," I said. "But I wish things were different."

"I understand, dear." Eugene patted my hand. "I hear you."

"What about you?" I said. "Do you have a girlfriend?"

"Who, me?" he said. "No, I'm just an old whore. I've got a wife down in the States. Couldn't live with her anymore, though." He sighed and looked around. "Sixteen years. So what else you got to eat here? I'm still hungry."

"Well," I said. "There's a roll of cookie dough in the freezer, but it's Ivan's, really."

"We should eat it, then." Eugene laughed. "Serve the arrogant bastard right." I looked at him. "Don't mind me, honey," he said. "You know I'm crazy."

I woke up once in the night, with Eugene snoring loudly next to me, and when I butted my head gently into his shoulder to quiet him down he wrapped his marvelous white arms around me. "Thought I forgot about you, huh?" he said distinctly, and started to snore again.

Sunlight forced my eyes open hours later. "Shit," said a voice near me. "What time is it?" The sun had bleached out Eugene's luminous beauty. With his pallor and coarse black hair, he looked like a phantom that one registers peripherally on the streets. "I've got a business appointment at noon," he said, pulling on his jeans. "Think it's noon?"

"I don't know," I said. It felt pleasantly early. "No clock."

"I better hit the road," he said. "Shit."

"Here," I said, holding out his knife.

"Yeah, thanks." He pocketed it and looked at me. "You be O.K. now, lady? Going to take care of yourself for a change?"

"Yes," I said. "By the way, how much does Ivan owe you?"

"Huh?" he said. "Hey, there's my jacket. Right on the floor. Very nice."

"Because he mentioned it before he left," I said.

"Yeah?" Eugene said. "Well, it doesn't matter. I'll come back for it, like—when? When's that sucker going to get back?"

"No," I said. There was really no point in waiting for Ivan. I wanted to conclude this business myself right now. "He forgot to tell me how much it was, but he left me plenty to cover."

Eugene looked down at his boots. "Two bills."

I put on the robe and counted out two hundred dollars from my purse. It was almost all I had left of the lively cash. "And he said thanks," I said.

I stood at the open door until Eugene went through it. "Yeah, well," he said. "Thanks yourself."

At the landing he turned back to me. "Have a good one," he called up.

I went back inside and put some eggs on to boil. Then I twirled slowly, making the stripes on the robe flare.

How on earth had I forgotten butter? The eggs were good, though. I enjoyed them.

After breakfast I rooted around and found a pail and sponges. It made me sad that Ivan had let the apartment get so filthy.

He used to enjoy taking care of things. Then I sat down with a mystery I found on a shelf, and by the time Ivan walked in, late in the afternoon, I'd almost finished it.

"Looks great in here," he said after he kissed me.

"I did some cleaning," I said.

"That's great," he said. I thought of my own apartment. There would be a lot to do when I got home. "Jesus. Am I exhausted! That was some trip."

"How's Gary?" I said.

"Well, he was running a little fever when I got there, but he's fine now," Ivan said.

"Good," I said. "Did he like his presents?"

"Uh-huh." Ivan smiled. "Particularly that game that the marble rolls around in. He and I both got pretty good at it after the first few hundred hours."

"I liked that one, too," I said.

"He's a good kid," Ivan said. "He really is. I just hope Linda doesn't make him into some kind of nervous wreck."

"How's she doing?" I asked.

"Well, she's all right, I think. She's trying to get a life together for herself at least. She's getting a degree in dance therapy."

"That's good," I said.

"She'll be O.K. if she can just get over her dependency," he said. "I'll be interested to see how she does with this new thing."

He would be monitoring her closely, I knew. What a tight family they had established, Ivan and Linda—not much room for anyone else. Of course, Gary and I had our own small parts in it. I'd probably been quite important in fencing out, oh, Micheline, for instance, just as Gary had been indispensable in fencing me out.

"Hey," Ivan said. "Who's been sitting in my chair?" He bent down and picked up a scarf.

"Someone named Eugene stopped by," I said. "He said you owed him money."

"Jesus. That's right," Ivan said. "Well, I'll get around to it in the next day or so."

"I took care of it myself," I said.

"Really? Well, thanks. That's great. I'll reimburse you. Sorry you had to deal with him, though."

"I liked him," I said.

"You did?" Ivan said.

"You like him enough to do business with him," I said.

"Yeah, I know I should be more compassionate," Ivan said. "It's just that he's so hard to take."

"Is any of that stuff true that he says?" I asked. "That he shot some guy? That he lived in the jungle?"

"Shot some guy? I don't know. He has a pretty extensive fantasy life. But he fought in the war, yeah."

"Oh," I said. "I see. Jungle—Vietnam."

"I keep forgetting," Ivan said. "You're really just a baby."

"That must have been awful," I said.

"Well, he could have gotten out of it if he didn't want to do it," Ivan said.

"He probably thought it was a good thing to do," I said. "Besides, people can't arrange their lives exactly the way they'd like to."

"I disagree," Ivan said. "People only like to think they can't."

"You know," I said, trying to recall the events of the day before, "I was having some sort of conversation with a butcher about that yesterday."

"A butcher?" Ivan said.

"Yes," I said. "And, as I remember, he was saying something to the effect that people are only free to the extent that they recognize the boundaries of their lives."

"Sounds pretty grim," Ivan said. "And pretty futile."

"Not exactly futile," I said. "At least, I think his point was that if I know that over here is where I'm standing, well, that's what gives rise to the consciousness that over there is where you're standing, and automatically I get a map, a compass. So my situation—no matter how bad it is—is my source of power."

"Well," Ivan said. "That's a very dangerous way of thinking, because it's just that point of view that can be used to rationalize a lot of selfishness and oppression and greed. I'll bet you were talking to that thief over by St. Lawrence who weighs his thumb, right?"

"Well, maybe I'm misrepresenting him," I said. "He was pretty enigmatic."

Ivan looked at me and smiled, but I could hardly bear the sweetness of it, so I turned away from him and went to the window.

How handsome he was! How I wished I could contain the golden, wounding hope of him. But it had begun to diverge from me—oh, who knew how long before—and I could feel myself already re-forming: empty, light.

"So how are you?" Ivan said, joining me at the window.

"All right," I said. "It's good not to be waiting for you."

"I'm sorry I missed Christmas here," he said. "Montreal's a nice place for Christmas. Next year, what do you say we try to do it right?"

He put his arm around me, and I leaned against his shoulder while we looked out at the place where I'd been walking the day before. The evening had arrived at the moment when everything is all the same soft color of a shadow, and the city seemed to be floating close, very close, outside the window. How familiar it was, as if I'd entered and explored it over years. Well, it had been a short time, really, but it would certainly be part of me, this city, long after I'd forgotten the names of the streets and the colors of the light, long after I'd forgotten the feel of Ivan's shirt against my cheek, and the darkening sight separated from me now by a sheet of glass I could almost reach out to shatter.

Broken Glass

As I exited through the terminal gate I thought, for an instant, that the plane had set me down in the exact spot from which it had lifted me up hours earlier, that I was distant only by some uniform tickings of the clock from the things I'd fled: the daily drive home from work past the hospital towers, the sight of the newspaper I'd combed every evening for articles that could penetrate the caul of pain and drugs in which my mother lay, the sounds of my own language, through which the furious chattering in my brain seemed to erupt with terrible force. Airports, train stations, hospitals—one looks much like another, whether it marks the beginning of a journey or the end; and when I reminded myself that I'd just flown several thousand miles, it was borne in upon me that my mother was going to be as dead here, now, as she had been in Chicago this morning.

Lovers and family members called to one another in the crowded lobby and embraced, and I was claimed by Ray, as he insisted on being called, the real-estate agent who had located a place for me in the town I'd chosen almost at random from a huge and uninformative guidebook. When I held out my hand to him, something like alarm flickered in his face. Had he expected some other sort of woman? No matter; I didn't want to know. We had about an hour's drive ahead of us, and I was determined to avoid the sort of intimate, confessional conversation that strangers are said to have. I had not gone into the circumstances of my trip in my letter or over the phone—I preferred to be considered simply a vacationer.

In the car I sat as far from Ray's damp heartiness as possible, and I looked out the window while he talked. I'd never been far from Chicago, and I'd chosen to come to Latin America because of its unfamiliarity to my imagination. All the alluring places that during my mother's lifetime I'd yearned to see belonged sealed now, I felt, in a completed past where they would remain contemporaneous with my mother.

The colors of the landscape that flowed around me were soft and dense, but the light itself was a rippling gold, and the clumps of trees and the sandy slopes and hollows seemed like moving islands tilting toward, then away from us in the fragile ocean of air. Eventually, we descended into a plateau ringed by mountains, and the disorienting glitter of the air melted in the low warmth, and soon distinguishable ahead of us against the tawny dryness was a tumble of feathery green and blossoms. Ray nodded. "Been a prime piece of real estate for something like a thousand years," he said soberly.

We drove downward into a maze of cobbled streets bordered by high, rosy walls, and we slowed to avoid a woman with several children who was crossing our path. On the woman's head was a bundle—wrapped in plastic, I saw, as a pickup truck veered around us, raising a wake of brilliant dust. In the back of the truck was a crowd of men whose copper-colored faces and black hair shone above their work shirts. I glanced at the rather spongy person beside me. "Oh, you won't be bored," he said. "We have a wonderful group down here. Very fine people from all walks of life. Tennis, golf, sites of historical interest, pools. Perfect climate, of course—anything you want. To tell you the truth, we think we're pretty clever. Not that we'd ever say so to our friends back home." He smiled playfully, buoyed up for a moment by his own wit, and I turned away, mortified, as if I had seen something disastrously personal.

We parked high up on one side of the town. I followed Ray through a large wooden gate and was astonished to see the lush garden that lay beyond the wall, just off the dry, dusty street. "You're upstairs over the garage," Ray said, leading me through the garden and across a slate patio to a white house with a tiled roof. "But we have to get the keys from Norman."

The front of the house was glass, and although the sun was too strong for me to see clearly into the unlit interior, I had the impression for an instant that a man, in something that looked like a bathrobe, hovered in back. "Mr. Egan. Mr. Egan," Ray called, and as a woman came to the door the man I thought I'd seen became shadows. "Oh, hello, Dolores," Ray said.

"Mr. Egan is not available," the woman said, smiling at me. The words had a fresh, odd sound in her accent, as if their meaning were not quite set. "I will take you upstairs."

"That won't be necessary, thank you, Dolores," Ray said. "Just let me have the keys and we'll manage."

Ray led me up a flight of whitewashed steps on the outside of the house to the door of what turned out to be a small apartment. "You needn't worry much about tipping, by the way," he said. "They don't expect it. Just meals and that sort of thing. Well—kitchen, closet, bathroom. Oh, bed—well, obviously. Water's generally potable, but you might boil to be on the safe side. We think it's a nice little place. Norman's wife used to use it as a sort of studio, I believe. I understand that she used to paint." He paused, and something seemed to strike him. "Nice fellow, Norman. Of course, we can all use the extra income."

"Is she still living?" I asked.

"Pardon me?" Ray said.

"Mr. Egan's wife," I said. "Did she die?"

"I see." Ray nodded, as if I'd made some sort of point. "Not at all, not at all. Well, looks like Norman's left you some provisions, but there are plenty of restaurants in town. Food's quite safe as a rule. Have to watch out a bit for the men, of course, but nothing actually dangerous, I mean." He held the keys out to me and then put them down on the table. "So," he said, and looked at me, his arms at his sides.

"Thank you," I said. "I'm sure everything will be fine."

So he left, and I stood still to let the sound of his voice drain away into the heavy, bright, humming afternoon. Then I opened my suitcase and put my things in the closet and arranged my jars of lotions and creams on the bureau.

What to do? At work I would have been finishing for the day, organizing my files for the next morning. And soon, at the hospital, the patients would be receiving little paper cups holding pills, like the cups of candies at a children's birthday party.

I went and sat on the small balcony that overlooked the garden. The air lapped against my skin with an unfamiliar silkiness, and scalloped rings of mountains surrounded me like ripples. Here and there, I could see softly rounded churches, with spires and crosses. My mother had been ill for so long that all time had flowed toward her death, and I feared that all time would flow backward to it as well. I had become thirty-four waiting for my own span to be placed over that fulcrum—an irrevocable placement.

Down below me a small white rabbit nosed out among the plants and zigzagged out of sight. Its pink eyes and the pink lining of its ears looked particularly sensitive to pain.

I noticed that my nice traveling skirt was already wrinkled and ingrained with dust, and a wave of sorrow engulfed me, as though I'd betrayed something placed in my care. This was only the strain, I understood, of the last weeks—the extra hours at the hospital, the extra hours at work to justify the time off I knew I would be taking, the funeral arrangements, the ordeal, especially, of sorting through my mother's papers and disposing of all the little things my mother had acquired over the years for one purpose or another, now also dead.

How thorough my preparations had been! My mother herself, though, had been utterly unprepared. For close to twenty-five years her life had consisted of little more than the miseries of a slow degenerative illness, but as her future declined in value and her suffering increased, her fear increased also. She had feared death greatly, and life clung to her like a burning robe.

I thought with sudden fury of the doctor who stood with me in the hospital corridor only a few days ago. He had been unprepared as well, and he looked helpless, like a little boy all dressed up in a doctor suit. Yet he must have known for a long, long time that sooner or later he would have to face someone the way he faced me that day, and say those things.

That night my sleep was shallow and unpleasant, and when I woke I had the queasy sensation of having been brought up short, as when one steps from a boat onto fixed ground, and that was how I remembered that I was finished for good with trips to the hospital.

Just as it occurred to me that I would have to plunge into an unknown universe merely in order to obtain some coffee a man with a trim silver beard appeared at my door. "Good morning, good morning. I'm Norman, your evil landlord," he said, holding out to me an armload of roses.

"Thank you," I said. The flowers, still richly furled and heavy with droplets of water, were a living, modulated, faintly sickening salmon color.

"Vase under the sink," Norman said. I judged him to be in his late fifties, and he would have been quite good-looking, I thought, except that his face seemed to have been stamped by a habit of geniality and then left unattended. Despite his jaunty white clothes, he seemed uncomfortable.

"My wife would have done a real arrangement for you," he said. "She has quite a flair for it. Gardening, too."

"Did Mrs. Egan do the garden here?" I asked.

"Sandra," he said. "Well, she doesn't do too much now. We have the boy handle it." Norman wandered over to the window and peered out, shading his eyes. "I suppose one gets tired of things." I remained standing, anxious to get on with my day.

"It's a shame," Norman said, turning to me. "Used to be, when we first moved in here, you could see the mountain from this window every day of the year. Sacred, you know. Of course, this whole area was considered special—conquered over and over again by different tribes till the Spanish came and grabbed it up. Cities right on top of other cities down there. But—it's fascinating—every one of those peoples used the same big pyramid up on the mountain to worship in their own way. Splendid ruins—Sandra and I used to take picnics. . . ."

I squinted out the window. "Oh, you can't see anything today." Norman dismissed with a little wave the blue sky and dazzling sun. "All kinds of industry now mucking things up. People coming in from the country—crowding, pollution, that sort of thing." He sighed. "Anyhow, nice to know you've got a view, eh? Whether you can see it or not. Well . . ." He put forth a mild, formalized version of a chuckle. "But we still love it. And, please—if you need anything, I hope you'll ask. There are always so many little things one doesn't quite know what to do about. One expects things to be one way, but then they turn out to be—not to be just exactly the way one expects."

"Yes," I said, from the depths of a sudden fatigue. "Perhaps you'd know where I might be able to buy some coffee."

"Coffee," he said. "Well—coffee. They'd have it in town, of course. Dolores handles that sort of thing for us. Oh, yes," he said, misunderstanding my look of surprise, "we're very lucky with Dolores. Down here we don't like to be very, *very* formal"—he winked at me—"but Dolores came to us very young. Husband disappeared—you know the way they do—and Sandra taught her everything."

"Really," I said.

"Well, we were in the restaurant business, you see. We had lovely establishments. New Orleans, Dallas, Cincinnati, Fort Lauderdale—all over. And in every one of those places we had a wonderful, cultivated clientele. Sandra and I always personally oversaw everything. Oh," he said. "I brought something else for you." He handed me a little book. "This might prove useful. And remember, don't feel shy. If you have questions, or you need something, you just come right downstairs and ask."

"I don't suppose I'll be bothering you often," I said, taking the opportunity to discourage further visits from him. "I'm really just here to—"

"Of course," he said. "You're young and adventurous. You didn't come here to hang around with a couple of old—a couple of old . . . people."

Young and adventurous, I thought irritably, as we went out together; young and adventurous. But as I closed the door behind us, I glanced back into the room, and I felt as if I'd been slapped. With the jars of cream out on the bureau, it was true that the place looked like a girl's first apartment, like the apartments my college roommates had gotten for themselves when we graduated and I'd moved back in with my mother.

When I opened the front gate, the town I'd driven through only the day before took me by surprise, as if my imagination had perversely reconstructed a fleeting hallucination. The concave whorl of tangled streets lay below me in a glaze of sun, and I wound downward, baffled by the high walls. How quiet all the people around me were! They spoke in low voices, and averted their heavy-lashed eyes as I passed by. Even the children made hardly any noise. Trucks and motorcycles and an occasional flustered chicken provided all the sound.

At the base of the town, I found a small square, and although I was anxious to do a few errands and get my bearings, its lacy little white iron benches looked so ceremonial and expectant that I felt obliged to sit down for a moment. I chose a spot in the shade of a broad-leafed tree and surveyed the odd patch of a park around me. Paved walks threaded through it, and it was dotted with tiny tiled fountains. Heavy prismatic beams seemed to converge on it from many different suns, giving everything an exaggerated dimensionality in which it was impossible to judge distances, and in the very center was a band shell, confected from curls of iron and pearly glass, whose dome rose above the leaves of nearby trees. Around the edges of the square, people who looked like dolls in costumes, with black yarn hair, sold things: painted toys, hardware, bursting red fruits, clothing, hideous stuffed dogs, or masks—a fantastic, impossible catalogue of items. Aromas of ripe—overripe—fruit, and dust, and some kind of peppery cooking oil swirled lazily around me.

It was hot. I looked at my watch and was dismayed to find that it had stopped. What ought I to do? I thought, standing hurriedly. But I forced myself to sit back down and relax. I opened the little book that Norman had given me—a compilation of phrases in English and translation which the author seemed to consider indispensable to travelers:

This dress is too long (too short).
" " is made to fit badly.
It is badly made.
That is more than I can pay for this dress (basket) (rug) (bowl).
No, thank you, I do not want it.
Good. That is a fair price.

"Is it something unpleasant that you read?" I heard, and I looked up to see a man standing over me. He seemed so close, in my alarm, that every detail of the medal lying on his exposed chest looked immense: the hair around it and the skin, glistening with sweat, appeared magnified.

"No," I said to the large, white teeth above me. I snapped the book shut and walked off on trembling legs.

Soon I had gotten myself back under control, and I paused to see where I was. Next to me an opening in the street wall gave onto something that appeared to be a sort of general store. Inside, past dusty cases of beer stacked along the buckling aqua-colored wall, I found coffee and other things I needed. At the counter, two almond-eyed little girls painstakingly picked what I hoped was the correct amount of coins from a heap I put in front of them. Supervising this proceeding was a large woman in long, ruffled skirts, who grinned at me. I was painfully aware of being the absurd tourist, and I stared at the woman, who only grinned with greater gusto.

It took me quite some time to find my way back to the square, where I stood looking helplessly at the streets that twisted up in a funnel around me. Eventually I managed to identify my route back, but at its mouth a row of women now sat, wrapped in shawls, and as I approached they stretched out their hands without glancing at me. There was no way to avoid them. I divided my change into equal portions and distributed it among the women, being very careful not to touch them.

The first thing I saw when I opened the door to my apartment was my heartless line of creams and lotions on the bureau. I quickly put the jars into the medicine chest, and then I examined the packages and cans of food that Norman had provided. Later I lay down to read. But instead of holding the book I was rising up to where I saw myself asleep. I dreamed of a cool, dark sleep that was ruptured almost immediately by noisy intruders who disputed and harangued for hour after hour in many guises and landscapes. Several times during the night they drove me into the solitude of wakefulness, at the boundaries of which they waited, shrieking and bobbing, until I was weak enough to be captured again.

In the morning I woke to see my few purchases of the day before on the bureau, where I'd left them. How odd this light made everything look—the coffee, the sugar, the soap—like menacing little idols. And later, when I opened the gate onto the street, I once again experienced a little shock, as if the town, simmering below me in the dusty gold, had just materialized to greet me.

I was determined to get a good start on the day, so I headed right down to the square, where I remembered having seen a news kiosk. Most of the publications for sale turned out to be comic books devoted to slaughter and tragedy, but there were several magazines with interesting pictures. I paid the older of the two boys who worked at the kiosk, while the other, who must have been around seven, stared at me, his face an upturned circle with a point at the chin.

In the heat of the afternoon, when shutters rolled down over the shop doorways, I inspected the restaurants and cafés that faced the square, but they were filled with roughly clothed men, drunk even at that hour, and foreigners speaking English or German at an arrogant volume. Sorrowful vendors circulated among the tables, and there were flies.

Persisting, I discovered a restaurant in a little courtyard that looked clean and quiet. After I settled at a table near a blossom-clogged fountain, I realized that the restaurant was part of a hotel, whose guests—small, ancient people in dressing gowns—spoke a language I did not recognize. I managed to order something from a young waiter, who encouraged my clumsy efforts with unwelcome enthusiasm, but when my meal came, steaming and covered with an assaultive spicy sauce, I could feel that the expression on my face replicated the one I had so often seen on my mother's when she confronted her tray of trembling sickroom substances. I watched, humiliated, as the wizened diners around me ate hugely, with evident enjoyment, and I reminded myself that if I were in Chicago I would have no trouble obtaining a nice, crisp salad and a refreshing glass of iced tea.

Norman was on his terrace when I returned, chatting with a man and woman who seemed to be about my age. The three of them sipped from frosty glasses, and a small boy squatted nearby, barking menacingly at a baleful setter. "Stop that, please, John-John," the man said.

"Oh, he's all right," Norman said, smiling at me in greeting. "Mister's used to children, aren't you, Mister?" The dog yawned with pleasure as Norman scratched his ear. "Mister and that old bunny rabbit belong to the people next door, but they like to come visiting."

"Excuse us," the man said as the boy sprinted off in tight circles, spluttering like a balloon releasing its air. "I'm Simon Peter Murchison, and this is my wife, Annette. And that dignified personage now disporting himself in the compost is our firstborn, John-John."

"Would you believe it?" Annette said. "We bought that little shirt in Florence for him."

"Don't be in a rush, now," Norman said. "Won't you sit down and have a drink with us, please? Dolores—" he called.

"Where has our son picked up these *habits*?" Annette smiled, inviting me to marvel with her.

"Yes, we've been all over since he was born," Simon Peter explained loftily.

"For pleasure?" I asked.

"For a pittance." He chuckled in the direction of his drink. "University salary."

"How nice to have a field that takes you around," I said obediently, as I craned to read his watch.

"History of Ecclesiastical Architecture in Colonial Countries," Simon Peter said. We all glanced up at the silhouettes of crosses that stood out on the peaks around us, black against the shining sky.

"These are so delicious, Norman," Annette said, accepting a fresh drink from Dolores. "What do you put in them?"

"Oh, just about any kind of fruit you can think of. And

then just about any kind of alcohol you can think of." Norman winked at me.

"Are you teaching here now?" I asked Simon Peter.

"I've picked up a semester," he said. "But essentially we're based in Europe for the moment."

Annette turned to me. "Do you know Europe?"

"No," I said.

"You should," she said. "You should try it. The things that are good here? They're even better there. Of course, prices have really soared since we first went. But now here, even with the devaluations, prices are a completely different thing than they used to be. We're priced right out now, on Simon Peter's salary." She cast a sour glance at the house. "You've certainly found yourself a bargain."

"I've just come for a short time. Besides," I said deliberately, "I inherited a small amount of money."

"There," she said. "You see?"

"Anyhow, we're glad to have you with us," Norman said.

"It seems like a wonderful place for children," I said.

"In many ways, yes," Simon Peter said with a vague judiciousness. "In many ways I suppose it is. At least they're happy enough."

"These children here can afford to be happy," Annette said. "They're spoiled rotten."

"Well, anyway," Norman said.

"No, it's a shame," Annette said. "I know these people. My parents came here every winter until I was twelve. These people are sweet, kind people; I grew up with them. They don't want to hurt anyone—they're Indians. But they're so irresponsible. They keep having children and having children—they just can't be taught to stop. And there isn't enough food, there isn't enough money, and so they starve. And now these people have become dishonest. You used to be able to leave them to take care of your house while you were gone, with all your silver or anything. Now they'll steal your wallet right on the street."

"They're a fine people, really," Norman said to me. "For the most part. And the little ones are darling."

"John-John," Simon Peter called warningly to his son, who towered over a plant from behind which the rabbit peeked out, twitching.

"No, I love these people, Norman," Annette said. "But you can't trust them anymore. Well, everyone has to eat, of course. I understand that. But they breed like—" Annette glanced with annoyance toward the shrubbery, where John-John now crouched holding a rock—"like I don't know whats."

"Well," Simon Peter said, "the climate's still perfect."

"Have you been up to the mountain yet?" Annette gestured toward the empty sky.

"I've really just arrived," I said.

"We'll go while you're here," she said. "There are some very good market towns up there. You can still get the most marvelous textiles and ceramics for practically nothing."

"How nice," I said. "Well . . ." I felt I had spent enough time on these witless marauders. "I really must be going upstairs now." As I stood, I realized how potent Norman's drink had been.

"Will anyone stay for some supper?" Norman asked.

"Don't you wish Mommy would let you?" Annette said to John-John. "Thank you, Norman. We wish we could."

"Well, please come back soon," Norman said. "Sandra will be dying to see you both."

"Hush now, honey," Annette said to John-John. "We're saying good night."

"She's due in at the end of the week," Norman said. We all looked at John-John as he tugged at Annette's hand and loosed a descending wordless whine. "Sandra."

"Well, isn't that wonderful, Norman," Simon Peter said, frowning.

So this was what was meant by "traveling," by "taking a vacation"—these unnavigable currents, this sudden immersion in the lives of utter strangers, their thin, dreadful lives.

That night sleep came for me like a great ship sliding between the dark sky and the dark water, and it bore me off to a territory that I recognized with horror, as I lost consciousness, from the night before. My dreams coiled and merged until I could no longer sustain sleep and woke exhausted, tossed by a shrill crowd onto the bed where I found myself.

The air was faintly sparkly, and a freshness drifted in through the open windows. While I lay there, trying to emerge into full consciousness, a memory permeated me like a single, low vibrating tone: My mother stood in the water, smiling at me. She would have been just slightly older than I was now. I wore a bathing suit the shade of vanilla ice cream, with the most special little candy-colored blobs—special, delicious colors. My mother held out her hand to coax me out farther. The cool sand where I stood became wet and wet again with a mild pulse of water. The sand gave beneath my feet each time a wave pulled back, then smoothed mysteriously before each return. I took my mother's hand and walked into the water to where the sand became round stones. I looked at my divided legs, and at the stones that wobbled when I moved, in the clear, different thing. My mother was happy. When had I ever seen her so happy? Where could we have been? I clung to her hand and edged in farther.

When I woke again, the sun was a yellow rayed circle over the garden.

For about a week I saw nothing of Norman, and the curtains of the main house were drawn. But Dolores continued to come and go, smiling her luminous smile, and a gardener appeared several times to redistribute mounds of dirt with an aggressive air of weariness and expertise which was surely intended for Norman's eyes. And so, as there seemed no need to inquire after Norman, I did not. In the mornings I hurried down to the news kiosk and then had my juice and coffee in the hotel restaurant while I looked at my magazines. I walked, then visited the dilapidated little museum in town, and after a midday meal I would join a busload of rapacious tourists to vist one of the nearby villages where Indians made textiles or worked copper, or I went to the square to read about the history of the area. Afterward, I shopped for the small evening meal I would assemble back at the apartment. I had no time to spare.

Then one morning, as I came downstairs, I saw Norman climbing out of his car with a load of parcels. He looked cheerful in his crisp white clothes, and he gave me a friendly wave as he headed toward the house.

"What have you brought me?" a woman called out to him from the doorway. "Treats," she said. "Good. And look—an American girl. He's wonderful," she said to me. "He does everything he can to keep me from—to keep me amused. You *are* an American girl, aren't you? You do understand what I'm saying?"

"This is our little tenant, Sandra," Norman said.

"Well, at least he didn't bring me the Van Kirks," the woman continued. "Or the Murchisons. Or, God forbid, the Geldzahlers."

"Oh, now, Sandra," Norman chuckled hesitantly toward me.

"But they'll be over soon enough. And besides," Sandra said, "we love them. They're our friends. Now—" she smiled formally at me—"are you going to stay and at least have a—a glass of juice with us, or are you one of those busy, busy people who have to rush off somewhere all the time?"

"Nowhere to rush to here," Norman said.

"I'll stay for a moment," I said reluctantly, "but I do have errands." What if the hotel stopped serving breakfast at a particular time?

"Dolores—" Sandra looked around and then left the room.

"So . . ." Norman said, sitting down.

I could leave my magazines until after breakfast, of course, but I hadn't brought anything with me to read. Furthermore, I'd planned to go to the museum right after breakfast, and the kiosk wasn't on the way.

"How nice," I said to Norman, "that your wife has arrived."

"Looks well, doesn't she?" he said vaguely.

"Tell me," Sandra said as she came back into the room, "do you play bridge? Or golf?" She was tall and athletic-looking, and her bright sundress suited her, but she had the hardened flesh of someone who has lain too long around a swimming pool.

"I'm not much for games," I said.

"Good," she said, pushing back her wiry bronze hair. She seemed exasperated by her own sensuous, slightly ramshackle vitality, and I felt grateful to have my orderly body. "Norman just plays to bore himself nerveless." Norman, who had been fussing with some small pieces of wood, smiled up at his wife cautiously, but she avoided looking at him. "He used to make such fun of them. Thank you, Dolores." She smiled brightly at Dolores, who set a glass of juice in front of each of us. "Alas. You must come and entertain me while he plays with his . . . *cronies*." She turned to Norman suddenly. "What have you got there?" she asked.

"Oh," he said, opening his hand to reveal a little dog he'd assembled from the pieces of wood. "One of these silly things. Cute, aren't they? Japanese." He and Sandra gazed at the little figure in his palm, perplexed and abstracted.

"What pretty glasses," I said, picking up my juice.

"Yes," Sandra said. She reeled her attention back from Norman's hand. "Those. Yes, they are quite pretty, aren't they? They're local work. It's a shame they don't make them any longer."

"Well, we've got ours," Norman said with a jolly lift of an eyebrow. "We got them years ago, and we still have them."

"Like everything else we got years ago," Sandra said crossly. She took a sip of her juice and set the glass down, pushing it away from her on the table. "They used to do such lovely work in this area," she said to me. "Norman and I used to bring carloads and carloads back home with us. Oh, those trips!" She looked at Norman for an instant. When she looked away again, she held out her hand, and he clasped it. I was decades away from them in the long silence.

"Would you like something instead of the juice, darling?" Norman said.

"Would I like something instead of the juice." Sandra looked at him and withdrew her hand from his.

"No, I just—" he said, and stopped. He set the little wooden dog on the table and watched it as if it were going to perform a trick.

"Well," Sandra said, seeming to remember me. "But I hope you're having a lovely, lovely time."

"She is," Norman said.

"We always do, ourselves," Sandra said. "Wonderful climate, wonderful friends—pool, sun, tennis . . ."

"And they're a happy people," Norman said.

My day, of course, was pretty well ruined. To salvage something of it I took an unfamiliar street into the square; although every street looked alike, and the walls, their colors softened by an aged, powdery bloom, hid most of what lay beyond them, each doorway and gate opened onto a little scene as precise and mystifying as a stage set, and today I walked slowly, to look. Here and there I could see part of a garden littered with fallen flowers, or the twisted trunk of a tree whose branches arched above the walls. I passed a shop where paper goods were displayed as proudly and elaborately as if they were precious rarities, and a tiny restaurant, consisting of several cheerfully painted tables and a stove, on which sat a stewpot. A jewel-colored parrot presided from his perch. Nearby in a roofed space, a woman leaned back against a polished sports car, resting, her eyes closed. She wore a little uniform with a starched pinafore, and she fanned herself slowly with a large, stiff leaf.

Stretching out behind her, on and on, I could see a slope covered with tiny shacks. Lines of washing crisscrossed it, and children played there. Several ponies—real ponies they were, of course—stood, flicking their tails. When the maid opened her long, obsidian eyes I was unsettled, as if something potent were being released through them. But she didn't seem to see me. Perhaps I was invisible in the strong light.

Later I wandered through an outdoor market I hadn't come across before. I was attracted to an array of miniatures spread out on a blanket, and I picked one up to admire it. It was a tiny scene exactly like the one I stood in front of at that moment: a woman wearing a shawl around her head and shoulders and a long skirt sat behind a display of her wares just like the woman who looked up at me now. But the miniature woman sold tiny foodstuffs—the smallest imaginable carrots and scallions and tomatoes and bottles of milk. I was charmed by the little tableau; but when I tilted it to inspect the toy woman's face, I saw that it was a skull, its mouth open in greedy bliss. Seeing my expression, the living woman in front of me broke into peals of laughter, and my hand seemed frozen to the nasty toy. I was shaking when I reached the news kiosk. Both boys looked at me with concern, and I was glad that it was not possible for us to communicate with one another.

Upstairs that night I took myself by surprise in the mirror. An American girl—no wonder Norman and Sandra insisted that I was young. I'd seen a small-featured face, unusually composed, and an almost aggressively fresh, pink-and-white complexion that seemed to have been acted upon by neither internal nor external weather. I had always assumed that life would start for me at about the age I had reached now; it was the age at which my mother considered hers to have started, the age at which she had married for the first and only time, had conceived her first and only child. But soon after that late, small budding of her life she had been left with only a wedding ring, a settlement, a disease, and a daughter, of course—a daughter who was now thirty-four years old.

. . .

After Sandra's arrival there was a great deal more activity downstairs. Sandra and Norman were often out sunbathing, or sitting on the terrace, where Dolores brought them elaborate little meals. In the evenings, they frequently had gatherings. The guests, often people who hardly would have spoken to one another in the United States, were bound together here by the conviction, based on the spending power of their dollars, of their own merit, and necessarily, therefore, the merit of their companions. They reinforced this conviction by continuous complaints about the town (and it was true that nothing ever happened on time, nothing was ever properly done, there were endless, inexplicable shortages of goods—it was a world of exasperating shrugs and smiles), and all conversations on these evenings were suspended in a medium of expatriate complicity, where no one had ever suffered any past indignity or disappointment, where no one, in fact, seemed to have any antecedents whatsoever. No one ever asked me anything about my own life. Any sharp-edged remnant of life "back at home" that might mar the smooth afternoons was washed away in the evenings' floods of alcohol. The morning sun burned off the hangovers. There was only one beautiful day and then another, and life being squandered.

During these parties of Sandra and Norman's I would go upstairs as soon as possible. But the loud voices and laughter seemed amplified in my little apartment, and after an hour or two I would feel weak with grief and rage, as one does when one is ill. When I managed to avoid an event of this sort altogether, Dolores would appear at my door with an invitation for me to join the company, and on those evenings that I sent her downstairs with excuses she would return with a tray of party food, decorated with flowers or paper constructions or carved miniatures. Usually I put the food into the refrigerator and saved it for several days before I threw it out, but once, as soon as I'd shut the door behind Dolores, even though I was terribly hungry I threw it wrathfully into the garbage. When there were no parties I sat inside with the lights dimmed, fearing the exhausting importunities what would surely ensue from downstairs if I were to be seen on my balcony.

One evening, to escape from Norman and Sandra I went to the square. And as I approached I was amazed to find myself in the company of the entire town. The street walls exhaled the retained heat of the day, and a sudden scent of honey was released into the air as people filed in from all directions, arm in arm, and perched on the embellished benches or the rims of the tiled fountains, or strolled along the little paths. The sky flowed pink to green, and across it birds convened in wide streaks, screaming, and settled, with the dark, down into the trees.

I found a spot for myself on a bench between two elderly women. Although the sheen of daylight hung over the sky high across from me, here under the canopy of trees and birds it was truly night. The steady, intricate play of the fountains wove up all the sounds, and small lamps spilled light onto the glossy leaves. All around the square the cafés filled with customers.

No one bothered me. No one spoke to me. I watched the children tumbling about, playing tag up and down the little paths or kicking large, bright, slow balls to one another. Two little girls in identical starched and ruffled dresses bought a balloon from a boy hardly older than themselves. Expertly he disengaged their choice from the massive cluster that bobbed above him. A group of little girls, with ribbons in their silky black hair, tottered, still rubbery with infancy, under a stream of translucent spheres that bloomed from the wand of a vendor of bubble liquid. Little boys ran up a flight of shallow stone steps and slid down its broad border over and over. Teen-agers sat entwined, kissing or reading comics, and older couples meandered hand in hand. Some vendors had spread out cloths to display their goods, and others sold sweets from carts, or glowing drinks made of crushed fruit. Musicians played—some in groups, others singly—without reference to each other, and then a band appeared in the little bonbon of a band shell, the brass of their instruments flashing more brightly than the sound. The porous night absorbed noises rapidly here, and activity streamed silently around one, like the sort of dream that binds the body and absorbs the voice as one struggles to break into the waking world.

After that, I often fled to the square in the evenings. It was like being part of a little music box. Every night the figures assumed their positions—the birds, the boys and girls, the parents, the grandparents, the couples, the vendors, and the musicians all took their places at the same time, and the men who sold bubble-making liquid sent their streams of bubbles tirelessly into the air while the tiniest children twirled, enchanted, beneath them.

Later the town would pitch and boil as I slept. Faces I'd hardly noticed in the square rose up around me and spoke urgently, but I could not understand the words. The flowery walls that lined the streets split open in the pale brilliance of my dreams, revealing broad veins of cardboard shacks where bodies tossed and groaned in their own sleep. Women sat wrapped in their shawls; they reached out, but when I put change into their open palms they threw it on the ground, shrieking. I was ill; I lay in bed, dreaming, with my hands on the covers, unable to move or call out. My mother stood with her back to me, moonlight sluicing down on her. She poured transparent juice from a pitcher into a glass, but it made no sound. She turned and walked toward me, grinning in pain, making a balloon dance on a string. Inside the balloon was a baby. Its face swam toward the surface, hugely distorted. My mother jerked on the string, grinning, making the balloon dance. I saw it was falling, I saw it was plummeting down toward the slate ground, suddenly a great distance away; but a roaring silence masked its impact.

I always awoke into the quiet before dawn with my heart pounding. I would pour myself a glass of water and swallow it slowly to regulate my breathing as I walked back and forth in my room. The moonlight that streamed into my dreams had given way to a softer dark, but how bright the stars were still—like tiny holes in a skin that hid a pure light beyond. Often I hardly knew where I was, as I drank my water and walked, so altered had the world been by my sleep. And all around me dream images of my mother—forgotten images from all the ages at which I'd known her—slipped into shadows. I myself was no age in my dreams, the age one is to oneself. Exhaustion would topple me back into the life of my sleep, which seemed to be flowing on independently of me, just like the life my body entered in the mornings. And after several more hours I could feel myself working free again, but just as I sped up toward a sunlit surface the picture would spin and I would wake plunging downward into a daytime world as protean as my dreams.

In the afternoons, when the sun had baked the town into opaque, reliable shapes, I sat in the square and refreshed myself by reading about the history of the peoples who had occupied the area. Throughout the history of the military struggles, the vanquished had absorbed, to some degree, the victor, and had ultimately asserted at least some subtle ascendancy. And although the stately cities thought to be buried beneath me in layers were as invisible as the mountain where the remains of the pyramid still stood, pockets of ancient languages and customs had survived intact among the people who pursued their quiet activities around me in the square. It seemed remarkable to me that these people were adrift at the margins of a history now generated elsewhere, and yet were the living descendants not only of the ultimate, fierce Spanish conquerers but also of the glamorous nations that had ruled here when this had been the center of civilization. I read about them all—the succession of vivid, vanished empires that ended during the reign of a bellicose, death-obsessed people, who had been technologically and martially accomplished but otherwise less refined than their predecessors. These final Indian rulers used the pyramid as an altar for human sacrifice, and I could not bring myself to visit the ruins. I wondered if Norman or Annette ever imagined the blood that had flowed down stone steps over his picnic spot, her marketplace.

One night when I came up the hill from the square I found Norman and Sandra on the patio with a young couple utterly unlike the reddened, tuberous creatures who were usually to be found there. "Come here," Sandra called. "I want you to meet Marcus and Eileen." The woman's skirt flounced out from her tiny waist, and her toylike high-heeled shoes were dazzlingly white and free of dust. "They're our neighbors."

"Yes, I am Marcos," the man said, standing. "And my wife, Elena."

"Now, where did I get 'Eileen' from?" Sandra said.

"For whom can I get something to drink?" Norman said, clapping his hands together.

"It's Dolores's night off," Sandra said. "God knows what she does."

"What is it you are drinking, Norman?" Elena asked, reaching out a slender arm.

"Water." Norman smiled sheepishly.

"Yes, certainly, but let me taste," Elena said. Her long red nails gleamed against the glass.

"A little water," Norman said as Elena took a delicate sip.

"A little water with a big gin," Marcos said.

"Yes, give me one of those, please, Norman," Elena said.

"And for me, too, please," Marcos said.

"Nothing for me, thank you," I said.

"Oh, come on," Sandra said.

"No, really," I said. "Thank you."

"These two live right next door," Sandra said, indicating the hedge through which Mister and the rabbit made their frequent appearances. "And *this* one"—she tucked my arm under hers—"lives upstairs. She came all the way from—from—America"—Sandra landed with relief on the word—"and now she's right here in this garden. She *hates* us, isn't that right?" Sandra winked at Elena. "We're bad neighbors and she hates us."

"You must forgive me, please," Elena said to me. "I do not speak very well English. Marcos, my husband, he speak it very well."

"You speak English like a princess," Sandra said. "Just like a princess. Isn't it odd, you know, how you can live right next door to people and never see them at all?" Marcos smiled, allowing a dark radiance to flow briefly out to Sandra.

"Here we are," Norman said. "Three waters, one water, and a nothing."

"Norman and I were just telling these lovely people about some of our other friends right here in town," Sandra said. "Now. You don't know Dr. and Mrs. Rafaelson, you said. Skipper and Lillian."

"Unfortunately, we do not," Marcos said with finality.

"Let's see," Sandra continued. "The Van Kirks, the Geldzahlers, the Murchisons—Oh! You must know the Dawsons. They do a lot of charity work at the church."

Elena's black hair seemed to flex and breathe as she smoothed it back. "I do not think so, do we, Marcos?" Marcos took a sip of his drink and shook his head without looking up. I feared I was to be condemned along with the other invaders from the U.S. without getting my own trial.

"Well, we're all very fortunate to be able to live in a town with such fine people," Norman said.

Mister squeezed through the shrubbery and seated himself between his owners. He looked up adoringly at Marcos, his tail beating on the ground, and Marcos raised his glass slightly in salute. "Poop on Mister," Sandra said as Elena bent down to stroke his fur.

"Poop on Mister," Norman said. "Mister Poops. We love Mister," he explained to me.

"Mister is a very good dog," Elena said. "To get Mister we have to go to the place where—how do you say, that place—"

"Pound," Sandra said. "Kennel."

"The place where they make the dog that have the history, the good family . . ."

"Dog breeder," Norman said.

"Yes, and now if Mister have good children they are worth very much in U.S. dollars."

"Oh, yes," Norman said. "Lovely things, setters. Sandra and I have had many fine animals ourselves."

"But we don't try, we don't try to have him, how do you say that thing?"

"That's a thing we don't say." Sandra nudged me. "We don't say it."

"Bred," Norman said, nodding.

"Yes, bred," Elena said. "We don't care about this thing."

"No, who cares?" Sandra said. "Dirty old dogs. Oh, Mister knows I love him."

"Yes, if they are healthy, the children, this is what we care," Elena said.

"Look." Marcos rested a finger lazily on my wrist. "Do you see?" And I could just make out, in the direction he indicated, the outline of a peak—flat, like a shadow cast from some original behind us—that rose above the others.

"The mountain," I said, pleased. "This is the first time I've seen it."

"It does not like to be seen often," Marcos said.

"No?" I responded reluctantly to his coyness, "Why not?"

"It is consecrated ground," he said, tracing a pattern on his frosty glass. "Young girls used to be sacrificed there." Perhaps he hoped to shock me, but of course I was already familiar with the facts. "Their blood was dedicated to the gods who made the sun rise."

"I know," I said. "Those poor girls."

Marcos shrugged. "Those poor gods," he said. "Compelled to make the sun rise, the days go around in their circle."

"Compelled?" I said. "I would have thought that gods could do as they liked."

"Oh, no." Marcos lifted his eyes to me. I was annoyed by the degree to which he and his wife made their good looks a public concern, but I was not able to look away. "There are advantages, I am sure, to being a god, but that is not one of them. After all, prayer forces gods to respond, does it not?"

"I suppose one could think of it that way," I said. "I don't happen to."

"No?" Marcos said. "But the rain, the revelation, the vision, the growth of crops, the investiture of wisdom or power—even salvation—these things have always been granted if the preparation is correct."

"Nevertheless," I said, becoming crude in my irritation, "it seems rather wasteful, doesn't it? All those girls hacked to bits to make the sun come up, when it seems to come up all by itself these days."

"Perhaps it does." Marcos smiled. Against my will I imagined him dressing in front of the mirror, buttoning his shirt (as far as he had buttoned it) over his muscular chest while his eyes narrowed with satisfaction. "Or perhaps we benefit from the unselfish labors of our predecessors. Here the past lives on in us. Do you not see it when you look at me? The raised basalt knife, the bound virgin, the living heart plucked from the breast—"

"Please," I said. "That's quite enough. Besides, everyone has a history. I suppose you're saying that I am a . . . that I'm a . . ." But I was too addled by his gruesome joking to think of an analogy.

"Yes," he said. "You see? You do not know what you are.

You come from a corner of America that eradicated its original population. For you the past is something that is terminated, because your own past is an erasure. What a sad thing, I think! You cannot look back and see your present, you cannot look inward and see your future—"

"That may be so," I said evenly, though I could feel myself flushing with rage—surely it was the presence of Sandra and Norman that had provoked this platitudinous sermonizing. "But I should think you would be grateful to have that particular chapter of your history shelved. Some people consider it barbaric, you know. Besides, it seems to me that you're making great claims for an area that itself no longer has an indigenous culture. The people here now come from all over."

"From all over," Marcos agreed, delighted. "Bringing with them civilized customs, yes? They come from wherever one can be indicted for tax evasion. Or war crimes. Or fraud. They come for the climate." He looked at me. "And for what have you come?"

"The climate," I said, tears stinging from behind my eyes as he laughed.

"I have upset you," he said. "But I am only playing." A spoiled, stuffy look came over him as he became bored with tormenting me. "My family, of course, is pure Spanish."

"Such a relief," I said, "to learn that it is your practice also to usher in the sunrise without all that . . . 'preparation,' I believe, is what you called it."

"Oh, I do not think we are suited for that now, in any case—that preparation," he said. "Because at the final moment all of it must be discarded."

Now that I was utterly beside myself, Marcos seemed to have forgotten me entirely, and he spoke as if he were musing in private. "I'm afraid I don't quite follow you," I said stiffly.

"Yes," he said. "Selecting the sacrifice, bending one's being to the desired thing, achieving the proper conditions for prayer—at the final moment this labor and struggle fall away like torn cloth, and the petitioner must face his goal unprotected. I do not think we, now, would be able to endure that."

"Endure what, you two?" Sandra said, turning to us. "What don't you think we could endure?" She gestured vaguely. "We can endure this. Anyhow—" She took both my hands as I stood up to go, and she looked into my face searchingly. "The main thing is, Are You Having Fun?"

"Yes," I said. "Of course."

"Good." She released me and shook her head slowly. "Because that's the main thing."

Now Marcos began to appear in my dreams. He was a jeering, insistent, impinging presence, but once, just before I awoke, he repented and took me, for comfort, into his arms. I showered immediately upon getting out of bed, but the feeling of him clung to me maddeningly throughout the day.

One morning soon afterward I was on my way out when Norman and Sandra called to me from the patio. "If it isn't just the lady we were talking about!" Sandra said. "Come have breakfast with Mr. and Mrs. Useless. Dolores—" she called, pointing at me.

"Of course, we don't want to keep you if you have things to do," Norman said, as I hesitated.

"Oh, she doesn't have anything to *do,*" Sandra said.

"No, the reason we hoped to see you this morning," Norman said, "is that some very old, very dear friends of ours, Gerald and Helen Moffat, have just come in from Minneapolis, and we're having a little party for them this evening. We thought maybe we'd forgotten to tell you."

"Are you from Minneapolis?" I asked.

"No," Norman said. "Our friends are."

"Norman," Sandra said, "have you spoken to Skipper and Lillian again?"

"Well," Norman said, "they'll do their damnedest to make

it, but apparently Skipper hasn't been feeling too well. Nothing serious. But," Norman said to me, "there will be plenty of lovely people, and you're a lovely person, and we know you'll enjoy the others."

"Thank you," I said. First my morning, and now my evening. "I'll certainly come, unless—"

"Now, where—" Sandra twisted around in her chair. "Oh, there," she said as Dolores appeared with a glass of juice and a plate of bacon and eggs for me.

Norman broke off a gardenia from a plant near him and put it on my plate. "Don't we do everything beeyoutifully?" Sandra said.

"Bee*you*tifully, bee*you*tifully," Norman chanted.

"And will the Moffats be staying with you?" I asked.

"No, no," Norman said. "They keep a lovely place here in town. Right out where our old place was. Just the other side of the golf club."

"Golf club," Sandra said. "Golf club, golf club. Who knows what anybody's talking about, with golf *clubs* and *golf* clubs? Anyhow, it sounds like some kind of expression, doesn't it?" I looked at her politely. " 'Those people live just the other side of a golf club.' It would mean, for instance, a tiny bit, but too much. Just beyond the pale, kind of." She laughed and clapped her hands together. "You would say, 'Oh, those two? They're lovely people, but they've gone just the other side of the golf club.' "

"Oh, yes," I said.

"Dolores," Sandra said, "we're *waiting* for our coffee."

Norman turned to pinch back the gardenia plant. "They have a marvelous pool," he said. "Just let us know if you want to use it. They'd be delighted."

"Is that to make it flower?" I asked him.

"Yes," Norman said. "I don't know. These silly things just flower in this climate no matter what you do." He got up to inspect some plants that made a border along the hedge. "That darned rabbit did a lot of damage, Sandra," he said plaintively. "We're going to have to get the boy to replace these."

"Well, anyhow," I reassured him, "I haven't seen it around lately."

"I'll bet you're dying for your coffee," Sandra said. "I know I am."

"Where do you suppose it went?" I asked. "The rabbit."

Sandra made a face and brushed some crumbs from the table. "Just look at this mess," she said.

Norman straightened up and sighed. "He had to take it out," he said, looking at the ground. "I don't know why."

As Norman wandered farther along, poking at the plants, Sandra spoke rapidly to me in a low voice. "I think those people next door ate the rabbit," she said. "But I don't want to say that to Norman. He'd have a fit. He loves rabbits. That rabbit was such a pest, though, wasn't it, eating all those plants. But it was cute. We don't have them at home. Well, we do, I suppose, we could, but people eat them here." She watched absently as Dolores approached, but then continued, enraged, "Oh, well, why not, after all? People have to eat." As Dolores poured our coffee, Sandra looked at me and raised an eyebrow. "Thank you, Dolores," she said with exaggerated graciousness.

I was embarrassed, but Dolores seemed oblivious of the sudden savage rudeness that Sandra would occasionally unleash. "We eat cows," I said.

"You don't happen to have anything like—a Valium, do you?" Sandra asked. "Or upstairs?"

"I don't," I said. "No."

"Well, good for you. Who needs that stuff? Yes," she said after a moment, "that's true. We do eat cows. And chickies. And piggie-wigs. But they're all revolting."

We sat and looked at Norman as he peered about among the plants. "This coffee is delicious," I said.

"Oh! If you want delicious—" Sandra said, jumping to her feet. She went inside and came back with a bottle. "Just try it," she said.

"What is it?" I asked. I looked from Sandra to Norman, who had returned to stand above me.

"Don't feel you have to, if you're not in the mood," he said.

"Oh, Norman. It's practically the national *drink,*" Sandra said.

"But if she doesn't want to—" Norman said.

Sandra opened the bottle, and we all listened while she poured some into my coffee. "It's just for her. To try."

I took a sip. "Lovely, isn't it?" I said, although I found it strong and peculiar.

Sandra watched me as I drank, her chin resting on the backs of her clasped hands. "Yes," she said.

She shook herself, as if from sleep and poured from the bottle into Norman's cup and then into her own. "Sandra—" Norman said. But she didn't look at him, and the three of us drank, our eyes lowered.

"Well . . ." Norman sighed. He raised himself up and shambled back to the border plants.

"He can't sit still," Sandra said. "It worries me."

Norman shook his head once again over the plants and then turned back to us, shading his eyes from the sun. "Can I give you a ride somewhere?" he asked me. "I've got to go down to the golf club for a quick game."

"You see?" Sandra called gleefully. "Well, stay this side!"

"I'm going into town," I said. "I don't think it's on your way."

"Got to drive anyhow," Norman said. "Just jump into the car, hippity-hop."

That evening the party glimmered below me with candles and lanterns. My room was like part of the evening, and as the rich murmur rose up to me I watched Dolores and a boy, who were both dressed in white with local weavings over their clothes, as they circulated, carrying trays among the guests. When I shut the door behind me to go downstairs, I could feel my apartment swell with dreams poised to overtake me on my return.

I made a quick circle through the garden—naturally, Marcos and Elena were not there—and I noticed Simon Peter heading in my direction. I turned away just in time and found myself facing a snub-nosed woman in a ruffled dress, with sticky-looking yellow-brown rolls of hair like varnished wood shavings. "You don't have a drink!" she said. "Well, I hope you can hold out for about an hour. The best thing to do is just to go in and pour yourself something, but it makes Norman so miserable if he sees. How long ago was it they moved from the big house? Nine years? Ten years? Still, I suppose it's a difficult adjustment. Sandra looks quite well, though, doesn't she?"

"Yes," I said.

"Sometimes it's worse when she's just come out of the clinic," the woman said. "It's hard to remember, isn't it, that she was the one who really ran the show all those years when Norman was such a souse. Oh, she was just as capable as anything! Of course, he was always just . . . *sweet,* wasn't he? A *gentle* man, Bob always says."

How dare she, I thought. How dare this stranger tell her friends' secrets to me. But as I thought it I realized that Sandra and Norman had already offered me this information about themselves, and I looked down to avoid the reflection in this woman's face of my own brutality and cowardice.

"Such a pity about this weather," the woman said. "All this haze. Or smog, whatever it is. We never used to have this." She patted her careful permanent. "Oh, I see that you're admiring my sash," she said. "Guatemalan. Old, the girl said, and she seemed honest. I think she was German."

"I'm sure," I said, looking around for Norman and Sandra. I would say good night and then leave.

"Excuse me?" the woman said.

"Pardon me?" I said. "Yes, it must be."

"Well, at least I was told it was," the woman said. "They still do marvelous things, of course, but I wouldn't recommend it. Bob and I were horribly disappointed ourselves last year. We had a wonderful view of the lake, but otherwise it was impossible. And the meals! Well, I'm sorry to have to tell you that it really wasn't food at all."

"Perhaps I will go inside and get myself something," I said, but at that moment the boy appeared with a tray of frothy drinks. He was very young, really a child, and he was absolutely radiant. He seemed delighted with his tray and his uniform.

"Uh-uh," the woman said loudly as the boy started to move off. "Hold still there." As the woman drained her glass and exchanged it for a full one, I realized that the boy looked exactly like Dolores—he must have been her son.

"Hello, hello," Norman said. He was crossing past us on the lawn, and he held firmly by the elbow a woman who walked unsteadily in high-heeled sandals. "All set up, I see. Good."

"Muriel," said the woman with Norman. "No one *told* me you were here yet."

"Just," said the woman I was talking to. "Barely a week."

"Marvelous," the other woman called back over her shoulder as she and Norman continued on their way. "And how's Bob?"

"Well, you know." Muriel leaned across me to answer her retreating friend. "He's been out on the course all day." Both women laughed and waved. "Actually," Muriel said to me, "he just can't stand to come to their parties any longer. He was so close to Norman, after all, and since they lost the Fort Lauderdale place Bob has hardly had the heart to see them. But I feel we just have to come out for Gerald and Helen, don't you?

You know—" she paused and turned on me a look of blind radar—"I don't remember you from Fort Lauderdale—"

"Isn't this lovely," said Sandra, arriving in a whirl of skirts. She put a bare, somewhat slack arm around Muriel. "Everyone all together."

"Just a moment, dear," Muriel said, reaching over with a piece of Kleenex to wipe a bit of lipstick off Sandra's tooth. "There. I was just telling your young friend here about your beautiful, beautiful place in Fort Lauderdale."

"We had such fun, didn't we?" Sandra said.

"Where do you two know each other from?" Muriel said.

"Oh, she's my darling," Sandra said. "Isn't she cute? But she's so busy. Full of important things to do." She crinkled her nose and put it against mine for a moment. "I hate you when you're busy," she said. She turned to Muriel. "Where's Bob?" she said. "I haven't seen Bob all evening."

"He was miserable not to be able to make it," Muriel said. "But he was simply exhausted. He spent the entire day on the course with Dr. Skip."

I realized that I'd never seen Sandra's face in repose before. She focused dispassionately on Muriel as Muriel carefully picked a fallen blossom off her dress, and when Muriel looked up again Sandra was still gazing at her. "He gets tired," Muriel said, glancing at me to enlist my support. "He's not as young as he used to be." But I was looking at her in just the way that Sandra had looked at her, and Sandra herself turned and walked off.

"There!" Muriel said. "Well, I suppose I've done something now, but that's just the kind of thing—" An expression of dull triumph spread across her face. "She blames us. She blames Norman. But what else can Norman do? He's the only one with the authority to commit her."

But over on the patio something was happening. Just as Norman reached down to take a drink from Dolores's son,

Sandra strode up. Norman seemed unable to move as he watched Sandra grip the child's shoulder and with her free hand take a drink from the tray, lifting it high above her head. The child stared, his huge eyes gleaming with fear, and the glass seemed to hesitate where Sandra released it, twinkling lazily in the air, before it shattered on the slate. The sound seemed a signal for the party to resume, more noisily than before, and the entire event was swallowed in the cleft of silence that closed behind us while Sandra raised the glasses one by one from the boy's tray and let them drop.

As I crossed the lawn, a pulpy hand grabbed mine. "You're not going to be all upset now, are you?" a voice said. The voice and hand belonged to a large man in Bermuda shorts. "It's over and done with," he said. "Tomorrow no one will even remember." I snatched my hand away and continued across the lawn.

I found Sandra in the living room leaning on Dolores, who comforted her as if she were a child. Her crying sounded like a small, intermittent cough. Norman stood several feet away, looking up at the moon. His face was wet with tears, I saw, and, like the face that looked back at him from the moon, it was indistinct, as if it were being slowly worn away. There was nothing I could do here.

Near the gate, Dolores's son was kicking listlessly at the wall. We pretended not to notice each other as I went out.

By the time I got to the square it was nearly empty. Four men still stood at equidistant points around the band shell conjuring streams of bubbles from their bottles of colored liquid, but the other vendors and the crowds had disappeared, and the last remaining people must have assumed, as I sat down on a bench, that I was waiting for something.

Had Sandra and Norman ever been aware of the life they were making for themselves? Probably not. It seemed that one simply ate any fruit at hand, scattering the seeds about carelessly and then years later found oneself walled in by the growth. I cast my mind back into my own past, straining to see any crossroad, any telling choice, that would indicate the destination toward which I was moving, but there was only the gentle clacking of the broad leaves above me and a slight scent of roses eddying through the night air.

If only I could be lifted up and borne off to someplace further along in time, to where the hours would move forward in a benign, steady procession and I would spend the modest coinage of daily life among pleasant people. I closed my eyes wearily for a moment, and when I opened them, a piece of chiffon seemed to wind around me, a billowing thing that had belonged to my mother's mother. I pored over it, studying the thrilling colors that were unfaded by previous exposure to memory. I held it up, filtering a cold afternoon light through its ravishing thinness. The patterns were larger, and the threads and the dark interstices between them, and then it was gone and the night was around me again. Yet I'd seen that forgotten scarf as perfectly as if some globe underfoot had rotated thirty years back, placing me right next to it.

And now there was another rotation, and I was crouching in the alley, where garbage cans clustered like mushrooms, and the brick apartment buildings rose up and up, casting a private weather around me. Most of the windows were dark and vacant, but in some, white shades were pulled halfway down. One cord and ring turned aimlessly, ominously, in a ghostly breath of air. I watched and watched until a tightening circle of darkness closed around it.

I sat shivering and miserable at the edge of a community pool where my mother sent me to swim on Saturdays. Lights, reflected from under the water, rippled on the dark walls and ceiling, and the tile room echoed with loose booming sounds. Chlorine stank, and burned in my nose and eyes.

During recess I leaned against the fence as classmates played tetherball—an awful game, dogged and pointless. Sharon, a bossy fat girl, came over and stood next to me. She had never talked to me before, but now she asked me to go skating after school. I looked at her uneasily. Had she felt sorry for me? As I stalled, I saw anxiety erode her self-assurance, and her purpose became clear—she thought I'd be easily acquired: "Sharon is making friends now," her relieved parents would be able to say. Well, I did not have to be her life raft. "No, thank you," I said. My strength had returned. "I have to get back to my mother."

In the university library I talked with a man from one of my classes. I was stricken with a fear that he was going to ask me to have coffee, and while I waited, trying to concentrate on what he was saying, his face became less and less familiar. Suddenly he checked his watch and turned away, leaving me confused.

My friend Pamela and I sat in our favorite café after an early Sunday supper, studying our check. We opened our purses, and each of us carefully counted out what she owed. The headlights of the cars that drove past were sulfurous yellow in a cold autumn drizzle. Time to go—the office tomorrow.

Well. Yes. That had been only last month. I blinked at the shapes of the foliage becoming visible against the velvety night. What random, uneventful memories. In any case, it must be terribly late, and I ought to be asleep, but as I rose to go, there was the sudden rush of entering a tunnel, and I sat with my mother, holding one of her hands. I traced with my finger the huge, adult bones, the fascinating veins that crossed it like mysterious rivers; I fitted my attention exactly to the ridgings of her knuckles, the wedding ring, her pale, flat nails. "Your hand is so beautiful," I said.

"My hand is hideous," she said, withdrawing it. "I have hideous hands. They're old." Later, in private, I cried until I felt sore. How old had I been then? Not more than seven, I suppose, but how well I knew those hands when I saw them lying, truly old, as frail as paper on the hospital coverlet. The light from the window fell across them, and across my mother's sleeping face, her skin soft, like a worn cloth, as I stood in the doorway wondering if I should make some small noise to see if she was ready to wake. But light was coming through the walls of the hospital room, and they faded, and my mother faded, into the sparkling dawn.

Heavens. Vanished. How quickly the long night had turned to morning. How little there was behind me. I got up from the hard bench, stamping slightly to bring the blood back into my feet. Colors began to pulse into the day, and a terror took hold of me at being out here in the open as, deeper and surer with every beat, colors filled up the leaves and the flowers and the steep walled streets and the circle of mountains all around me, and the sky, too, where a round, yellow sun was rising.

People were appearing in the square, quietly preparing for business, and I saw that there was a row of women already sitting cross-legged on the sidewalk, waiting for change. As I quickly distributed mine among them, one of the women said something to me. How thin she was, that woman—there was practically nothing left of her. At the correct moment she would need only to shrug off her ragged shawl in order to ascend from the sidewalk, weightless.

When I passed the news kiosk, only the little boy was there. My terror intensified; where was the boy's brother? I wanted badly to ask, but of course I was not able to, and as the child waved to me I caught a sudden glimpse of what those gods of Marcos's would see if they were to look down now at their former venue: a dying beggar; a little boy beginning his working life in earnest; a community of refugees from failure, ravaged by their pursuit of some deadly spectre of pleasure; a lonely woman moving into middle age. We would be a pretty sight, I thought, rocketing along our separate courses—tiny shooting stars burning out in space. But they were not going to look down, those gods. They had been released, and now they were free behind the screen of smog and pollution that protected them from the clamor of their new, unskilled petitioners, and as the day carried the people around me toward whichever of the positions they were to assume that night in the square, I would have to search unaided through my raucous sleep for the dream in which my mother would take my hand and step into the moving current.

All around me the tin shutters were rolling up, and the streets grew crowded and noisy with traffic, and people with bundles of goods poured down into town like cataracts of melting streams, and in what seemed to be no time I'd been flung upon this tide back at the gate, breathless and disheveled. But as I headed for the refuge of my apartment, a gleaming from among the stale litter of ashtrays and dishes drew me over to the patio. Oh, so many of the beautiful glasses—a little heap, I thought, of something over and done with. How sorry Sandra was going to be when she woke up!

I bent over the flashing splinters, and when I raised my eyes again I saw to my surprise that the living-room curtains were open and that Norman and Sandra were already awake. I peered cautiously into the dim interior, and I watched, shading my eyes, as they moved slowly about, making an ineffectual attempt to neaten up after the party. When they came to the door to answer my knock, I was shocked to see how old they were in this morning light, and seedy in their worn robes, like people just come from a hospital. They looked at me bewildered, as if they couldn't quite place me—and, goodness knows, I had never come to them before—but I wasn't able to explain myself or to speak at all. And as we stood and stared at each other, I saw on their faces the record, which was changing right in front of me, of countless challenges met and usually lost, and then, understanding what they must do, they composed themselves and invited me in.

A NOTE ON THE TYPE

The text of this book was set in a film version of Garamond No. 3, a modern rendering of the type first cut by Claude Garamond (1510–1561). Garamond was a pupil of Geoffroy Troy and is believed to have based his letters on Venetian models, although he introduced a number of important differences, and it is to him we owe the letter which we know as old style. He gave to his letters a certain elegance and a feeling of movement that won for their creator an immediate reputation and the patronage of Francis I of France.

Composed by Brevis Press, Bethany, Connecticut
Printed and bound by Fairfield Graphics, Fairfield, Pennsylvania
Typography and binding design by Dorothy Schmiderer